The imag she balled her fists against her eyes to blot them out. Those faces. That sound. *Drip, drip . . .*

Would another sleeping pill make the dreams go away? Or would it simply make her more helpless against them? Wouldn't it ever be over?

She squeezed her eyes tightly shut, trying to focus her thoughts. . . . Something about a valley and a shadow of evil. She groped for the words. *Yea, though I walk through the valley of the shadow of death, I shall fear no evil.*

Fear no evil . . . what next? *I shall fear no evil . . .* But try as she might, the rest of the verse eluded her . . . She couldn't concentrate. She couldn't remember . . . and she couldn't stop feeling as though the worst had not even begun.

DARK ANGEL

Donna Ball

A SIGNET BOOK

SIGNET
Published by the Penguin Group
Penguin Putnam Inc., 375 Hudson Street,
New York, New York 10014, U.S.A.
Penguin Books Ltd, 27 Wrights Lane,
London W8 5TZ, England
Penguin Books Australia Ltd, Ringwood,
Victoria, Australia
Penguin Books Canada Ltd, 10 Alcorn Avenue,
Toronto, Ontario, Canada M4V 3B2
Penguin Books (N.Z.) Ltd, 182–190 Wairau Road,
Auckland 10, New Zealand

Penguin Books Ltd, Registered Offices:
Harmondsworth, Middlesex, England

First published by Signet, an imprint of Dutton Signet,
a member of Penguin Putnam Inc.

First Printing, March, 1998
10 9 8 7 6 5 4 3 2 1

MAY 1, 1996

One

Durham, North Carolina

The evil in the city was sometimes so thick he could taste it. The miasma of it rose up from the streets and the sewers, from the parks and alleyways, threading its way up the sides of highrises and seeping into air vents. It clung to every bush and vine, every signpost, vehicle, and building like an oily yellow film, clogging up pores, cutting off oxygen. Its stench made him nauseous.

In the midst of this fog of human filth he had found her, breathing the noxious air, absorbing the putrescence through her skin; stepping in the offal, soiling herself in the mire. She had red hair and the face of an angel. He had killed her, not because she deserved to die, but because she deserved better than to live.

He disposed of her personal belongings in the incinerator, because he was thorough, and it was necessary. The scalpel with which he had cut her throat was disposed of in the same way, because he never used a single instrument twice. The body he wrapped in a clear plastic drop cloth and buried in a deep water cove on Lake Cummings. He knew that her spirit was no longer within and that what became of the body was immaterial, but he observed the rituals. Purification by water was essential to eternal salvation.

When he had completed his task he stood by the lake shore in the dark night and wept. The sorrow, once the deed was done, was always immense. Emptiness and loss filled him, and his soul was as cold as the bottom of the lake.

He was not sorry for the life that was gone. The girl whose spirit he had freed to its destiny had already left his mind, though she had never weighed very heavily upon it, and she at any rate was the fortunate one. It was he who had to stay behind, confused and in pain, wondering what he had to do to make the emptiness go away. The souls he released were mere tokens, he knew that, crumbs tossed to the yawning hunger inside him, and they were never enough. A greater good waited to be satisfied, a larger beast roared to be fed. No matter what he did, no matter how many he killed, always something was missing; it was never quite right. Still he was a failure.

And that was why he wept.

APRIL 17, 1997

Two

Later, Ellen Cox would play the "what-if" game. What if she hadn't overslept? What if she had showered the night before, instead of that morning? What if she hadn't misplaced her keys and had to spend over three minutes searching for them? Or what if she hadn't found the keys so quickly, or what if she had slept a little longer or decided to take another route? And the biggest what-if of all—what if none of it would have made a difference?

Ellen Cox taught third grade at Branson Academy, a private school for the hearing impaired in Norfolk, about twenty miles from her Virginia Beach home. Her classroom was bright, noisy, and chaotic—creative expression at maximum output for six hours a day. Perhaps because her work environment was so unstructured and unpredictable, she appreciated order in her home. She disliked surprises, changes, or breaks in her routine. She absolutely hated to be late.

She took a cup of coffee with her and settled it in the cup holder of her blue Honda Accord as she backed quickly out of the driveway and left her residential area for the feeder road that led away from the beaches. Though the worst of the rush-hour traffic had already passed, what remained was moving slowly. Class at Branson started at nine. Ellen glanced at the dashboard clock and made a decision. At the next stop light she turned right onto Broad Bay Road toward the expressway. It wasn't the most direct route but at this time of day it should be faster. Finally, away from the congestion of traffic lights and residential neighborhoods, she relaxed enough to turn on the radio and pick up her coffee cup.

It was eight thirty-six.

Ben Bradshaw finished his rounds at eight o'clock, spent a few minutes dictating discharge summaries at the nurse's station, and picked up a ham and egg croissant to go in the hospital cafeteria. It was a truism everywhere that doctors—especially those just out of residency with enough outstanding student loans to finance an emerging nation—had the worst dietary habits in the world. He left Doctor's Memorial at eight-thirty, driving with one hand and absently munching on the sandwich with the other, and turned left onto Broad Bay Road, toward the beaches where the clinic was located.

He was thirty years old, single, gainfully employed, and he still had a hard time adjusting to the fact that, for all intents and purposes, his life was just beginning. He still drove the eight-year-old car that was the first he had ever owned. He rented a condo instead of buying a house, and it was beach view instead of beachfront. One of the inducements

the clinic had used when recruiting him for their staff
was the fact that a predictable ten-hour day would
leave him more time for a personal life, and at the
time Ben hadn't realized he didn't have a personal
life. At the time it hadn't mattered.

He practiced family medicine from eight to six—
sometimes seven—four days a week, which he liked
more than he ever thought he would. He played tennis when he could find a partner, visited his parents
in Suffolk every other weekend, spent a great deal
of time avoiding being "fixed up" by female relatives
who had an inflated estimate of his present income
and future prospects and who were unable to rest
easy in their beds at night with the certain knowledge that Benjamin Bradshaw, M.D. remained single
and uninvolved. The evenings were devoted to cater-
ing to the every whim of two Great Pyrenees dogs,
and, until he took the time to think about it, which
he rarely did, he was satisfied with his life.

Today he found life a little more satisfying than
usual. The twelve-year-old girl he had admitted with
encephalitis two weeks ago was going home today,
no permanent side effects. The young secretary he
had referred for surgery had returned a benign bi-
opsy, and the harridan in Medical Records with
whom he had been arguing over insurance forms for
the past month had allowed him to pass through her
corridor unmolested this morning.

At the traffic light just past the bridge he saw a
pretty woman in a blue Honda, which was a good
omen for the rest of the day. She didn't notice him,
though, which was not. All in all, he figured he was
still ahead of the game.

When the light changed he beeped his horn lightly at her just for the hell of it, and grinned to himself as they drove off in opposite directions. He reached down and turned on the radio.

It was eight forty-seven.

"Good Thursday morning, sailors and surfers, it's coming up on eight forty-eight in the A.M. and if you were supposed to be at work at eight-thirty, hey, you're late! You're listening to Big Don Jackson on WSRF, 93.8 on your FM dial, and if your workday doesn't start till nine o'clock, you lucky dog, you've got about ten minutes to sneak in under the clock. To help you get there let's check in with WSRF-Radio's Sky Watch Traffic Chopper with Captain Jake Skinner. How's it looking up there, Captain Jake?"

The tinny sound of static and helicopter blades replaced the D.J.'s voice and Ellen reached down to turn up the volume. She sipped her coffee as the voice of the traffic reporter announced, "Not too bad for a Friday morning, Big Don. We've got all west-bound lanes of 264 clear, I-64 moving pretty freely after you get past the downtown exits. You might have a little slowdown on Virginia Beach Boulevard moving westbound, but the Broad Bay Road is moving pretty steady . . ."

"Hallelujah," muttered Ellen, and that was when the world began to rumble and heave and collapse beneath her.

It was eight-fifty in the morning. April 17, 1997.

Three

From the air it looked like this: The two-hundred-foot concrete bridge was one moment arched serenely over the gray-green waters of Broad Bay. The morning sun glinted off the windows and hoods of traffic moving at normal speed. In the next moment the bridge seemed to sag, shifting so subtly it almost could have been an optical illusion but it wasn't because a second later—too quickly for any driver to react, too quickly for an observer to even draw breath—a cloud of dust arose from the concrete support that buckled under its own weight and a gap appeared in the decking as the two sections of the bridge swayed apart.

On the eastbound side, a ten-foot slab of decking pulled loose and took two cars with it as it tumbled eighty feet into the water below. On the westbound side another car, caught in the gap when the bridge pulled apart, went over soundlessly while two others were flung through the guardrail by the momentum of the swaying bridge.

Chaos exploded. In the westbound lane, cars began

to fishtail, spinning and rear-ending one another as the as yet unseen obstacle up ahead brought the previously fifty-mile-per-hour traffic to an abrupt halt. In the eastbound lane, traffic slowed as drivers gave their attention to their rearview mirrors and the upheaval behind them, and horns began to blast from that lane when rubbernecking resulted in near-misses. At the intersection the light changed, allowing traffic from the side streets to turn on to Broad Bay, and more horns trumpeted as those drivers found the intersection blocked by accidents and stalled cars. A few determined drivers pulled out anyway, trying to inch past the congestion on the shoulder, compounding the tangle of traffic.

The worst of it was over in under fifteen seconds.

The sound was horrendous. The screeching and tearing of metal, the rumbling of shattered masonry, the roar of wind through the newly created gash; the blare of horns and scream of tires and the fainter, yet more penetrating, screams of human beings. From the air, however, the event was silent. The helicopter pilot who looked down on it all could hear nothing above the sound of his own screams.

Ben had stopped to make a left turn against traffic some fifty feet from the stoplight, which was the only reason he was still in the vicinity. The first thing he knew of the situation was the squeal of tires and the blare of multiple horns from the bridge and he thought, *Oh, shit. An accident, and it sounds bad.* He glanced in his rearview mirror, adrenaline already pumping as he prepared to pull out of the left-turn lane and over to the shoulder of the road, and that was when the traffic reporter on the radio started screaming.

He had been saying, "There seems to be a problem developing on Bay Bridge Road, we're just swinging around to take a look . . ." Then, "Oh Christ, oh no—" in a tone that grew more shrill with every breath—"I'm not seeing this, oh no, it's the bridge, it's falling, *the bridge is collapsing into the bay*! Get off the bridge, get off—"

Ben laid his hand on the horn and executed a blind wide right U-turn, swinging across two lanes of traffic and onto the grassy shoulder of the road facing the bridge. He narrowly missed slamming into a pickup truck and a red Jeep—in fact thought his fender might have scraped the Jeep—but that was the least of the accidents that were happening all around him.

People started to get out of their cars, their faces registering shock, anger, fear. Ben opened his door and pulled it quickly closed again as he was almost broadsided by a motorcyclist who, trying to weave his way through the traffic, had lost control and skidded onto the shoulder.

Ben realized then that his engine was still running, the gear in drive. He turned off the engine, grabbed a handful of rubber gloves from his glove compartment, and popped the trunk of his car. Opening the door more cautiously this time, he got out and grabbed his medical bag from the trunk.

He remembered a lecture in medical school about the "new ethics" of the physician in a world of sky-rocketing insurance costs, out-of-control malpractice suits, and Good Samaritan laws. Most of his classmates had privately agreed that no doctor, particularly one just starting out, could afford the potential consequences of rendering emergency aid outside a licensed facility, and that the most prudent course of action would be to call 911 and quietly go on one's way. Ben had agreed with them. None of them had taken into account, of course, the adrenaline factor.

That he acted now out of impulse more than reason, excitement rather than compassion, was evident—and inconsequential. He just acted.

He quickly examined the motorcyclist who had skidded out and found him dazed but uninjured. In the next few cars he found bruises and scrapes, some hysteria, a lot of confusion. Instinctively he knew the worst injuries would be beyond the intersection, and that was the direction in which he headed. He wasn't the only one on foot. Other Good Samaritans were going from car to car, inquiring about the injured. Ben saw two people with car phones, dialing for help. A helicopter hovered overhead, and the sound of beating blades in the distance heralded the arrival of at least one more. People were sobbing, babbling about the bridge. Ben caught no more than broken fragments of sentences.

At the intersection cars were wedged together like pieces of a jigsaw puzzle, and he had to crawl over bumpers to move between them. He found a woman bleeding from a head injury and a child with a broken arm, along with a Navy corpsman and an off-duty EMT, both of whom were making themselves useful. The road was filled with the sound of the emergency room—sobbing and moaning, the occasional sharp cry of fear or horror, pleas for help—in addition to roadside confusion, shouts of anger and impatience, stuck horns, hissing radiators. Ben bandaged the woman's head and used one of his inflatable splints for the child's arm. In the distance he heard sirens, lots of them, and his stomach began to unknot a little. The helicopters were hovering just ahead, over the bridge, adding their din to the general confusion.

Ben had done his internship in emergency services and had participated in three disaster drills; he knew how to work under fire. This was field medicine at its rawest, a battlefield of pain and helplessness that had no boundaries. He was aware of a sense of timelessness, of detachment that lent an almost surreal quality to the scene. Sometimes his own voice seemed half a second behind the words he spoke; sometimes he treated a victim without ever seeing his or her face. He kept moving until he reached the edge of the intersection.

Ben climbed up on the hood of an empty Celica with a crushed rear end and tried to see over the melée. He climbed to the roof and stood cautiously.

The bridge, or what was left of it, looked like a carnival ride gone bad. Cars had plowed into the guardrail and into each other; they were twisted together, lying on crushed roofs, turned on their sides. Ben looked at the scene and saw death there. But even that did not chill him as much as what he saw beyond the graveyard of automobiles.

Where once a concrete bridge had spanned the expanse of water eighty feet below now there was only empty air. Blue sky, blue water. Steel girders popping out like broken ribs, cables swinging in the wind. The sight of it, perhaps combined with the knowledge that he had been on that bridge only moments before, left Ben feeling sick and dizzy.

But that was not the worst of it. Because just then his eyes found and focused on the blue Honda. He felt the remaining blood drain out of his face.

"Good Christ," he whispered.

The car was balanced on the edge of the bridge, its back two tires on solid concrete, its front portion hanging out in empty space over the water. And someone was still inside.

9:16 A.M.

When Ellen was a little girl she had lived in a big white house with green shutters and a lilac bush in the front yard. The bush must have been ancient; it grew halfway up the side of the porch and dropped low branches to the ground tall enough for a five-year-old girl to create a make-believe playhouse underneath. Ellen had spent hours in her sanctuary under the lilac bush, giving tea parties for her dolls, dressing the cat in petticoats, spying on her mother's friends as they came to call, and making up elaborate stories about their activities. The days of her childhood were sunny and simple and filled with the scent of lilacs.

Ellen opened her eyes after the accident, and she saw sky, and smelled lilacs.

It took her a moment to realize, after a time of

fuzzy rumination in which nothing, really, made much sense, that she was pressed back into the seat by gravity at an unnatural angle. Her car seemed to be stopped uphill. Wincing a little at the pain in her shoulder caused by the constriction of the seatbelt, Ellen tried to sit forward. The car rocked alarmingly.

A voice at her ear said, "I wouldn't do that, lady."

Ellen gasped and turned to her open driver's side window, and the car shifted once again. She stiffened. The young man at her window raised a staying hand, as though he could physically steady the car by holding it, and there was alarm in his eyes.

Ellen eased herself back against the seat, breathing hard. The car stopped rocking.

The man said, "I'm a doctor. Are you hurt?"

Ellen said, "The rabbits. They're all dead."

"What?"

She turned her head cautiously against the headrest to look at him. He was frowning. "I spilled hot coffee on my leg," she said.

"Anything else?"

"No. It wasn't very hot." Cautiously, she raised her hand to her sternum. "My chest is sore."

"Can you breathe okay?"

"Not really. I'm scared to death."

His expression relaxed a little. "Understandable. Try wiggling your toes for me."

She did.

"Good. Just try to stay still now. What's your name?"

"Ellen." Her throat was dry, and she swallowed. "Ellen Cox."

"Well, Ellen." His eyes shifted forward, then back

21

to her again. "The good news is, you had a narrow escape. The bad news is, your car is balanced like a matchstick with two wheels over the edge of the bridge, so please, be very, very careful about how you move. Your driver's-side door is pretty banged up, but I'm going to try to get it open. When I do, unfasten your seatbelt, but not before, okay?"

Ellen watched him, eyes wide, nostrils flared for slow, deep breaths. She dared not part her lips for breath even though she felt as though she was smothering. If she opened her mouth she knew she would start screaming.

Slowly, she nodded.

He gripped the door handle and pulled. The car dipped and Ellen cried out. He shoved his weight against the door, and Ellen squeezed her eyes shut, gripping the sides of the upholstered seat until the car straightened up again.

He said, breathing hard, "Well. I won't try that again." His face was white and shiny with sweat. He got down on his knees again, so that his face was even with the window. "The door is jammed," he explained. "Or at least it's stuck too much for me to get it open under these circumstances."

Ellen held herself pressed rigidly against the seat, her eyes fixed on his face. It was a nice face, she noticed with a faraway part of her mind. An open face, easily expressive, framed by sandy hair that was curly with sweat, and accented with hazel eyes now dark with worry and fear. She fixed on his face and her breath came a little easier; she found her voice long enough to inquire, "What about the other door?"

He shook his head. "It's too far over the edge. I don't think I can reach it, and even if I could I don't want you moving, shifting the balance. We've got to find a way to get this car stabilized."

"Sounds good to me."

He smiled at her in what was no doubt meant to be a reassuring way. "My name's Ben, by the way. Ben Bradshaw."

He stuck his hand rather awkwardly through the window. She shook it, resisting the impulse to hang on to it like a lifeline. "It's a pleasure to meet you," she said.

"It would have been, I promise," he said, "under different circumstances."

They just looked at each other for a moment.

Then, Ellen said, "So, Ben. I don't suppose you thought you'd be doing this when you got up this morning."

She saw surprise in his eyes, which was gratifying, then he smiled, which was even more gratifying. He answered, "I'll bet you didn't, either."

"You got that right."

She concentrated on another few deep breaths, and moved her eyes away from his. Nothing but sky was in front of her. She couldn't think about what was beneath her.

He said, "Listen, I'm going to go back and see if I can get some help. Are you going to be okay for a few minutes?"

"No!" she gasped, and the cry was out before she could stop it. She knew the proper response was *Yes, of course, you go ahead, I'll be fine*, and in her mind she actually said the words but the sound that came out was an almost inarticulate expression of horror. She flung up a hand as though to grasp him, to keep him from deserting her, and she was suddenly, irrationally convinced that if she were left alone she would die. "No, don't leave, God, don't leave me—"

"It's okay, I'm here." Swiftly he slid his hand through the open window and grasped hers, holding it tightly. "Don't worry, I'll stay. I'm not leaving."

Ellen's breath was quick and shallow and so was her heartbeat. She pressed her head back against the headrest and tried to focus, to reclaim the mature and rational woman she once had been, to bring order to her tumultuous thoughts. And she wondered if, in all of human experience, there had ever been words to express what it meant to clasp another human hand at a time like this.

She said, staring straight ahead and trying to keep her voice from trembling, "I'm sorry. I don't mean to be hysterical. I'm usually much more self-sufficient than this."

"It's okay. You're allowed to be a little hysterical under the circumstances."

She tried to draw a deep breath. It caught in her throat. The sky seemed enormous, as huge and as fathomless as what lay below her. The beating of helicopter blades blended with the sound of screaming sirens, blaring horns, and sobbing people to form an audio map of a nightmare. Her heart pounded against her chest and a cold dampness bathed her face and she knew if she had to listen to those sounds another minute she would start screaming, and she would scream until she had no more breath. To block the sounds out she said rapidly, "Talk to me, Ben. Could you just talk to me?"

He seemed to understand. His grip on her hand was firm and steady. He said, "Sure. How about we start with the fascinating story of my life? I was born in Hampton Roads, which is not something too many people can say, to a displaced family of horse lovers from Kentucky. My dad was in the Navy, big surprise, and ended up retiring to Suffolk, where he lives with my mom even now, raising horses instead of kids. I went to the University of Virginia, pre-med, and medical school at Columbia, along with half the free world. The only reason I'm still allowed to come home weekends is because I have two brothers who followed their father's advice and joined the military. How do you like it so far?"

She managed a shaky smile. Her breath was coming a little easier. "I like it. Thank you."

"Help is coming, Ellen." His tone was gentle but serious. "The place is swarming with flashing lights and blue uniforms. They've just got to work their way up to us, that's all. You're going to be okay."

Slowly, she nodded her head. She tried to swallow. Her throat was so dry it hurt. "I'm usually—much better than this," she managed.

"At what? Driving off bridges?"

The edge of light amusement in his voice almost made her laugh; she could feel the hysteria rising up in her like a musical note yearning to be set free. She had to force it down with an effort. She said, tightening her fingers on his, "It's just the noise, you know?" Her voice sounded high and unnatural. "All the sirens and the helicopters . . . it's like being buried alive."

She saw by the slight frown in his eyes that she had done something wrong, and then she realized that her nails were digging into his hand. She quickly released the pressure and flexed her fingers; small white crescent marks appeared in the flesh on the back of his hand.

But he barely seemed to notice. He said, "Ellen, are you in any pain?"

"Yes. Everywhere. Why?"

Now his smile seemed forced. "Because I'm a doctor and if I don't ask that question at least six times a day I lose my license. I wish I could get a better look at you."

The helicopters. They were beating in her ears like drums. She pressed her head against the seat again and said, "Talk to me some more. Tell me about medical school."

"No, it's your turn." A gentle, encouraging squeeze of her fingers. "Tell me about you. What do you do?"

"I teach . . ." A catch in her throat surprised her. She had to swallow and draw a breath. "Teach at Branson Academy in Norfolk. It's a school for the hearing impaired. Third grade."

"No kidding?" He seemed genuinely interested. "How did you get involved in that?"

But Ellen was distracted by a gust of wind that seemed to come from nowhere, battering the car from the closed window on the passenger side and seeming—surely she didn't imagine it?—to rock the car. Her hand clenched around Ben's spasmodically.

He said firmly, "Where did you go to school?"

She shook her head against the seat, breathing hard.

He insisted, "Work with me, Ellen. Where did you go to school?"

"Okay," she whispered, trying to calm the racing of her heart, trying to concentrate. "Okay. Just don't leave. Don't leave me alone."

"I'm not going anywhere."

The most beautiful words she had ever heard.

"Now, talk to me. Where did you go to school?"

She took a couple of deep breaths and in a moment managed, "High school or college?"

She could hear the smile in his voice. "Either one."

Four

The Naval Academy
Annapolis, Maryland

11:30 A.M.

Matthew Graham took off his glasses and rested his forearms on the podium, leaning forward a little to address his audience. For this part of the lecture he did not need notes. "Let me close," he said, "with a summary of one of our most remarkable failures. May 1, 1980: An eight-year-old female Caucasian was riding her bicycle home from a church function outside of Charleston, South Carolina when she disappeared. Two days later her body was found in the Ashley River, enclosed in a clear plastic garbage bag. Hair color red, eye color blue. Her throat had been cut with what the lab later determined to be a surgical scalpel.

"May 1, 1981: A ten-year-old female Caucasian is abducted from a church school parking lot in Edistoe, South Carolina, hair color red, eyes blue. Her body washes up on the beach three days later, wrapped in clear plastic, throat cut with a scalpel. May 1, 1982,

Jacksonville Florida: Same M.O., a twelve-year-old girl. Seattle, Washington, May 1, 1983 and 1984; San Diego, California, 1985. Only by now, the victims have reached their mid-teens.

"The FBI became officially involved in 1986 when the body of Lucy Adams, age 17, was found on the banks of the Chatooga River in the Chatahoochee National Forest of North Georgia. As you know, the FBI has automatic jurisdiction in all cases of crimes committed on or involving federal property, but we had been profiling this guy for years. We already knew he was a white male, who began his killing— at least the ones we knew about—between the ages of eighteen and twenty. Serial killers are almost always male, and they tend to choose victims from their own race. He was strong, energetic, precise— what we call an organized killer. He had a strong religious background and was possibly connected with a church in the community as a volunteer or in some other, informal way. All the girls were abducted from or close to churches, and the fact that all of them were disposed of in the water has a definite religious connotation.

"Finally, you've probably already noticed a familiarity to the pattern of the location of the crimes— Charleston, Seattle, San Diego, even the Chattahoochee National Forest is only a two-hour drive from NAS Atlanta. Our man was definitely in the Navy, enlisted but not an officer, possibly a corpsman, probably assigned to or near the infirmary.

"By tracking the location and the frequency of the murders we were able to track the killer's transfers and eliminate a good three-quarters of the United

States Navy, which only left some 200,000 or so suspects. By considering only enlisted men we narrowed the field further; by focusing only on medical personnel we reduced the suspects even further. We feel certain we have interviewed the subject in relationship to these crimes in the past. We have yet to make an arrest.

"In 1989 and 1990 there were no killings. It is possible the killer was stationed overseas, but we think it's more likely that the bodies simply were never found. The killer's preference for disposing of the remains in water—particularly in the ocean—make this likelihood more possible than not. In 1991, in Jacksonville, Florida, a twenty-two-year old woman, red hair, blue eyes, was found in a swamp sixteen miles from the naval base, her throat cut, wrapped in plastic. In 1992, the victim was twenty-five, same general physical appearance, discovered in the Savannah River. The 1993 victim was never found, although a twenty-eight-year old woman matching the general physical characteristics of previous victims disappeared when her car broke down in front of a community church just outside of Fairfax, Virginia.

"In 1994, our killer took an early out from the Navy. If we knew where he was discharged it would be a simple matter of matching names and places, but we don't. On May 6, 1995, the body of the tenth known victim was found in a lake in the Raleigh-Durham area of North Carolina. The woman was thirty years old, red hair, blue eyes. Her throat had been cut with a scalpel, her body wrapped in plastic. She disappeared on May 1 after attending an A.A. meeting in the basement of a local church."

Matthew straightened up and tucked his glasses into his pocket, never losing eye contact with his audience, which was, as they almost always were by this time, rapt. "So there you have it, gentlemen, the spectacular frustrations of an FBI profile. For fifteen years we've tracked a killer. We know who he is, we know where he works, we know what he does, we know when and how he's going to kill and we know, for the most part, why. What we don't know is how to catch him. We're not perfect. Sometimes they get away. Don't ever forget that.

"Thank you for your attention, gentlemen. I'll answer questions for—" he glanced at his watch "—another six minutes."

Hands went up across the lecture hall. Fresh-faced midshipmen in starched whites asked intelligent, respectful questions. As he began to wind up the question-and-answer section, Matthew was aware of a sense of satisfaction with the day's work, which was something he had not known in months. Years.

Then a female midshipman got to her feet and Matthew decided this would be the last question. "Sir," the young woman said in that clear, strong voice he so admired in Academy students, "if you could name one characteristic essential to the success of your work as an investigator specializing in the behavioral sciences, what would it be?"

Matthew could not prevent a faint, wry smile. Somehow the kids always knew, and saved the hard questions for last.

What did it take to spend twenty years crawling inside the head of the most twisted, degenerate, conscienceless so-called representatives of the human species? What it did take to put not only your life but your mental health on the line over and over again? To lose more than you won, to keep going back long after the desire to win was gone? He could have given a list of answers: Persistence, sacrifice, singlemindedness, determination. Stupidity, selfishness, ruthlessness. A strong stomach. A touch of masochism. Maybe even a death wish.

He said, "Compassion."

He stacked his notes and left the podium, leaving the midshipman looking puzzled and surprised.

Matthew did four or five of these guest lectures a year at various universities around the country, in addition to the special request seminars for regional law-enforcement agencies and the regular classes he taught at the FBI Academy. When he first joined the FBI the classroom had been an anathema for him, almost a punishment; now it was his sanctuary. And it was the only place he ever felt effective anymore.

Matt didn't linger to chat with the cadets or socialize with the officers, and he had already refused, with feigned regret, the commander's invitation for cocktails. Social functions made him uncomfortable, and he considered small talk with strangers a waste of time. His job was finished and he wanted to go home.

On his car radio, Matthew heard about the collapse of the bridge, and he turned up the volume. He lost interest when he realized the disaster was in Virginia Beach and would not affect his drive time home.

Compassion. He had used up his store of it years ago.

* * *

"This is Allison McCarthy reporting live from the scene of the Broad Bay Road bridge collapse. Already officials are calling this the most devastating disaster in recent Tidewater history. A confirmed eight are dead, and thirty-seven have been transported to area hospitals. As you can see behind me, the automobile that has been so precariously balanced on the edge of the bridge all morning is still holding on, so to speak. The car has been secured to the bridge with heavy marine chains, but attempts to free the driver have so far failed. Apparently the door is jammed closed, and as you can see the position of the car makes it impossible for rescuers to get cutting equipment in. There was some talk of going in through the back window but experts decided the risk of overbalancing the car was too great. The occupant of the vehicle, Ellen Cox, a teacher at Branson Academy in Norfolk, is said to be uninjured and in good spirits, despite the fact that she has been trapped now for almost four hours . . ."

"380 Jericho Street," Ellen said, "Wintersville, West Virginia. That's where I was born." Her voice was hoarse from talking and her vocal cords actually felt swollen, but she didn't dare stop. Speech, the sound of her own voice and the certainty that someone was hearing it, was her only connection to reality now and she had a superstitious conviction that when the backward recitation of her life ended, so would her life. So she kept talking, leaving out no detail.

"Never heard of it," Ben said. His face was sunburned and shiny with sweat, for as the sun grew higher in the sky he had taken the brunt of it. He never left her, except for a few minutes at a time to talk to rescue workers or restore the circulation in his legs. He always came back.

Ellen said, "I'm not surprised. Population 861; I remember seeing it on a sign." She was tired, and it was so hard to keeping talking, to concentrate long enough to force the words out. Her back ached and her legs were growing numb from the long hours of forced immobility. Ben had wrapped a cervical collar around her neck—"just as a precaution" he had said—and someone else had made her put on a life jacket. Both were hot, and the cups of chipped ice rescuers kept bringing her did little to alleviate her discomfort. She had to keep fighting that feeling of disassociation, as though she were floating far away, watching this horror happen to someone else, and the only way to do that was to focus, to make herself remember who she was and where she was. To keep talking.

She said, "It was at the corner of Broad, a big old white house with a wrap-around porch painted dark green, and a lilac bush by the steps. I used to play under the lilac bush. God, the smell. Right after— the first thing I remember after the accident was the smell of lilacs. It's a good memory. I walked to school, two blocks away—Nathaniel Hawthorne Elementary—and to church on Angel Street."

Ben said, "Sounds perfectly Norman Rockwell."

"It was." She wanted to close her eyes and surrender to exhaustion. She wanted to weep and surrender to defeat. She struggled to do neither. "I don't suppose many kids get a chance to grow up like that— not these days, anyway."

But her voice cracked on the last words and for no good reason at all she felt tears stinging her eyes. Ben said swiftly, "It's okay, Ellen, you're doing great. Don't give up on me now. Come on. Tell me more. Tell me what it was like being little Ellen Cox in Wintersville, West Virginia. Tell me what you remember."

Ellen swallowed hard. She took a few ice chips into her mouth and let them melt. She took some breaths. "The smell of chalk dust and stained-glass windows. Thanksgiving pageants and the sound of Easter hymns at sunrise and rain on a tin roof and the scent of lilacs. I played Pocahontas in the third-grade play. And there was this lake with swans, and picnic tables and swings set up around it, kind of a community park. My dad used to take me there to play on the swings and once I did something to make the swans angry and one of them started chasing me. They're mean, you know, and really terrifying to a little girl with all that hissing and squawking. Daddy picked me up and held me high over his head and I remember I felt so safe . . ." Again her voice broke. "So safe."

Ben said, obviously trying to distract her, "Do you always do that? Talk in sign language?"

Ellen clenched her hands self-consciously. "Only when I'm upset or excited or—yeah, I guess I do. It's a habit."

He smiled. "I like it."

Ellen swallowed hard. "I'm getting scared, Ben. Do you think it will take much longer?"

"Give me your hand, Ellen."

She did, and Ben threaded his fingers through hers, holding on silently. She closed her eyes.

"My throat hurts," she whispered. "I'm so tired."

"I know."

She turned her head, as much as the cervical collar would allow, to look at him. "I'd guess you got an 'A' in bedside manner."

He smiled. "You bet."

"Why are you doing this, Ben? You don't have to. You've got people waiting for you, depending on you—"

"Nobody more important than you."

"That's nice—to say."

He said, "You want to know the truth? I haven't been a doctor very long and I've never lost a patient. I don't want you to be the first, okay?"

Ellen looked into his eyes—good, gentle eyes—and saw that he was serious. She said, "Okay." Then, "But I'm not your patient."

"I still don't want to lose you. Now, go on. Do your folks still live in Wintersville?"

It was a moment before she could find the strength to answer, "No. We moved to Virginia the year before I started high school. My dad had a fatal stroke when I was in college and my mother died of cancer two years ago. I was a midlife baby and they were both elderly. But it's hard being an orphan, just the same."

The silence between them was brief and tense and Ellen could tell Ben regretted his choice of topic and was searching for a new one. But she had to go on. She said quietly, "My only living relative is Gencie Kellog, an aunt. She's in the Clara Barton Perpetual

Care Center in Williamsburg. It would mean a lot if someone could—break the news in person, just in case . . ."

His hand tightened. "Come on, Ellen."

She continued determinedly, "And my headmistress at Branson, Diane Virion. She must be going crazy, wondering what's happening. I wouldn't want her to hear it on the news if—well, you know."

Ben nodded, his face sober. "I'll take care it."

And then, in the heavy silence that followed, he forced a smile. "All right, my turn to talk. Did I tell you about my dogs?"

Ellen closed her eyes. "Yes."

"Well, you get to hear it again. Samson, he's the biggest, is also under the delusion he's the smartest. He couldn't catch a ball if it hit him in the face. Now Delilah, who's six months younger and twenty pounds lighter . . ."

His voice droned on, their hands held on. Telescopic lenses focused and helicopter-mounted video cameras zoomed in. Across the nation soap operas were interrupted for live footage of the unfolding drama; shoppers in appliance stores gathered before the banks of television sets to catch the hourly updates.

Matthew Graham arrived home at 3:00 P.M. after a brief stop at the office; he turned on CNN and watched.

Ben's parents, retired in Suffolk, watched the story from beginning to end, and didn't know until after the fact that the "hero doctor" on the bridge was their son.

Ellen's headmistress, alerted by the media librarian, turned on the television in her office at ten and sank, weak-kneed, to her chair when a video camera went close-up on the familiar, terrified face of one of her teachers.

The rescue was finally accomplished at four o'clock. After almost eight hours on the bridge, it took less than ten minutes to tow the car back on level ground and pry open Ellen's door. When the door squeaked open and the fireman with the crowbar stepped back, an enormous roar went up, which Ellen later realized was the applause of a cheering crowd.

The first thing Ellen saw when her rescuer stepped back from the open door was Ben. Laughing and weeping, Ellen reached up for him. He extended his arm to help her out. A photographer snapped the picture.

6:35 P.M.

Like thousands of other Americans, Daniel Nichols came home from work that evening and turned on the news. The story of the bridge collapse in Virginia Beach was on all three networks and he listened with sad fascination while he put his frozen dinner in the microwave. He thought about wars and rumors of wars, earthquakes and plagues and famines and pestilence; hallmarks of the time, heralds of the end. Every day the headlines sketched tragedies, catastrophes, and disasters in proportions greater than any since the beginning of history. People hardly even noticed anymore.

Daniel was no better than the rest. He was interested, in the way he would be by any dramatic television program, but none of it affected him; he was not involved. Then he poured himself a diet cola, set the timer on the microwave, and turned around to look at the television set . . . and he was involved.

"And so, after eight hours of hovering between earth and sky, between life and death, Ellen Cox, a thirty-year-old teacher of the hearing impaired from Virginia Beach, is safe again. She was taken to a local hospital where doctors say she is in remarkably good shape after her ordeal. So at least there's one happy ending in the midst of this enormous tragedy, and the profile in courage and hope that's represented by this scene is destined to become a part of our consciousness for a long time . . ."

The scene to which the reporter was referring faded from the car, poised precariously over the edge of the bridge, to a still shot of the woman who had been rescued from it. He moved closer to the screen; he knelt beside it. He stared at the photograph. Still he did not believe it. Arms upraised, laughing, crying, curly red hair blowing in the wind, moist blue eyes. Her face. Her unforgettable face.

There was no mistake. It was her.

Daniel lifted an unsteady hand and touched the screen. His face was radiant with quiet wonder and gratitude. "Ellen," he whispered. "Angel."

Suddenly, everything made sense.

FRIDAY, APRIL 18

Five

The dream began with the sound of dripping water and the sure, sick certainty that she had been this way before. Ellen was passing from sunlight into shadow, into a small dark cave that was horribly familiar, and she tried to wake up, she resisted going, but with the dread inevitability of dreams she was compelled forward. The cave was cold and filled with candles, like a stage set for *Phantom of the Opera*, and there were other people in the cave: a round-faced man in a blue plaid shirt, rimless glasses pushed high on the bridge of his nose; a woman with curly black hair pulled back in a ponytail, wearing a white sweater; a young man with a sharp nose and blond hair slicked back; a boy in a red-and-white-striped polo shirt . . . many, many people, none of them looking at her, all of them with flat, dead expressions on their faces, like dummies in a wax museum.

And that was where the dream became confused. She was sitting in the small dark place with all those people around, faces so clear, people she knew, but none of them could see her. She was wearing a white dress, petting the rabbits on her lap. The sound of water dripping grew louder, and louder still was another sound—heartbeats? footsteps? It terrified her. Then she looked down and the bunnies in her lap were all dead, their necks broken, their fur matted with blood. That was when she awoke, heart pounding, drenched in sweat, and knew that she had had the dream before.

She pushed herself up in bed, fighting off a heavy-limbed grogginess, and the alarm that thumped in her throat with the unfamiliar surroundings was a second too late, so that by the time it registered she had already remembered: She was in a hospital. The dim yellow glow that bathed the room in ugly phosphorescence was from the nightlights that lined the room at floor level, the metal guard her hand struck when she stretched it out was from the rail of the hospital bed, the dull-witted lethargy was from the sleeping pill they had given her. The smell. Surely that smell, the surface antiseptic odor that disguised the desperate battle to keep death at bay, was strong enough to penetrate even a drug-induced sleep and give her nightmares.

Ellen sat up, breathing shakily, and drew up her knees beneath the skimpy hospital sheet. It all came back: the bridge, the rescue, the doctor called Ben. The day that had started so normally and ended so explosively, with a huge rip across her life on this side of which nothing would ever be the same. Less than twenty-four hours separated the woman she had once been from the woman she was now, but she knew that already. *Nothing would ever be the same.*

Everyone had made such a fuss. Cameras and news people had been waiting for her in the emergency room and she looked awful. She had watched some of the film coverage on the eleven o'clock news and even now she cringed with embarrassment. The doctors and nurses had been almost worse than the reporters, telling her over and over again how lucky she was, making her feel almost guilty for having survived. And when she looked around at the blood-stained gurneys and dazed, battle-shocked faces, she did feel guilty.

She had managed to get a call through to Aunt Gencie, and the nurse who took the phone to her gushed with excitement and relief. The hospital public relations woman had come to talk to her, asking all kinds of questions about her life and her background and how it felt to have been thrust to national attention, which she said she would compile into a brief statement for the press. She was extremely sympathetic and gentle, but Ellen found the entire interview uncomfortable and exhausting. Diane, Ellen's headmistress from Branson, had managed to get through before the switchboard disconnected her phone, which was overloaded from all the calls from media, well-wishers, curiosity seekers, and just plain cranks. And somewhere in the midst of all the craziness, she had lost sight of Ben.

She knew it was probably just a symptom of post-traumatic stress, or whatever they called it, but that moment—when she looked around and saw that her guardian angel was no longer there—was the darkest one in the entire insane, out-of-control day, and the only time she had ever been truly afraid.

She hadn't even been here eight hours and already her room was filled with flowers. The hospital had posted a guard outside her door because people—patients, staff and visitors alike—kept wandering by to look at her, to say hello, to ask questions. They treated her like a heroine. She just wanted to go home.

Ellen was a list maker. Her day, her home, her classroom were all carefully organized and compartmentalized, activities planned, needs prioritized. True, sometimes—oftentimes—the lists were ignored, the plans fell through, and the priorities rearranged. In fact, nothing could serve as a better example of the futility of trying to organize anything than the events of yesterday. Nonetheless, lists were Ellen's way of trying to exercise some control over her life, and lying there alone in the hospital bed, with the remnants of the dream still clinging to the roof of her mouth, the most comforting thing she could do for herself was to make a list.

They said she could go home tomorrow. The first thing she would have to do was call someone to pick her up. No, a taxi. *Call a taxi. Send flowers to one Dr. Ben Bradshaw, a dozen roses. A hundred roses.* She smiled a little, beginning to relax. *Rent a car. Call the insurance agent.* She could handle this. It was going to be okay. Life would go on, a string of lists and chores to be done, lesson plans and staff meetings; nothing, really, was changed and she could handle this.

She was alone in a biliously lit hospital room in the middle of the night, sweating from a dream so vivid she could still smell the blood, and she felt small and afraid and chilled to the bottom of her soul. The dream. It was a stupid dream, a child's

dream, and of course she should have nightmares—
who wouldn't? But she couldn't get the images out
of her mind. The rabbits, broken and twisted in her
lap. Her hands, wet with blood. She squeezed her
eyes tightly closed, but the picture wouldn't go away.
She remembered then, the last time she had had the
dream. It was the night before her mother died.

"Oh, shit," she said out loud, softly, unsteadily.

She drew a deep breath, tried to concentrate on
her list. Groceries. Did she have groceries for the
weekend? No, she had been planning to stop on the
way home from school yesterday. *Buy groceries: milk,
coffee, bread, milk . . .*

The images kept flashing in her head and she
balled her fists against her eyes to blot them out.
Those faces. That sound. *Drip, drip . . .*

She looked at the call button on the edge of her
bed. But who was she going to call? Would another
sleeping pill make the dreams go away? Or would it
simply make her more helpless against them? She
wanted to go home. Why couldn't it just be *over?*
Wouldn't it ever be over?

She squeezed her eyes tightly shut, trying to focus
her thoughts. From deep within her childhood a talis-
man rose up, arcane and comforting, the last resort
of countless night terrors and demon dreams. Something about a valley and a shadow of evil. She
groped for the words. *Yea, though I walk through the
valley of the shadow of death, I shall fear no evil . . .* That
was it. Shadow of death, not shadow of evil. Was
there a difference?

Fear no evil . . . what next? *I shall fear no evil . . .*
But try as she might the rest of the verse eluded her,

phrases slipping through her grasping fingers like beads of oil. She couldn't concentrate. She couldn't remember. And worst of all, she could not get the picture of the rabbits out of her head, and she couldn't stop feeling as though the worst had not even begun.

Sometimes he dreamed about her, his red-haired angel. In his dreams she was young and sweet and she yielded like clay beneath his hands. In his dreams her eyes were big and blue and grateful when they looked into his.

But he knew the difference between dreams and reality and now there was no time to waste on foolishness. For the first time in his life he knew exactly what to do. He had a plan, and he was triumphant with the freedom that knowledge gave him, powerful with the calm of certainty.

At four in the morning, he had awakened from a sound sleep, dressed in jogging sweats and dark running shoes, and had set out on a morning run. He was not a runner. This was not part of his routine, but his feet were weightless, his lungs made of iron. He could have run for hours.

He did not have to. His route took him around the small lake on which his apartment was located, down a wooded path and across a pasture with a picturesque white fence and horses on one side, and into a quiet community known as Cherryville. He had always liked that name. The Cherryville First Methodist Church was on a corner across from a bank and a bakery; the streets that angled off from the corner led to upper-middle-class neighborhoods and shopping districts. Cherryville was the bedroom community for the salaried working class of Durham. Nurses lived there. Upper-management types. Computer salesmen. Jogging was a favorite pastime there.

Daniel took Magnolia Street, which made a semicircle behind the church for six blocks, and within two blocks he was rewarded. It was nearing five-thirty but still pitch black; a neighborhood like this wouldn't start stirring for another hour at least. But a light came on in a white brick ranch at the corner of Magnolia and Cherrywood. He slowed to a walk and when he came around the block a second time she was just coming out the front door. Her dark curly hair was pulled back in a ponytail and she was zipping up the jacket of a running suit over her turtleneck sweater. In the porch light, he could see the color of the sweater was white. Her name was Judy, and he knew her.

He turned back toward the church, where Ariel was waiting for him. Ariel smiled at him. "See?" he said softly. "I told you."

Daniel knew then he could do no wrong.

Of course she would turn east instead of west; of course she would circle behind the church, skirting the dark, empty parking lot for the safety of the mercury vapor lamps on the street corner, the blind eyes of the bank and the bakery gazing across from the other side. There was a security camera at the ATM in the bank parking lot, and lights were on in the back of the bakery, but Daniel wasn't worried. He could do no wrong.

When he heard her footsteps approaching, her smooth runner's stride, his pulse quickened. Ariel gave him a faint encouraging nod and a subtle thumbs-up. Daniel matched his pace to hers and came out of the shadows behind her a hundred yards before the corner. He heard the change in the pace of her breathing, the catch of alarm, and without warning she whirled on him.

The relief in her face was a joy to see. "Daniel!" she gasped. "Good heavens, you scared me to death! What are you doing out here?"

He said, "Hi, Judy," and slit her throat with the scalpel he had concealed in the palm of his hand.

She died quickly, effortlessly, and with a great deal of blood. He carried her into the front door of the church and placed her carefully in a sitting position on the aisle of the third row left. He unzipped her jacket, which was slick with blood, and tossed it aside. He arranged her hands folded in her lap. Her head, with the supportive neck muscles now severed, lolled forward on her chest, which was fine. She looked as though she was praying. Daniel left her to light the altar candles with a book of matches from his pocket. Then he had to take a moment to step back, breathing deeply, and try to comprehend what he had done.

It came upon him suddenly, with black descending wings. He was shaking with awe and terror and the aftermath of physical exertion; the candles pulsed and pounded before his eyes. Dread gripped his spine with a cold hand. He had not expected it to feel this way. It wasn't supposed to feel this way. His head was spinning. He was nauseous.

Ariel laid a quiet, calming hand on his shoulder. "She's beautiful, isn't she?"

"No," he whispered. Even his voice was shaking. "No."

Fingers tightened on his shoulder, pressing the sharp tendon that traversed to his neck. "She is," Ariel repeated firmly.

Daniel knew he was right. He tried to recapture the feeling with which he had awakened that morning—the power, the purpose, the certainty. An hour ago he had been omnipotent. Now . . . "I'm afraid," he said, and it was a great relief to say it, to have the words out where they couldn't hurt him any more.

Ariel's grip on his shoulder gentled, his hand stroked and soothed. "Is that all?" he said tenderly. "Don't you know? Have you forgotten?"

Daniel felt weak, foolish, but no longer quite as afraid. "What?"

Ariel stroked his neck, warm fingers supple and comforting. "Fear no evil," he murmured into Daniel's ear. "For I am with you . . ."

Daniel relaxed as the familiar words came back to him. " 'Thy rod and thy staff, they comfort me, thou annointest my head with oil in the presence of mine enemies . . .' "

Ariel rested his head on Daniel's shoulder, his gaze fixed lovingly on the altar before them, and they finished together, softly, "Surely goodness and mercy shall follow me all the days of my life, and I shall dwell in the house of the Lord forever."

Six

Matthew Graham lived a deliberately ordered, precisely regulated life that he tended with the care of a gardener for a hothouse orchid, and protected as fiercely as a Doberman on patrol. His three-bedroom townhouse was a model of controlled light and structured spaces, furnished in dark fabrics and shiny surfaces, glass and brass and ebony lacquered wood. It was a cop's dream crime scene, commented the few of his compatriots who had ever visited him there—provided, of course, the crime was not committed by Matthew Graham. No smudge or fingerprint had ever lingered on a surface more than a few seconds before being polished away, no mote of dust or fiber or trace of surface soil was allowed to accumulate from one hour to the next. He had even been accused of vacuuming up his own footprints as he crossed a room.

He had a sliver of a view of the Potomac and a glass-doored bookcase filled with leather-bound volumes of Milton and Tolstoy and Dante. He didn't read the books and the glass doors were kept locked because he didn't want dust to damage the covers, but he liked looking at them. The books he read were neatly alphabetized and arranged spines up in the two drawers of his nightstand.

He arose each morning at six, even on weekends. He had tea and biscotti from the Italian bakery two blocks down, and in fair weather watched the world come alive from his balcony with its sliver of a view of the Potomac. He did not look at the papers or turn on the morning news until he had finished this ritual, which Polly termed his "meditation hour."

Polly. She was still the only person he had ever known who could make his knees go weak simply with the thought of her name.

He glanced at the clock on the microwave as he washed and dried his teacup and saucer and put both of them away. Six forty-five. She would be in the shower now, washing her thick auburn hair so that it would dry into the cascade of frizzy curls she liked by the time she had to leave at eight. She went through more shampoo in a week than most people did in a month and Matthew often complained about it, but if the truth were told he liked the frizzy curls too. He missed her desperately, particularly in the mornings. He missed her more the nearer the time drew when he would see her again, for he was superstitiously convinced that anticipation was the harbinger of disaster, ushering in the demons that would somehow, at the last moment, prevent their reunion.

Matthew shook out the crumbs from his wine-red napkin into the trashcan and deposited the napkin in the hamper in the adjacent laundry room. He wiped off the counters, rinsed out the sponge, then used it to polish the last of the water droplets from the stainless-steel sink. A quick, almost careless glance around showed him a kitchen that was as antiseptic and undisturbed as it had been before he entered it.

He knew, of course, that his behavior was borderline obsessive-compulsive—sometimes he thought he might even have crossed the border—but one small lapse in mental health was his only indulgence, and he allowed himself that indulgence gladly. No one had greater need of external control than someone in the midst of internal chaos. And no one had seen more internal chaos—had waded deep into it, had wallowed in it, had eaten, slept, lived and breathed it, had almost choked to death on it—than Matthew Graham.

At six fifty-two he sat down on the sofa and dialed her number. She answered on the third ring.

"Good morning, Sunshine," he said.

"Captain, oh my captain," she returned, and he grinned. It was a private joke between them, and hearing it never failed to make him smile. Sometimes she could make him feel twelve years old again, sometimes as old and as wise as the first man who had ever walked the earth.

"So how's my favorite academic and why is he calling me at this ungodly hour of the morning?"

He could picture her in a white terry robe, phone held to one ear while she massaged a towel over her damp hair with the other hand. *It must be love,* he thought, *when they can break your heart long-distance.* "And when else am I going to be able to snatch a moment from your busy schedule? I miss you, baby."

"Well, I hardly think about you at all."

"Lucky for you, I happen to know you're a chronic

liar. Listen, I talked to the R.V. rental place yesterday and—"

"No, no, *no*," she said, and now he pictured her sitting up straight, dropping the towel, frowning at the phone. "I told you, I'm not going camping with a wuss. It's backpacks and pop-up tents or nothing at all."

"It gets pretty cold in the Shendandoah Valley this time of year."

"That's why God made campfires."

"You're going to miss all your favorite TV shows."

"They're in reruns."

"What about bugs and snakes?"

"I'll keep them away with the force of my personality. Face it, dude, you're going to have to get down and dirty if you're going with me."

He chuckled. "Okay, just remember who offered when you've been two weeks with nothing but freeze-dried food and it's pouring-down rain and you're down to your last pair of clean underwear. A camper could have been yours for the asking."

"Two weeks from today," she said firmly, "you, me, Mother Nature. Be there."

"It's on my calendar."

"Okay. I'm looking at a Delta flight, arriving Richmond two thirty-three in the afternoon. Is that too early for you? Or would you rather me fly straight to Washington and drive down with you? It's cheaper to fly to Richmond," she added conscientiously.

He smiled as he jotted down the numbers on the telephone pad. Her frugality was one of her most endearing traits, despite the fact that it sometimes frustrated and always baffled him. "Sweetheart, if you managed my budget I'd be a rich man today."

"Hey, I've offered."

"The Richmond flight sounds fine. Somebody told me about a B&B just south of town I think you'd like. We can spend the night and get an early start for the wilderness in the morning."

"B&B is it?" She pretended to stifle a groan. "God, you're turning into such an old maid."

"Watch your mouth, young lady. I'll have you know you're talking to one of J. Edgar Hoover's finest."

"*The* finest," she corrected softly, and the pride and affection in her voice made his throat tight.

Then she said, in a tone that was a little too casual, a little too carefully nonchalant, "So, we're definitely on, then? Thursday, May first, two-thirty-three, Richmond? Because this is a nonrefundable fare, you know."

And because he had only spent half his life breaking promises, missing appointments, making a reputation for preferring the company of twisted, psychotic killers to that of the ones he loved. Because Polly knew better than anyone that he could not be counted on and that truth twisted in his gut with dull knife-points of guilt.

But that was the old Matthew. This was one appointment he intended to keep. "I'll be there," he said. "Just make sure you are."

"Wouldn't miss it." Her voice was cautiously relieved. "I'll make the reservations today."

"Call me with the flight number."

"Sure thing."

He smiled, holding on to the connection for no other reason than that he couldn't bear to let her go. "I love you, sweetheart."

"Back at you, Captain. More than life."

He hung up the phone, still smiling, and turned to the morning papers. He was ready to face the day.

Ben was awakened by a raucous ringing that wouldn't stop. Two huge dogs bounded from the bed and left the room, barking. The ringing persisted. He picked up the phone and got a dead line, then remembered he had unplugged it. He fumbled for the clock radio and knocked it over. He found his beeper and turned it off. Swearing, he stumbled to the front door in his boxers and wrinkled teeshirt, shoving dogs aside as he went, and saw George Wayhill standing on the stoop, brandishing a stack of newspapers and a white paper sack from the deli. Ben let him in.

"So how does it feel to be a hero?" George demanded. He made his way inside holding the deli sack out of the dog's reach.

"Like a three-day hangover." Ben leaned on the open door, ran a hand over his face, and stared at George dully. The dogs, having thoroughly inspected the visitor, lost interest and went outside. Ben closed the door. "Am I wrong, or is this my weekend off?"

"You're wrong." George tossed the newspapers on the dining table and opened the sack. "But you're covered. We figured it might have slipped your mind."

Ben said, "Shit."

"Well spoken. May I quote you on that?" George

took two large cups of coffee from the sack, popped the lids, and offered one to Ben.

George Wayhill was one of the senior partners in the clinic, which meant that he spent more time on his boat than he did practicing medicine. He had recruited Ben, and in the six months he had been on board Ben had come to like George despite—or perhaps because of—his cavalier attitude toward business, medicine, and life in general.

Ben took the coffee and sprawled in a low chair, rubbing a hand over his face one more time to clear the cobwebs of sleep. He winced a little at the irritation of sunburn that brought back the incredible events of the day before. "I didn't get to bed till after three," he said, and took a careful sip of the coffee. "You wouldn't believe the people who called after they saw me on the news."

"Oh, I might." George's tone was bland as he rummaged in the deli sack and brought out an oversized muffin. "One of them wouldn't happen to have been Dan Rather, would it?"

Ben sat up straight. "As in *the* Dan Rather?"

"And I can't vouch for it, but Marian claims she talked to Oprah Winfrey's personal assistant yesterday." Marian was their receptionist.

"You're kidding me."

George shrugged and took a bite out of the muffin.

Ben grinned, only a little self-consciously. "Well, what do you know? Celebrity doctor. I kind of like the sound of that."

"Don't get too used to it. The practice has decided to consult a publicist—we'll split the cost fifty-fifty with you—but we're definitely leaning toward the low-profile position on this. No talk shows, no tabloids, no television interviews. A general release statement, maybe a tasteful sidebar for *Newsweek*— that's it."

Ben stared at him. "Wait a minute. You're serious."

"Have to be. Corporate image and all that." He glanced at his watch, popped the last bite of the muffin into his mouth, and went on. "Steddle's taking your shift Monday. We'll have a staff meeting tonight—you're invited, of course—about seven. We've got Lynn and Shelly working on your messages, but drop by and pick them up sometime today, will you? Oh, and the lawyers want to meet with you at three about exposure."

Ben felt his day—hell, his life—slipping out of his control. He repeated blankly, "Exposure?"

George, slick and tan in tennis whites and gold Rolex, crossed his ankles and sipped his coffee. "You treated a lot of people on that bridge. Very much against the rules, by the way; read your employee handbook. Some of them might not be as nice as the schoolteacher. The ones you didn't treat might be even less nice. The lawyers think we're covered, but they want to get the facts anyway."

"From hero to liability in five minutes flat," Ben said. "Thanks for the ride."

"You bet." He looked again at his watch and put down the coffee cup. "I've got a game in twenty minutes. I stopped by the hospital this morning, by the way, and the girl is doing fine. I signed the discharge order."

It only demonstrated Ben's state of mind that for a moment he did not know who "the girl" was. "Oh.

Thanks." In fact, he was a little irritated. He didn't like the partners overseeing his patients, and he had intended to make Ellen's hospital room his first stop this morning. "Let the dogs in, will you?"

At the door George paused. "Just between you and me," he said, "and keeping in mind that my opinion doesn't necessarily reflect that of the practice or the partners—good job."

Ben waited until he was gone to comment on that with a half-rueful, half-incredulous shake of his head.

He gave the dogs their breakfast and found a couple of banana-nut muffins in the deli bag. He sat down at the table and opened the first of the newspapers George had left. He stared at the front-page photograph. He reached for the next paper. And the next.

"Holy shit," he said softly.

He was beginning to understand.

At the editorial meeting of the *Wintersville Herald* in Wintersville, West Virginia, Ray Mischler, editor in chief, looked at his top reporter and inquired, "Why is there a hole in the middle of my front page? You know, the one that was supposed to feature what is no doubt the most famous photograph in the country right now and the headline, 'Local Woman in Dramatic Rescue.' What happened to that story, Mike? Please don't tell me you misplaced it."

Mike Bethune, lead reporter on a three-reporter paper, chewed laconically on the end of a pencil for another moment before answering, "Didn't lose the story. Lost the girl."

Mischler took off his glasses and polished them, waiting.

"Somebody once told me to check my facts before printing them," Mike explained. "Turns out Miss Ellen Cox of Wintersville, West Virginia wasn't born in Wintersville after all. Not only was she not born here, she never even lived here."

"Maiden name?"

"Never been married."

"Another Wintersville?" His tone was heavy with defeat.

"Not in West Virginia."

"Well, hell. Why would she lie?"

Mike shrugged. "If I was going to make up a place to be from, I sure think I could do better than Wintersville, West Virginia. You get this from Associated Press?"

"Along with every other news organization in the country. Come on, Mike, don't do this to me. We're a town with a population of thirty-five hundred. This may be our only claim to fame this century. Track it down, will you?"

Mike stood up. "You want to authorize a trip to Virginia Beach?"

His editor returned a dry look. "*Without* any travel expense, if you don't mind. And get it nailed by noon tomorrow, we can still make this week's edition. Be sure to interview everybody who knows anybody who ever knew her—schoolteachers, neighbors, babysitters, boyfriend from the third grade. You know the kind of thing."

"You got it. The impossible is my daily fare."

"Hell, talk to old Doc Parson. He's delivered every baby in this town since 1946. He's bound to remember her."

"Bet he didn't deliver this one."

"Well, talk to the woman herself. How hard can it be? Tell her we're naming a park after her or something."

"I imagine her phone's pretty tied up these days. You know these press sharks."

"Yeah, and every one of them with a park in his back pocket. Just get the story Mike, will you, for crying out loud? And don't screw it up or you can kiss your chance at a Pulitzer good-bye."

Mike sauntered toward the door. "I'm telling you: Wrong woman, wrong town."

"Why would she lie?" repeated Mischler, a little plaintively now.

And Mike replied, "Maybe *that's* the story."

Seven

Diane Virion was a fifty-six-year-old African-American woman with a comfortably expansive girth, a penchant for colorful flowing scarves, and a complete lack of inhibition about speaking her mind, loudly and clearly, on any subject whatsoever. She was not only Ellen's headmistress, she was her closest friend, and the strongest woman Ellen had ever known. She had lost most of her hearing to nerve damage at age ten.

"Hell, sweetie, doctors were ignorant back then—colored *and* white," she had told Ellen once. "Breaks my heart to think how many sweet children lost their hearing on account of that ignorance. They told my mama I had a bad cold and what did she know? What I had was diphtheria, can you believe it? Diphtheria in 1950 in the United States. The fever didn't burn out my brain—though my second husband would sometime set to arguing with me about that!—so I'm lucky all I lost was my hearing. I tell you the truth, with eight brothers and sisters to take care of it was a month or two before I even noticed and when I did I was grateful for the quiet."

She liked to tell people that she had gotten the job

at Branson because the administrators considered it politically correct to hire a deaf black woman, but five minutes in her presence was all that was required to dispel that myth. She *was* Branson, its heart and soul, its commander and its navigator, mother to every staff member and student who walked through its doors.

Hearing aids had restored partial hearing, enough to allow her to drive and use a telephone with an amplifier, and to distinguish most sounds in the middle frequency range. It was an imperfect improvement, however, and except when the occasion specifically demanded it she did not wear the hearing aids. For the most part, Diane preferred to deal with the world the way she had always done—through excellent lipreading skills and force of personality.

When she strode through the door of the hospital room, arms open wide and long purple and black scarves fluttering, Ellen felt for the first time since the accident as though there might be a chance to return to the life she once had known. Ellen stepped silently into her embrace and let herself be enfolded.

"I was so scared," she whispered against Diane's shoulder, knowing she couldn't hear and needing to say it for precisely that reason. "So scared."

Diane pushed her away and held her face, looking at her severely. Ellen smiled weakly. "I said I was scared," she said.

"Of course you were," pronounced Diane in that perfectly enunciated, only slightly overloud tone that was the result of her deafness and a trademark of her personality. "Be a fool if you weren't. Now look at you." She stepped away, dropping her hands to

Ellen's shoulders, and raked her eyes over her critically. "What in the world are you wearing, girl? Do you have any idea how many people are down in that lobby waiting to talk to you?"

Ellen gestured to the wrinkled sweater and skirt she had been wearing when she left the house yesterday morning, a century ago. "It's all I have." Automatically, she began supplementing her words with American Sign Language, which was a habit when she was with Diane—and because she always felt more comfortable expressing herself with the secret language of her hands than with words. "The nurse told me there were reporters in the lobby, but they can't be wanting to talk to me. Diane, I didn't do anything! What do they want with me? God, do you know how many people died yesterday? How many were maimed and crippled for life right here in this hospital? I heard someone say they turned the lounges into overflow wards and transferred patients to as far away as Portsmouth to make room for all the injured! My God, what do they want with *me*?"

Diane smiled tenderly, her own hands moving in her subtle signature style, reflecting her words. "Darling girl, they want to touch you. They want your magic to rub off on them. You survived, that's all. You beat the odds, and that made you important."

Ellen drew a breath for more protest, but then changed her mind, hugging her arms to choke off the words. She wished it were as easy to push back the images that had been bombarding her from the television all morning. Broken bodies on stretchers, people weeping and holding each other, broken concrete and smoky dust rising, and her own car balanced so precariously on the edge.

In a moment she managed, turning so Diane could read her lips, "Do you think I'll ever get over this?"

Diane answered, "No."

But Ellen took strength from the other woman's gaze, and after a moment she felt the tight knots of tension begin to seep out of the muscles of her shoulders. She said, "Thanks for coming, Diane."

Diane snorted. "Like I wouldn't? It's not as though you could exactly drive yourself home, now is it?"

Ellen smiled. "I was going to call a taxi."

"Save your money. Now, do we have to wait for that sweet young doctor to say it's okay, or are you ready to go?"

Now Ellen's smile turned a little wan. "Actually, I haven't seen that sweet young doctor since the emergency room. The nurse said his partner was taking his rounds today, so I don't guess I'll see him again. I wish I could, though. I'm not sure I thanked him for what he did."

"You did."

The voice came from the doorway and Ellen turned, a delighted smile breaking over her face. Diane followed her expression and nodded approvingly when she saw Ben standing at the threshold with a bouquet of roses in his hand.

"I was going to send you roses!" Ellen exclaimed.

And he said at the same time, "I was hoping I would get here before you left."

They both laughed a little awkwardly, then Ben said, gesturing, "Should I keep these and save you the trouble?"

Ellen came forward quickly. "Thank you, it was sweet." She took the roses as his gaze traveled to the dozens of vases and bouquets that already crowded every surface. "They're from people I don't even know," she explained, still feeling warm-cheeked and awkward. "I don't know why. I asked the nurses to distribute them to the patients who really needed them."

Diane came forward, her hand extended. "Diane Virion, and it's a pleasure to shake your hand, young man. What you did yesterday should serve as an example to every man, woman, and child in this country, and besides, you saved the life of someone mighty precious to me."

"I didn't save her life," Ben said. He seemed embarrassed. "But it's a pleasure to meet you anyway."

He turned to Ellen. "Just in case you were allergic to roses, I brought you something else." He produced a small flat package sloppily wrapped in Christmas paper. "I thought you might like it for your scrapbook."

Ellen shifted the bouquet to one arm and curiously unwrapped the package. It was a framed photograph clipped from a newspaper. The photograph was of her at the moment of rescue, the wind whipping back her hair, her face awash with tears of relief and gratitude, her arms extended as she reached for Ben. A chill went through her, a dread and nauseating sense of déjà vu, and another image flashed before her eyes, another girl—*rabbits, splashed with blood*—then it was gone. She swallowed hard and made herself look up at him, not knowing what to say. She wouldn't have been able to speak if she *had* known.

"It was on the front pages of at least seven newspapers this morning," he said, "probably a lot more around the country."

Ellen looked at the framed clipping again and tried to imagine hundreds of thousands of people looking at this photograph, thinking about her, thinking this was all there was to her. She wasn't even sure how she felt about that; she couldn't possibly put her feelings into words. "My fifteen minutes of fame, huh?"

Ben looked a little uncomfortable now. "Maybe it wasn't a good idea. I just thought you might like to have it."

"No." She looked up at him again. "It's important." She wished then that her hands weren't full, that she could have used them to embellish the statement with what she really meant—the moment was important, the memory was important, the symbol was important; it was important that she have this life-shattering event reduced to a five-by-seven framed photograph that she could hold in her hands. Of course, even if she could have signed the words Ben would not have know what she meant, but oddly, when she looked at him she had the feeling he already understood. So she finished simply, "Thank you."

Then she said, "I'm glad you came."

He made a deprecating gesture with his wrist. "I should have gotten here earlier. It's been kind of hectic."

She smiled. "How are the dogs?"

"Big. Loud. Hungry."

"I'm glad you came," she repeated.

He said, "Me, too."

Diane watched the interchange with interest. She said, "So, Ben. You're a doctor. Family practice or specialty?"

He turned to her politely, though Ellen liked to imagine it was with a certain amount of reluctance. That made her smile.

He told Diane, "General medicine. I work for the Hillsborough Medical Group. We have a clinic beachside."

She nodded approvingly. "The world needs more good old-fashioned family doctors. Do you live near here, Ben? Own your own home?"

"Condo, actually. North side of the beach."

"Well, a single man doesn't need much more."

Ellen was becoming embarrassed. "Diane . . ."

Diane signed, *So far, so good*, and addressed herself to Ben. "You've never been married, Ben?"

He was clearly amused. "No, I never had the time."

"Neither has Ellen. You have a lot in common that way." She looked smug and signed, *Good catch*.

Ben signed back, *Actually, I was more interested in you*.

Diane burst into laughter and Ellen looked at him in astonishment.

"Sorry, I should have told you," Ben said, grinning. "I worked summers at a center for handicapped children during college, and I learned to sign. It's been years, though. I'm surprised I remembered."

Diane chuckled. "He'll do, Ellen, sweetie. Now, Ben, how about giving the lady a ride home? I believe I heard she was having trouble with her car."

Ellen protested, "But I thought you—"

Diane waved a dismissing hand. "All part of the plan. I'm meeting a couple of the teachers at your house; we thought you might need help dealing with all the pies and cakes and tuna casseroles folks will be bringing over." She turned to Ben confidentially. "I don't know what it is about neighbors that makes them think whatever the problem, food's the cure, but Lord, it sure is nice to have them! So don't you worry," she added to Ellen. "We'll deal with all your company until you get there. Take your time."

Ellen realized what a truly large service Diane's thoughtfulness was providing when she remembered all the reporters in the lobby, and the cameras that were sure to be following her every move—even to her doorstep and beyond. Her eyes flashed with grateful tears and she hugged her friend hard. "Thank you."

They walked on the beach, carrying their shoes. The wind was cool off the Atlantic, the water icy where it lapped at their toes. The sky was as blue as it had ever been, the sand so bright it hurt their eyes. Ellen did not know why they had ended up here, or how long they had been walking, or whether they had talked at all.

She said, "Isn't there something called survivor's syndrome?"

"Do you mean where the colors are brighter and the smells sharper and everything you see makes you happy?"

"I feel like the first woman to ever walk the earth. I feel so powerful I could fly . . . and so scared, sometimes, I can hardly breathe."

"What are you scared of?"

She shook her head. The wind tossed her hair across one cheek and then blew it back. She squinted her eyes in the sun to avoid looking at him. "Nothing. It's stupid. Bad dreams. And that photograph— it made me feel weird. As though I was looking at someone else and . . ." She struggled for the words and, even when she spoke, knew they weren't precisely right. "As though what happened to that girl, the one in the photograph, was somehow worse than what happened to me. It frightened me." She shrugged self-consciously, and pushed at her windblown hair. "I told you it was weird."

"I think it's probably pretty normal." He hesitated. "You know the Red Cross and the hospitals will be setting up counseling centers to deal with the problems of survivors. If the dreams get too bad, it might help."

She glanced at him. "What about this thing with us? Will counseling help that?"

He was studious and silent for a time. "You must mean the thing that's making me try to figure out some way to keep you here all day when I know your friend expected you home an hour ago."

"After what happened we shouldn't want to be around each other any more. We shouldn't want to be around anything that reminds us of the bridge. But I didn't feel safe until I saw you again. Is this going to turn into some kind of weird dependency disease?"

"Very possible," he allowed. "And I suppose I'll be the codependent."

"Or maybe you'll just develop a hero complex. You

71

know, where you don't feel validated unless you have someone to rescue."

"Fortunately, both conditions are treatable. I'm just not sure I want to be cured."

She smiled. "You might be sorry. You don't know anything about me."

"Are you kidding? I probably know more about your life story than you do."

"You're right. What I meant to say is that I don't know anything about you."

"You know the important parts."

"I didn't even know you could sign."

"But I'm a good catch."

"So I've heard."

He said, "I'd like to see you again."

She just smiled as they walked back to the car.

When Ben pulled into the driveway of her house— a two-bedroom cottage in a neighborhood that catered mostly to Navy families—a banner constructed of butcher paper was stretched over the small entry porch that read "Welcome Home Ellen." The house was filled with people from school and people from the neighborhood, most of whom she had never met, with food and drink and Diane presiding contentedly over all. Ellen wept because until that moment she had truly never realized there were that many people in the world who knew she existed or cared what became of her one way or the other at all.

Ben stayed. They filled their plates with pasta salads and cream-based casseroles and ate on the small back deck in the sunshine. The neighbors were kind and cheerful and didn't stay too long. She told the story more times than she cared to, listened to far more accounts of other people's experiences than she wanted, but in its own way that, too, was therapeutic. The telephone never stopped ringing, but it wasn't until the party was beginning to wind down—when only Diane, a couple of the neighbors, and Ben remained to help with the clean-up—that Ellen, banned from kitchen duty and feeling guilty over all the attention she was receiving, answered it herself.

The voice on the other end sounded relieved when she confirmed, however cautiously, that she was indeed Ellen Cox. "I've been trying to reach you all day," he said. "I've left several messages. This is Mike Bethune from the *Wintersville Herald* in Wintersville West Virginia."

Ellen almost groaned out loud when she realized she was talking to yet another reporter, and then she recognized the name of her hometown paper. Still, her voice was carefully restrained as she said, "Yes?"

"First of all, I want you to know that the hearts of everyone in the town were with you yesterday on that bridge."

"Thank you."

He wasted no more time with small talk. "I'm covering the story for the paper and well, this might sound like a crazy question, but the information we have is that you were born here in Wintersville, right?"

"That's right."

"Wintersville, West Virginia," he repeated, with a slight emphasis on the "West." "Colquitt County."

"That's right," she replied, a little amused. "Why do you ask? Is there another Wintersville?"

He was silent for a moment. "No. You're sure it was West Virginia, not Virginia."

Now she was puzzled. "Of course, I'm sure. You don't mistake your birth state. We moved away when I was twelve, and people used to tease me about my coal miner's accent."

"There's hardly a trace of it now," he said graciously.

"Thank you." She wasn't sure why she was thanking him, only that she wanted to end the conversation. "If that's all—"

"Actually, I was trying to get some background information on you—you know, talk to some of the people in town who had known you as a child—and we couldn't find any trace of you. Was your name changed by any chance?"

Ellen frowned. "Of course not. I was born in Wintersville and I lived there until I was twelve years old. My parents were Jim and Rita Cox. My daddy worked for the telephone company."

He seemed to be writing this down. "So there are probably people there who remember him?"

"I suppose. I don't know. It's been a long time." Now she was growing a little uncomfortable. "Listen, I don't know why you want to talk to my parents' friends anyway. Both of them passed away some time ago and—"

"But the people here are very concerned with your story, Ellen," he assured her. "It's such a small town everyone has connections with everyone else and when something like this happens everyone is involved. You went to school here, then?"

"Nathaniel Hawthorne Elementary," she confirmed. "And I went to Blessed Hope Community Church, right there on the corner of Broad and Angel Street. The pastor is bound to remember my family. My parents were very active in the church. But I really just want to say I don't see the point of your story. I didn't do anything except happen to be in the wrong place at the wrong time. I'm not a hero. I'm not the one you should be writing about. There were dozens of people on that bridge who were saving lives, risking themselves to help other people. Those are the ones you should be writing about."

He was silent long enough for Ellen to begin to feel a small, vain sense of satisfaction in the belief that her noble speech had made him reconsider. Then he said in an odd, remote tone, "Ellen, there is no Nathaniel Hawthorne Elementary School in Wintersville. No Blessed Hope Church, either."

She was taken aback. "You must be mistaken."

"I'm looking at a city directory right now."

"Well . . ." Her mind stuttered with confusion. "Then, I guess the names must have changed. Names change, don't they?"

Mike Bethune said, "There is one elementary school, one junior high, and one high school in this county. None of them are called Nathaniel Hawthorne and I should know. I've lived here all my life and I went to all three. I'll tell you something else. We have a Broad Street, but no Angel Street."

Ellen didn't know what to say. She was vaguely aware of Ben's questioning look as he entered the room, and she half-turned from him, unable to meet his eyes. Her heart was racing and she felt a dim and inexplicable sense of dread that reminded her of the way she had felt when Ben presented her with the framed photograph. She swallowed hard but still couldn't speak.

The reporter's voice was kinder now, although that expression seemed forced. "Ellen, I'm just trying to get my facts straight. Imagine how embarrassing it would be for us—for *you*—if we've got the wrong hometown. If you could just give me something to work with here—"

Ellen heard Diane come in, talking to one of the neighbors who had two empty casserole dishes in her hand. She felt suddenly crowded, breathless, out of control. She couldn't deal with this reporter now. He was obviously mistaken, possibly insane, and maybe not even a reporter at all. She said abruptly, "I'm sorry. I'm afraid I can't help you." And she hung up the phone.

For what seemed like a half-second too long Ellen simply stared at the telephone, and that was enough to bring a worried frown to Diane's face and to cause Ben to ask, "Something wrong?"

She managed an unconvincing smile as she turned away from the phone, gesturing. "That was a reporter from my hometown paper."

"Wintersville, West Virginia," supplied Ben promptly, and Ellen felt a ridiculous surge of relief, as though hearing him saying it was more of a validation for her birthplace than her own memory.

"That's right," she said. "Only he claims I wasn't born there at all."

Ben arched an eyebrow. "That is strange."

"Turn off the phone," Diane advised.

"Not only does he say there's no record of my birth there, he insists that the school and the church I went to don't even exist."

"It's got to be the wrong town," Ben said with such matter-of-fact confidence that Ellen felt a little foolish for her own uneasiness.

Still, she felt compelled to argue, "Not according to him. He had the right county. It just makes me feel weird."

Diane repeated, "Unplug the phone." Then she held out her arms. "Have to go, sweetie. You have yourself a nice rest and if you need more time off you just let me know."

Ellen hugged her hard, then stepped back to allow her friend to read her lips. "Thank you, Diane, for everything. I never knew . . ." But she couldn't quite finish that, both because her voice choked and because she did not know how to put the depth of her emotion into words. She signed instead, "How much it means to have a friend."

Diane smiled and patted her cheek. "Then it's about time. I'm glad you're still with us, dear heart."

When she was gone, there was only Ben and Ellen. Ben said, "If it's still bothering you about that reporter, why don't you just fax him a copy of your birth certificate?"

Ellen looked at him, grateful not only for the suggestion but for the sensitivity that had prompted him to make it. "It does bother me," she admitted. "I know it's silly, but it does. It was as though he was accusing me of lying."

"A lot of towns have the same name, or sound alike, and as widely publicized as that picture has been, everyone is going to want to believe they have the inside scoop. Probably it was an honest mistake."

"Maybe." Her tone was a little grudging. "But I like the idea of sending him my birth certificate. Gosh, now he's got *me* wondering if I know where I was born."

Ben smiled. "Do you know how long it's been since I knew a girl who said 'gosh'?"

Ellen said, "Do you know how long it's been since I allowed anyone to call me a girl?"

He grinned. "Sorry."

"Would you like to stay for dinner?" She knew how foolish that sounded the moment it was spoken, since they had only just finished lunch, and she flushed with embarrassment.

"Yes," Ben answered, "but I can't. I was supposed to be somewhere half an hour ago. I have the rest of the weekend off, though, and Monday, I think. Do you like to sail?"

"Do you have a boat?"

"I can get one."

"Then I like to sail."

He smiled. "I'll call you in the morning."

"I'm glad I met you, Ben," Ellen said. "And for more than the obvious reasons."

His expression gentled. "Me, too. But you still don't know anything about me."

"I know you're a good catch."

He laughed and turned for the door. "So I've heard." Then he looked back. "I gave you my card, didn't I? You know you can call if you need anything before tomorrow."

Ellen felt a surge of emotion—pleasure, contentment, wonder, and gratitude—that was so intense she was almost giddy. She had never been much of a philosophical person, but was it possible that something this good could happen from something so bad?

She said, "Yes, I know." And that was the most miraculous thing. She did know.

His expression was tender and amused. "I'll see you tomorrow, then. Meanwhile, take care. And stay off of bridges."

"You, too."

The euphoria she had named "survivor's high" was easily recaptured then, and overcame even the irritation caused by the reporter from Wintersville. It lasted the afternoon and well into the evening, until she went into the bedroom and discovered Diane had arranged Ben's roses in a vase on her dresser, and beside them the framed photograph from the newspaper.

Ellen couldn't sleep that night until she put the photograph away, and still she had nightmares.

Eight

Daniel discussed it with Ariel, and they agreed there was no reason to inconvenience anyone by varying his routine. He made his rounds, went to the bank, took care of the myriad small details that were required for an extended absence.

At the hospital he picked up a supply of scalpel blades and surgical gloves, slipping both into his briefcase and making the necessary adjustments on the inventory list from Central Supply. Then, following Ariel's instructions, he slipped a single capped hypodermic syringe into his pocket—such a small item would not be missed—and accessed the controlled substances inventory to disguise the loss of one vial of Seconal. It bothered him, taking the drug, but Ariel had insisted. And the actual theft was easier than he had expected. Hospitals didn't have security cameras, and the pharmacy was appallingly lax about restricting access to their supply shelves. He simply dropped the vial into his pocket and walked out. No one stopped him, despite the fact that he was sweating with guilt, his heart pounding so loudly it should have been audible to police cruisers three blocks away.

"Next time, you do your own dirty work," he told Ariel angrily when he arrived home. "I'm not a petty thief."

Ariel examined the bottle Daniel removed from his pocket with amusement. "Certainly not. This is possession of a narcotic, and that makes you a felon."

Daniel glared at him. "I don't have to listen to you, you know. I don't have to take you with me."

"You'd be lost without me," Ariel returned impatiently. "What about the other things? Did you get them?"

But Daniel set his jaw stubbornly. "I'm not a thief," he repeated. "I don't have to do what you say."

"You're not a thief," Ariel allowed, forcing reason into his tone. "But you *do* have to do what I say. You know that, don't you?"

Daniel hesitated.

"Don't you?"

Daniel turned away, a tacit admission of his own inability to argue with what was so obviously true. "I got the other things," he said. "I don't understand what we need them for."

"You want everything to be perfect, don't you? Let me see."

Daniel unpacked his purchases and spread them across the dining table. A gold-plated cross on a chain. A child's polo shirt, red and white striped. A man's plaid shirt. A teddy bear with jointed limbs. Other things, odds and ends, the pieces of perfection. Ariel touched each one of them in turn, smiling with approval.

"You'll be glad I remembered these things when the time comes," Ariel told him. "You wait and see."

"It seems like a lot to keep up with."

"That's what you have me for. I'll help." And when Daniel wanted to object again he added, "It's for her. For Ellen, and for you. It has to be perfect. You won't get another chance."

After a moment, Daniel nodded. He knew Ariel was right. He always was.

At noon he made a point of watching the news, not for his own small part in it but because he knew the airways would still be filled with images of Ellen. And he was right. The rescue photograph had become a logo for the tragedy; snippets of the film were shown over and over again, highlighting clean-up efforts. On the local front, the bizarre death of one Judy McFarlane, a thirty-two-year-old nurse at Regional Medical Center, didn't even make the first five minutes of the broadcast.

Daniel washed and dried his lunch dishes and put them away, sponging off the counters and sweeping the kitchen floor. He didn't like to leave a mess, no matter how long he was going to be gone. Even though he knew that this time the likelihood was that he would not be coming home at all.

He packed a small bag of necessities, including the items he had purchased. He unplugged his appliances, closed the blinds. These small rituals were empowering, calming, a confirmation that the time was indeed at hand, the miracle was about to unfold, his destiny was near. He was in control.

At his desk he hesitated. He even went so far as to unlock his drawer and take out his collection of photographs, touching each one in turn with an almost superstitious reverence. He wanted to take them with him, but Ariel put a staying hand over his. "Leave them," he advised softly. "You did well to get this far with them, but you don't need them any more."

Once again, Ariel was right. Daniel closed the drawer.

He took out the trash, put his mail on hold, unplugged his phones. He was on the road in good daylight, well before rush hour.

At dusk, Ariel made him stop at a roadside tavern, where he met a thin blond young man who said he was on his way to Chapel Hill and could use a ride. What he was really proposing was sex. Daniel said he thought they could work something out.

They were in Virginia before dark.

SATURDAY, APRIL 19

Nine

Ellen was a little shy about seeing Ben again until she saw the two massive white canine heads peering out from each of the Jeep Cherokee's two windows: one was wearing a straw hat with sunglasses fastened to the crown, the other a stylish gray fedora. She burst into laughter.

"They're also great at parties," Ben admitted with a grin.

Ellen looked up at him, still laughing, as they walked to the Jeep. "You always know just what to do, don't you?"

He said with a shrug, "I thought we might need an icebreaker." Then, hesitantly, "It still seems a little weird, doesn't it?"

Ellen didn't flinch from his gaze or try to make light of the question. She agreed simply, "Yes."

The drive to the marina was a hilarity of dogs and sunshine, and Ellen's mood skyrocketed. She could not help wondering whether every laughter-filled moment of her life from now on would seem this precious, this remarkable . . . or whether it was only those moments spent with Ben.

At the marina she got out of the car and took off

her sunglasses in awe as she gazed at the thirty-foot cabin cruiser Ben had indicated they were to board. "Wow," she said, a little reverently, "you surely do know how to go in style, Dr. Ben. This is what you call a boat?"

Ben, busy with leashes and water bowls, replied ruefully, "This is what my boss calls a boat. I call it a luxury liner."

"And he lets you borrow it?"

"Sure. As long as I don't bring the dogs." He handed the leashes to Ellen and proceeded to set up the boarding ramp for the dogs.

"What I mean is, are you sure you know how to drive this thing? It *is* awfully big."

"I come from a Navy family, remember? I was born on the water."

Ellen's apprehension eased once they were out of dock. Ben was obviously at home on the big cruiser, and so were his dogs, who, now relieved of their funny hats, joyfully paced from one rail to the other, heads turned to the wind. As soon as they were out of the main traffic areas, Ben cut the engines and let the boat drift. Ellen stretched out in a wooden deck chair and turned her face to the sun.

"Who is this boss of yours, anyway?" she murmured appreciatively, letting her eyes drift closed behind the dark glasses. "I'll have to remember to send him a thank-you note."

"Do me a favor, though, and don't mention the dogs." Ben sat down beside her, two frosty tumblers of orange juice in his hands. He offered one to her, and then stretched out in his own deck chair.

Ellen tasted the drink and lifted an approving eyebrow. "Champagne," he noted. "Nice touch."

Ben lifted his glass to her. "Old George does have style, I'll say that for him. And he keeps a very well stocked bar."

"I never knew a doctor who worked *for* anyone before," Ellen said, taking another luxurious sip. "How did that happen?"

"It's a sign of the times. Most of the larger practices are set up like law firms now, with senior partners and associates. It's the only way they can hold off the HMOs. I have an employment contract that guarantees salary, benefits, office space, equipment, and things like that, and provides for me to buy into the partnership after a certain length of service. It's not a bad deal, especially for someone just starting out."

Ellen rested her cheek on the weatherproof chair cushion to look at him. "So tell me, Ben. Why hasn't a guy like you been snapped up already? Are you involved with anyone?"

Ben, squinting into the sun, made his expression wistful. "Relationships," he murmured. "I remember those. Seems like the last time I had time for one was in 1983." He took a sip of his drink. "I was seeing someone, up until last year. Another doctor, if you can believe that, as though one of us in residency wasn't crazy enough. She bailed out six weeks before I got this job offer, which only goes to show what a lack of vision can do. Another few months and all this—" he waved the hand that held the glass "— could have been hers."

"Her loss."

"You bet. What about you? Any present or former relationships you want to talk about?"

"You asked me that before." She couldn't bring herself to be more specific than that. She didn't have to.

"Did I? What did you say?"

"Present relationships, none. Former relationships not worth mentioning."

"What a coincidence."

She smiled. "Yeah."

They were silent for a time, baking in the sun and riding the gentle roll of the surf. One of the dogs—Samson, Ellen thought it was—flopped down beside her chair, panting heavily, and she lowered her hand to stroke his thick fur.

Then Ben said, "You know what we haven't talked about once."

"Yeah." Ellen kept her eyes closed, and her voice was as lazy and as unconcerned as she felt. "It's been nice."

"As though we might actually have something in common besides disaster."

Ellen opened her eyes and looked at him. "As though we can be around each other without being reminded of something horrible."

Ben nodded soberly. In his casual white ducks and open windbreaker, with the sun spilling over his wind-tossed hair and bronzing his face, he looked good to her, better than she remembered, and different somehow. He was more than the man on the bridge now; he was starting to become a whole person. That was a good thing, she knew, and it excited her—and frightened her.

"It's good to get away for a while," Ben said. "To pretend it didn't happen, even if only for an hour or two. This is the only place I could think of that would be possible."

"I feel guilty," Ellen said quietly, looking into her half-empty glass. All morning, and until this moment, she had been able to keep that feeling at bay. She realized now that the guilt was not something she wanted to deny, or that was healthy to ignore. "I can't really pretend it didn't happen, you know. It's always lurking there in the background, something that's going to be as much a part of me from now on as the color of my hair or the memory of my first piano recital. And I feel guilty for trying to walk away from it."

Ben said, "The partners won't let me work this weekend. Both of the hospitals we admit to have put out a call for help but I'm off the list. It's frustrating as hell."

Ellen said, "They probably think it would be too stressful for you."

"That might be part of it," Ben agreed grudgingly. "But mostly they're just trying to cover their asses from liability. I was with lawyers three hours yesterday. They finally decided I might not have done irreparable damage to my professional future or the partners' insurability by practicing medicine when it was most needed." He took a swift drink, then frowned at the glass as though disappointed it contained nothing more potent than champagne. "It makes me crazy."

"I'm sorry," Ellen said, with genuine feeling. "When I think of all the people you helped and how much it meant for them just to have you there—and then to be censured for it—it must be hard." She dropped her eyes to her glass again. "It's hard for me to think how many more you might have helped if you hadn't stayed with me all day."

Ben made a stifled sound of bitter amusement. "According to the lawyers, the only thing I did right was stay with you. It kept me from 'extending the exposure,' I believe was the term."

Ellen looked at him for a moment, searchingly, from behind her dark lenses. "Whatever the reason, and however selfish it is, I'm glad you did stay."

Then she forced brightness into her tone. "Hey, is that why your boss let you borrow his boat? To ply me with champagne so I wouldn't sue?"

Ben chuckled. "Rats. You found us out."

He got up to refill their glasses; just orange juice this time, poured from the carton. Ellen appreciated that. She liked the fact that she didn't have to tell him when enough champagne was too much, and she liked that he dressed his dogs in funny hats to put her at ease, and she liked the long, comfortable silence that settled between them before he said, "Was it hard for you last night, being alone?"

She thought about that for a moment. "Not really. After you left, three reporters came to my door, can you believe that? And they never stopped calling. I ended up unplugging the phone."

Ben nodded sympathetically. "Me, too. It's amazing what the media can find to focus on. They should be interviewing the policemen and off-duty firemen and the divers and rescue teams who came from as far as three states away—" He cut off his own lecture with an apologetic shrug. "Which they are doing, I guess."

Ellen said quietly, "I couldn't even turn on the news this morning."

"Me, neither."

In a moment she went on, "Anyway, I guess it's all a blessing in disguise because by the time I finished dealing with all the camera lights and phone calls I was exhausted. I was asleep almost before I was out of the shower." She hesitated, then felt compelled to add honestly, "It didn't last long, though. I had terrible nightmares."

"That's to be expected for a while," Ben assured her. "I've had some pretty weird dreams myself. Let me know if they get too bad and I'll write you a prescription for something."

"Thanks, but I'm not one for chemical solutions. The hospital sent some sleeping pills home with me, but they make me groggy. I don't even like to take aspirin."

"Careful, now. You're talking to a professional aspirin-pusher."

She smiled and sipped her orange juice. "You know what is really strange? My nightmares, they weren't about the bridge. I don't remember most of them, but I do remember one dream was about my hometown being swallowed up by a monster—with me in it. Dreaming about monsters, at my age."

"I don't think we ever stop dreaming about monsters," Ben said. "Their faces just change over the years, that's all."

"I think it was because of that reporter. The one

who said I wasn't really born in Wintersville after all."

"I wonder what he ended up writing about you."

"That's what's giving me nightmares."

Ben smiled. "How far away is this place, anyway?"

"Wintersville? I don't know, I'd have to get out a map. I haven't been there since I was twelve. It was such a hokey little town, to tell the truth I'm surprised it's still in operation."

"It might make you feel better to drive out there one weekend and face down this reporter yourself. Also, to put your mind at ease that a monster didn't really eat your hometown."

She laughed. "Maybe. But I'll tell you what I am going to do. I'm going to call the hall of records and get this whole confusion about my birth certificate cleared up." She hesitated. "Am I fixating?"

"Probably. But there are worse things to fixate about."

He patted her knee lightly as he got up. It was an easy, friendly gesture, and she liked it more than she had expected to.

"Cold chicken and potato salad for lunch," he said, "courtesy of the Twelfth Street Deli. I'll set up under the awning."

She suppressed a moan of pure luxury. "Speaking of dreams, this must be one. I've never been so pampered in all my life."

"Enjoy it while you can. You're washing the dishes."

Ellen just laughed and sank deeper into the chair and hoped the day would never end.

Highborn, Virginia

10:15 P.M.

The wedding at the Rehobeth Pentecostal Church was over at 7:15. The reception, which was held in the adjacent social hall, ended at 8:30. Janet looked beautiful in a swath of white satin, and Derrick Bleckly had to admit the two candle stands and all those flowers flanking them had looked right pretty, despite the fact that he had been bitching and moaning about the cost for the past six weeks.

Janet and her new groom, the needle-nosed Howard Walker, were on their way to their Myrtle Beach honeymoon, the women had finished sweeping up the rice pellets and silver and pink ribbons an hour ago, and the mother of the bride was at home with her sister, sniffling and packing wedding cake into Tupperware containers. Derrick didn't know what all the crying was about. Tonight would be the first quiet night they'd had in that house since Janet was born, and he for one was looking forward to it.

Or at least he had been until he remembered the fancy-assed candle stands that would cost him fifty dollars extra if he didn't have them back at the rental place by nine o'clock the next morning to accommodate another wedding at the country club on Sunday afternoon. So he got back in his car and drove all the way back out to the church at ten o'clock at night, cursing under his breath but half glad to be out of the house with all its tired post-wedding glitter and weeping women.

The lights were out but the sanctuary doors were unlocked, as they always were. He'd been a layman in the church for twenty years and knew it inside and out; he didn't even have to search for the light switch as he entered the auditorium. He started straight down the aisle toward the glitter of the two candle stands that caught the reflected street light, and drew up short, startled but not alarmed, when someone stepped out of the shadows in front of him.

"Evening!" he said, peering to recognize what he was sure was a familiar face. "Didn't expect anyone to be here this late!"

"That's okay," replied the voice, mild and smooth and not the least bit familiar. "I was just leaving."

He walked past Derrick.

Derrick started to turn. "Hey—"

The scalpel blade was sharp and the stroke powerful; he died instantly and with no time for regret. Daniel held him as the life flowed out of him and pooled on the floor, and he thought, *Fear no evil, fear no evil . . .* until the terror that fluttered inside was replaced with a kind of reverence, an awe. It was so perfect. How could he not be amazed?

He carried the body to the sixth pew on the left-hand side, center seat. He removed the jacket and the tie, which weren't quite right. The church did not have a baptistery—so many of these small churches did not—so he had to go to the water fountain to wash his hands. Then he returned and lit the candles in the candle stands, and stood by to observe the effect.

Ariel stood beside him, his expression critical. "Forget something?" he prodded.

Daniel glanced at him. His voice was hoarse. "No. He's perfect, just like you said."

"Not quite." Ariel held out his hand, and in the flickering candlelight Daniel saw the glitter of a cross on a gold chain. He caught his breath. *Of course*, he thought, and he took the chain from Ariel.

"I told you you'd be glad to have it." Ariel sounded a trifle smug.

Daniel took the cross and edged down the pew. He draped the chain and cross over the man's head, and resumed his place at the end of the aisle.

"Now," he whispered, almost overwhelmed with the beauty of it. "*Now* it's perfect."

Ariel slipped an arm around his shoulders. "That's what you have me for," he said.

MONDAY, APRIL 21

Ten

Charlie Fontana—short for Charlene—was a tall, slender, ebony-skinned woman whose exotic beauty could have been her ticket to the world of high-fashion runways or Hollywood lights, but which had instead resulted in her spending the first four of her ten years with the FBI in undercover roles as call girls, drug molls, and porn queens. When she joined the FBI with a degree in criminal law and a background with the Secret Service, she was only one of two black women in a bureau that was not known for favoring either women or minorities. Today she was only one promotion away from heading up her own field office and, it was grudgingly agreed by most everyone who had ever worked with her, could probably have outshone any ADIC on the job if she was given half a chance.

While most of the other women in the bureau had come in through "side doors," with specialized degrees that made them valuable in the sci-crime lab or other special units, Charlie's specialty was investigation, good old-fashioned law enforcement.

She had worked herself up through the ranks the hard way, and in the process had garnered either the respect or the resentment of every other agent in the Bureau, but very few friends. The other female agents didn't quite know what to make of her, and the males were, if the truth be known, a little afraid of her. There was little argument that she was one of the sharpest investigators in the Bureau, and for that reason Matthew would be sorry when she was promoted out of the field. He liked to think her supervisors felt the same way, because that promotion was becoming dangerously overdue.

Her makeup always looked professionally applied—dark berry lips, pencilled brows, taupe lids, perfectly blushed and arched cheekbones. She wore her rich black hair cropped close to the scalp in a way that emphasized her long neck and the sleek, sharp angle of her jaw. The tailored suits and plain white shirts she preferred only enhanced the subtle sexuality that she wore as casually as perfume, and Matthew was not the first agent to reflect that if J. Edgar had ever guessed what someone like Charlie Fontana would look like in the regulation haircut and uniform he would have rewritten the dress code without delay.

She sat across from Matthew's desk now, one long leg crossed over the other, swinging her foot impatiently as he took his time flipping through the file she had delivered to him three hours previously. "I don't like looking over another agent's shoulder," he told her, "especially without his permission and especially when there's no call for it."

"Any other agent in this building would kiss your ass to have you look over his shoulder."

Matt murmured, "Please be sure to mention that's not necessary."

"Mark Hayes did the profile and I told him I was bringing it to you. He's cool with it."

"He's a good profiler."

"He should be; you trained him. But this isn't his speciality. He wants your opinion."

"Then he should have brought it to me himself."

"Jesus Christ, Matt, will you stop being such a goddamned tight-ass and tell me what you think? Why does everything have to be such a production with you?"

"It's a power thing." He glanced down at Mark Hayes's report, scanned the police report and preliminary autopsy. He had gone over the file once already; he repeated the motions now more to stall for time than to refresh his memory. "Thirty-two-year old nurse disappears while jogging. Her body is found propped up in a pew of the Methodist church by the youth minister who came to prepare for an afternoon basketball game. Her throat was cut. Altar candles had been lit and burned down. She wasn't a member of the church. Her jacket had been removed and was found in a dumpster behind the church."

"Hairs and Fibers has it," she responded a trifle impatiently to his questioning look. "Nothing yet."

"I don't see anything here that requires a second opinion." He turned over color crime scene photos one by one, his face impassive. "The profile is by-the-book. White male, age thirty-seven to forty-five; five feet, eleven inches. One hundred seventy-five pounds, athletic. A respected member of the community, possibly even a member of this church, works a steady job in a hospital or medical-supply facility. He hangs out with cops, may even be an ex-cop or military policeman. He drives a Chrysler or Ford Taurus, brown or dark blue—again emulating a policeman by choosing the most common type of police vehicle." He glanced up, removed his glasses. "It's all pretty routine. Most likely occupation: hospital security guard. Probably at the same hospital in which the victim worked, just like Hayes said. You didn't need me to review this."

"You're our foremost authority on the assassin personality, not to mention religious ritual killings. Who was I supposed to ask?"

He closed the file and pushed it across the desk to her. "What's the deal, Charlie? We've known each other too long for games."

"Could it be a copycat?"

"Of what?"

"Come on, Matt! Throat sliced, church, the second one in Durham in a year—did I mention the murder weapon was a scalpel? Does any of this sound familiar to you at all?"

"Ah, so this is another Mayday alarm." He had known as much the moment he looked at the file, and now he tried not to let his irritation show. "You guys are never going to let me go on that one, are you?"

"Why should we? You know more about the Mayday Killer than anybody in the world."

"This is not the Mayday Killer. And I don't know anything about him. If I did he'd be in jail right now, wouldn't he?"

"God should've made you a mother, Graham, you're

so goddamn good at being in charge of the world. Maybe you'd like to confess to being responsible for the Holocaust now."

"It would just be nice to be famous for something other than the ones that got away."

"Just answer the question, please. Copycat or not?"

Matthew patiently ticked off the list on his fingers. "One, the victim is the wrong age. Two, the victim had brown hair, not red. Three, the murder occurred two weeks before the anniversary date. Four, the body was not disposed of in water. Five, I'm a full-time teacher now, not a case agent. This is none of my business."

"What about twinning?"

He lifted an eyebrow. "I'm impressed. You always were one of my best students." Then he shook his head. "Twinning is an entirely separate phenomenon, wherein the subjects would feed each other's fantasies by committing similar crimes. There simply aren't enough similarities here."

"So you're saying coincidence."

Her dark gaze pinned him mercilessly. He met it without blinking. "I'm saying until we have something better, that's the best anybody can do."

"How's this for better?" She reached into her pocket and took out a folded sheet of fax paper, shaking it open with a snap of her wrist. "This just in."

Matthew read the fax with outward impassivity, although a superstitious chill gripped his spine midway through the report. It was a standard homicide report from a little town called Highborn, Virginia, just off Highway 58. A fifty-two-year-old man, his throat slashed, was found sitting in the pew of a rural church where his daughter had been married only hours earlier. The candles in the candelabra had been lit and had burned down to pools of wax on the carpet by the time the pastor came in for Sunday services and discovered the body.

"What do you think?" Charlie asked.

Matthew handed the fax back to her, his carefully trained expression unrevealing. But his heart was pounding hard and with each beat a voice in the back of his mind was cursing, *Damn, damn damn . . .* "I think you've got yourself a spree killer," he said. "And a shitload of trouble."

Charlie snatched the paper away from him. "That must be why they pay you the big money."

"He's getting bolder," Matt said. "He got away with it once, a woman jogger who knew him on sight. Early morning, no one around, plenty of time to get away. This time he took on a man, a perfect stranger, and a good-sized one, too, from the police report."

"What about the necklace?"

The report had indicated the victim had not been wearing any jewelry when he left the house, but a gold cross on a chain had been around his neck when the body was found. Evidence indicated the necklace had been placed there after the man's throat was cut, and police were withholding mention of the necklace in hopes that it might lead them to the killer.

Matthew said, "It's more positioning, like the removal of the jacket with the victim in Durham, like placing them upright on the pews."

"This one's jacket was removed too."

Matthew nodded. "The police are thinking the

necklace has some kind of personal significance—that it belongs to the killer or has meaning for the victim. I think if they check they'll find the necklace was recently purchased in a Walmart or drugstore, it's gold plate not gold, and it was purchased precisely for this purpose."

Charlie was taking notes. "So he went to some trouble planning this."

"In some respects, yes. The use of props, the removal of clothing, the positioning of the bodies, that shows some forethought. But did he stalk the victim or stake out the church, waiting for the wedding guests to go home and the father of the bride to come back? I don't think so. He couldn't have known that he would. He might have known that the first victim jogged every morning at the same time and he might even have lured her to the church, but I frankly think both victims were crimes of opportunity. They were in the wrong place at the wrong time."

"So you're saying the Durham victim and the Highborn one were both chosen completely at random."

Matt hesitated. "Not completely. This guy has an agenda. He's playing out a fantasy, and these two had their own special roles in it. The key is to find out what that fantasy is, and right now I don't have enough to go on."

"I can get you more."

Matt took off his glasses. "How'd you get this, anyway? I don't see anything that gives us jurisdiction here."

"Chief Walker in Durham took one of your

courses," Charlie explained. "He requested the unit's involvement with a profile."

Matt nodded. That was common enough.

"Then the Highborn case came in through VICAP, and the similarities were chilling enough to warrant an alert. Right now we're just involved on an informal basis." She held his gaze. "So tell me, Matt. What's the likelihood that this thing is going to get formal?"

He answered, "High."

"I want you with me on this one, Matt," Charlie said.

His chest began to tighten again, but he was shaking his head before she finished speaking. *Pound, pound* . . . "Not my gig anymore, you know that. Besides, you don't need me. The guys in Investigative Support are the best the unit has ever had."

"Since you, you mean. I've got a feeling about this one, Matt, and you know I wouldn't ask if it wasn't a big, bad feeling."

She held his eyes for a moment. Then the phone on his desk rang and he was relieved to excuse himself to answer it.

It was Polly, with her flight information. He copied down the numbers and they chatted for a few minutes. When he hung up the phone, Charlie was sitting back in the chair in a relaxed stance, a knowing smile on her face. The business portion of their meeting was apparently over.

"Let me guess who that was," she said.

Matt realized how transparent his face must have been when he recognized her voice and he shrugged, a little embarrassed. "That obvious, huh?"

"You're letting that girl make a fool of you."

He grinned. "I'll tell her you said so."

Charlie nodded toward the telephone. "Planning a little getaway, huh?"

"She's flying into Richmond the first. Then we're driving down to the Shenandoah Valley for two weeks of big trout, great sunsets, crackling campfires."

She chuckled. "Leave it to you to get yourself a girl whose idea of a big time is trout fishing and campfires."

"That's why I picked her."

Charlie studied a chipped spot on her nail. She wore the palest pink polish and no one but she would have noticed. "A quick survey of the crime sites wouldn't take till the first. You wouldn't miss your vacation."

"You're right, because I'm not going."

"As a courtesy."

"As a courtesy, leave me out of it."

She looked at him steadily. "What's the real reason you asked to be reassigned out of the field, Matt?"

"I found out there were more important things than twenty-four hour workdays."

"Like Polly?"

He said, "This is the only relationship in my life I haven't managed to screw up. I'm giving it one hundred percent."

"And you can't do that with serial killers and child molesters crawling around in your head."

"You got that right."

"Well, nobody can blame you for that." She tapped the case folder against her knee, as though straightening the papers, and added, "Of course, some people say you left because you lost your nerve."

He replied blandly, "That, too."

She looked at him. "We're all casualties of war, Matt, the innocent as well as the guilty. You can't keep blaming yourself for what happened to Eleanor, and you can't be everything to everybody all of the time."

He almost didn't answer. He resisted invasions of his privacy on any level, by anyone, possibly because he had spent so much of his life invading other people's privacy. But it was Charlie, and she meant well, and ignoring her would only give her tacit permission to try again. So he agreed, "Right. Just another one on the list of those who got away."

"And you're going to carry every goddamn one of them to your grave." She said it without rancor; merely as a statement of fact. She stood up. "You break my heart, Matthew Graham. You really do."

"Thanks for stopping by, Charlie."

"Just thought I'd brighten your day."

"Listen . . ." He hesitated. "If you want to keep me informed, on a completely informal basis, go ahead."

From the doorway she looked back at him. "What's he going to do next, Matt?"

"He's going to kill again," Matthew answered. "Who or where I can't say yet."

"We can't stake out every church in the country, or even the state of Virginia."

"Take it back to Investigative Support," he advised. "Let them do their jobs."

She twisted her face into a brief grimace of disgust. "You've got oatmeal for balls, Graham."

He grinned. "I should've married you a long time ago."

"Yeah, and lucky for you I don't date skinny white boys or your ass would be mine by now."

"Always a pleasure, Charlie."

She was out the door when he added, "That wasn't the reason."

She poked her head back in. "What?"

"It wasn't that I lost my nerve," he said. "It was that I didn't care whether I lost it or not."

She considered this for a moment, then nodded and left.

WEDNESDAY, APRIL 23

Eleven

"*Another body has been found today in the bizarre case of the Church Pew Slayings, and that story tops our news at this noon hour . . .*"

Ellen jerked her attention away from the television screen as a human voice interrupted the dead silence of "hold" that emanated across the telephone lines from the Division of Births, Marriages, and Deaths in the state records department in Charlottesville, West Virginia. She was in the teacher's lounge on her first full day back at work, using up most of her lunch hour on a long-distance credit-card call that was supposed to have put her mind at ease but was in fact only making her more tense than she had been before.

"Yes ma'am, good afternoon," she responded quickly to the fourth bored female voice who had inquired how she could help. "As I was telling the person before you, I'm trying to track down a birth certificate—"

"We only honor requests that are made in writing. The charge for a photocopy is—"

"I know that," Ellen said impatiently. "I don't want a photocopy, I want—" She broke off with a breath. "Look, this a complicated story and I've told it four times already today. What I really want is to speak with a supervisor."

"I am the supervisor," replied the chilly voice. "And I'm afraid you'll have to put your request in writing."

"No, wait, please don't hang up!" Sensing a hesitance on the other end of the line, Ellen took the only tack left to her, and the one to which she had sworn she would not resort. "My name is Ellen Cox," she rushed on. "Maybe you recognize me—I was the one trapped on the bridge in Virginia Beach?"

"Is that right?" The voice sounded skeptical, and Ellen felt foolish.

"I really am," she insisted, and when she realized the two other staff members in the room were finding her telephone conversation even more interesting than the grisly noon news she felt even more foolish. "But that doesn't matter," she added, lowering her voice a fraction. "All I'm trying to do is find out whether or not a birth certificate was filed on me from Colquitt County, West Virginia. Surely you have that kind of information on microfilm or computer or something? I'll make the proper request in writing, I promise, but right now I just need to know whether or not you have the birth certificate."

There was a silence. "It would be faster to contact the county of your birth."

"I tried that. They had no record of my birth and told me to contact you."

Another silence.

"Please," Ellen said. "I know it's a lot of trouble,

but it would take such a load off my mind. Couldn't you please just ask someone to check for me?"

Eventually, in a tone that was edged with exasperation, the woman demanded, "Full name at birth, mother's maiden name, date and place of birth."

Gratefully, Ellen gave her the information and resigned herself to another stint on hold.

Helen Myers, the front office manager and Diane's personal assistant, patted Ellen's arm sympathetically on her way out. "If you need me to write some letters and kick some butt, you just let me know."

Ellen smiled, albeit a little tiredly. "You'll be the first."

"To recap our top story," the lady anchor of the noon news was saying, "a third victim of the so-called Church-Pew Killer was found late yesterday afternoon in an abandoned church building in Roanoke County near the North Carolina line. It is believed that twenty-two-year-old Peter Lincoln, missing since Friday from his Henderson, North Carolina home, has been dead since Saturday."

"Lord help us," murmured Diane as she entered, "what is this world coming to?" The television, of course, was closed captioned, and she paused to watch it with growing despair on her face.

Ellen started to reply but was distracted by the brisk impatient voice in her ear. "Colquitt County, West Virginia, May 1, 1964, there is no record of a birth being registered to Rita Cox."

For a moment Ellen was too nonplussed to speak. Then she said, "Wait! Did you look under neighboring counties? Maybe—?"

"I searched by maiden name and date. We have

no record of that birth anywhere in this state. For further information you'll have to go to the county in which the birth was supposedly registered. I'm sorry."

Ellen hung up the telephone, an uneasy frown on her face. "Well, that settles it," she said. "I officially don't exist."

"You'd have a hard time convincing anyone in this state of that," Diane answered, and gestured to the television screen.

Above the anchor woman's right shoulder was a color copy of the photograph that had become an epigram for disaster. Blue sky, blue car, her own weeping face, grainy and skin-toned, wispy strands of wind-blown red hair, arms upstretched and reaching. The impact was powerful enough to stop her breath in her throat, and Ellen tried to push back queasiness as she turned away.

The newscaster was saying, "Federal inspectors were on the scene again today to try to determine the cause of last week's tragic bridge collapse . . ."

"You know something?" Ellen said. "I don't care if I ever see that photograph again."

Diane gave a grunt of acknowledgment and lowered herself to the chair opposite, a diet soft drink in her hand. She looked at Ellen assessively. "So other than that, you doing okay?"

Tuesday she had only come in for a half day, but the euphoria of being back at work—of being alive—was still strong enough to make her want to smile all the time for no reason at all. The memory of walking into her classroom to see the children lined up to welcome her, signing, "We love you, Miss Cox" still made her cry. She still had nightmares, she still got the occasional call from the media or the curious, and she sometimes was seized in the middle of the day for no reason at all with an inexplicable sense of dread, depression, or anxiety. But for the most part, life was almost back to normal—or as normal as it would ever be again. The other teachers no longer treated her with kid gloves and her insurance claim was being express-processed; her classroom was recovering from the holiday feeling of having a celebrity for a teacher and her lesson plans were back on track again. She didn't know why she should let this ridiculous business with the birth certificate bother her.

"I talked to the clerk at the Colquitt County Court House," she explained. "He said my birth certificate wasn't on file there. I asked him where it would be. He said it would be filed in the county where I was born. I said I was born at Colquitt County Hospital in Wintersville, West Virginia. He said . . ." She paused for effect. "There was no such place."

Diane lifted an eyebrow. "Sounds like your memory is playing tricks on you, honey. Either that or there's been some kind of screwup at the Hall of Records. Do you mean this is the first time you've ever had to request your birth certificate?"

She nodded. "I suppose I had it when I applied for my driver's license or social security card, but Mother would have taken care of that and it wasn't in with any of her papers when she died. Am I being obsessive about this?"

Diane poured a measure of the diet drink into a plastic glass; she never drank from the can. "A little."

"So then I called the state," Ellen went on, "thinking, as you did, that I must have had the hospital or even the town wrong. I *do* remember that this was a really small rural town and it's perfectly reasonable that women would have had to go out of the county to give birth. Not that the clerks in Charlottesville were exactly anxious to be of service, but I finally convinced someone to look up the records and *she* told me there was no record of anyone by my mother's name having given birth in West Virginia on that day."

Diane sipped her drink. "I'm not sure how much of my emotional welfare I'd allow to rest on the infallibility of bureaucratic records, my dear."

"It's just . . ." Ellen pressed her hands tightly together, choosing her words, then began to sign. "Since all of this—you know—happened, I've felt as though everything about my life was different, as though I were different, and that nothing I can ever do will make it the same again. I don't suppose anyone who was on that bridge will ever be the same, whether they were actually involved in the accident or not. It's just—it's difficult to explain but it's an odd sort of identity crisis. And then, when that reporter called and said, more or less, that I *wasn't* who I said I was—that I wasn't even from where I thought I was—well, of course I know it's just some giant misunderstanding, but that missing birth certificate almost seems symbolic somehow." She stopped suddenly, then gave an embarrassed little shrug. "I know, it sounds crazy."

Diane smiled. "Other than crazy, how are you?"

Ellen took a moment before replying. "Fine, I

think. Okay. I still have nightmares—odd dreams, about people on the bridge, I think. Faces so clear I could draw them with a pencil, and details—like one of the women was wearing a red blouse, and there was a man with a gold cross pendant, and a little boy with a red and white polo shirt, and a woman with a baby. I mean, listen to me. I could pick them out of lineup. The dreams never have any point, they're just haunting, and I wake up terrified. Ben says he has nightmares too, about the ones he couldn't save. He thinks it will pass."

Diane nodded. "And what does the young doctor have to say about your identity crisis?"

Ellen smiled ruefully. "I'm not sure he's noticed." Then she glanced at Diane and added a little shyly, "I really like him, Diane. I keep waiting to wake up and find out that I'm tired of him or he's tired of me, that the only thing we have in common is what happened on the bridge and that when we get over that we'll get over each other. And who knows, maybe we will. But for now, I really like him."

"My mama always said God never shuts a door but that he opens a window."

Ellen chuckled. "Mine, too. Everybody's mama always said that." Then she frowned a little. "I just wish my mama had said where she put my birth certificate."

The overhead lights flashed, signaling the beginning of fourth period, and Ellen got to her feet. "I have a suggestion," said Diane. "Why don't you and Dr. Ben take a ride up to Wintersville some weekend? Have yourselves a look around, set your mind at ease, have a nice romantic picnic."

Ellen laughed. "Maybe we will," she said.

But she had the nightmare again that night.

God, Ariel told him, was in the details. Daniel's mind was full of detail and his eyes missed nothing and it was difficult to resist the temptation toward perfection. He was aware, however, that it was the ritual that was important, for Ellen's sake; everything else was just embellishment, vanity, an appeasement of his own sense of symmetry.

He watched the woman drop off the toddler at the church day-care center and he knew these were two he had to have. Even though it meant the loss of an entire day, waiting, even though there were others equally appealing he could have chosen, this was too close to perfect to resist. To walk away from them would be to spit on the gift his dark angel had given him.

Now he understood the reason for the purchases on which Ariel had insisted. He apologized for doubting.

Daniel left his vehicle in the small shopping center six miles distant and walked back to the church, waiting in the woods until mothers began to call for their youngsters around five. She arrived at five-thirty. She was wearing a navy skirt and a white blouse with a floppy bow, and her brown hair was pinned at the nape with a blue chiffon bow. Even the hair was right.

She left her car unlocked, and why shouldn't she in a church parking lot while she ran inside to pick up her child? She wasn't gone five minutes. But during those five minutes Daniel slipped inside the car and lay down on the floorboard in back. The carseat was in the front, which was another sign his angel was watching. If it had been in the backseat, as regulations required, his plan would not have been so easy to execute.

He waited until she was out of the parking lot and had turned onto a brief stretch of deserted highway to sit up and make his presence known. He held the scalpel to her neck and told her to pull over. Her eyes were big and dark and terrified in the rearview mirror, the eyes of a woman who has stared her nightmare in the face and knows it's not a dream. She pleaded for her life, and the life of her child. He told her everything would be okay if she would just pull over. She did, and he slit her throat.

He waited until he returned to the church to do the child, though. It was full dark, and only the security lights were on in the vestibule. There were cars in the west parking lot, and one of the ancillary buildings was fully lit for some function or another. The place of worship, however, was deserted.

Daniel carried the mother, in her navy skirt and blood-stained white blouse, into the sanctuary, and arranged her on the eighth pew from the front, three seats toward the center. He took the chiffon bow out of her hair and pulled her hair down, loose and lank, around her shoulders. The child had begun to cry when he returned to the car, so he killed him there. That was hard to do, and at first he didn't think he could; he panicked and thought he would fail looking into that fat, red little face, swollen with angry tears. His courage was gone, his hand was shaking, he was sinking into humiliation and helplessness; he was going to fail.

Then Ariel quietly covered the face with a cloth diaper from the bag of baby paraphernalia on the passenger seat floor, and he covered Daniel's hand with his. "Fear no evil," Ariel murmured, and Daniel felt a peace come over him unlike any he had known since childhood, a strength that enabled him to do what he must. Ariel's hand guided the blade, but Daniel's will brought it home.

He wrapped the head in the diaper and carried the small body inside, arranging it on its mother's lap. Lastly he tucked a fuzzy brown, jointed-limbed teddy bear into the baby's arms. He stepped back and admired his work.

Ariel stood beside him, nodded with approval. Daniel knew he had done well.

He was growing stronger every day.

It began as it always did with the sound of dripping water and the candlelit cave. Ellen was wearing a white dress, cradling the rabbits in her arms. As she walked along, she gradually came to realize that the cave was not a cave at all, but a wax museum with wax figures sitting in perfect alignment to one another, as though seated on rows of a bus. When she moved past them she could see their features, planed by the flickering candlelight. Every step she took increased the dread. There was the fat man with the gold cross around his neck. Next to him was a woman with salt-and-pepper hair and glasses on a chain—his wife?—and another man, in his twenties, with short blond hair and wearing a pink shirt. One row behind them was a boy, perhaps ten years old, with red hair like her own, wearing a red and white polo shirt. She turned her head and saw other faces— the thin-faced woman in a red shirt with lank black hair, a fat man wearing a gold cross on a chain around his neck, a pretty girl with curly blond hair, a teenaged boy with bad acne. There was a young woman in a blue skirt balancing a toddler on her knee. The child was holding a teddy bear with jointed arms and legs. The more she looked, the deeper the dread became, until she was suddenly convinced that if she didn't leave this place right now the wax dummies would come to life and start chasing her with knives, and they wouldn't stop until she was dead. She turned to run but she couldn't move, and when she looked down her white dress was covered with blood, and the rabbits in her arms were all dead.

Ellen awoke shaking and damp with sweat. She stumbled out of bed and made her way to the bathroom in the dark, where she turned on the faucet and desperately tried to scrub the blood from her hands.

THURSDAY, APRIL 24

Twelve

The first thing Sheriff Lelan Camp knew of the very bad day he was about to have was the way the color drained out of his dispatcher's lips when she first took the call. He happened to be standing near the switchboard, enjoying the morning's first cup of coffee and glancing through the overnight calls—one drunk-and-disorderly and two fourteen-year-olds caught joyriding in a stolen car—and the horror of that call seemed to come through the telephone lines like a living thing, so that he froze with the cup halfway to his lips, staring at the dispatcher and knowing, somehow *knowing* before she said a word.

He remembered thinking, *You never think it's going to happen to you.* Not in a place like Pendleton County, where a busy night meant hauling in a drunk and two kids. Not to your neighbors, your friends, not at six fucking o'clock in the morning.

The dispatcher disconnected and turned to him, eyes big, face white. "That was Reverend Michaels from the First Methodist. He was calling from the church. He said there was—he'd found—oh, God, Sheriff, I think you better get over there."

He was already moving toward the door, the words echoing in his head, *Not in my town, Jesus, not my town.*

Branson McCall had been unit chief of Investigative Support/Behavioral Science while Matt was still handling active cases; when McCall had been promoted to assistant director, Quantico, Matt had been offered his old job. McCall was one of a handful of people who understood why Matt had turned it down, and later, when Matt had requested a full-time teaching assignment, had asked no questions. But Matt knew why he had been called into McCall's office before a word was spoken, and the history between them only made the knowing more difficult.

McCall didn't waste time with small talk. As soon as Matt was seated he said, "You've been following this Church Pew Killer business."

Matt nodded. "Unofficially. Mostly what I read in the papers."

McCall made a dismissing gesture with his hand. "Agent Fontana submitted a report on her conversation with you."

Matt's mouth tightened. That wasn't protocol. That was, in fact, damn near to subterfuge. If she had wanted a formal statement of opinion, why the hell hadn't she just come out and asked for it?

McCall said, reading his mind, "She had to, after we opened a case file. You know the drill with something like this, Matt. Gum wrappers stuck to the shoe, conversations overheard in a hall, fingerprints taken off a goddamn washroom stall—if it's about, around, or near anything having to do with the case it goes in the file, and let me tell you, with this one we need everything we can get."

Matt felt dread sink into the pit of his stomach. Even though he had known it was coming, the actuality was a cold thing. "So it's official, then. We're in."

"As of three forty-five yesterday afternoon, when two kids taking a shortcut home from school found the body of Peter Lincoln stiffening up among the cobwebs and a bank of burned-down candles in Roanoake County, Virginia. Lincoln was last seen in North Carolina, so there's every reason to believe this represents a kidnapping across state lines. Forensics suggest Lincoln might have been the first or second victim. What do you think?"

Matt nodded slowly. "It would fit the profile. First a woman in a neighborhood that's familiar to him, low risk. Then a young man, slightly built—was he gay? Our guy might have posed as a potential lover. Leaving the body in an abandoned church in an out-of-the-way area, again taking no chances. It wasn't until he attacked the 250-pound man in a church that had been occupied only a few hours before that he started to show confidence."

"Which means we can't expect him to lose his nerve now."

"That could make him easier to catch."

"Maybe. But how many victims will it take before he gets reckless enough to screw up?"

Matt said, "I wouldn't want to be the one waiting around counting."

McCall said, "Good. Because as of right now you're back in the field."

Matt felt every muscle in his body stiffen, but he did not reply or react visibly in any way.

"We slugged the case Churchpew, and Fontana is heading up the team. We're throwing everything we've got behind her, and the first thing she requested was you." His gaze was steady, anticipating Matt's reaction. "If she hadn't, I would have."

Matt said carefully, "You know I'll do whatever I can from here—"

"Not good enough. I know how you work—hell, how we all work. I want you on site."

His heart was pounding, pounding. "I've been out of it too long. I'm out of practice, out of shape. I'd only be a liability to the team."

"If I thought that I'd fire your ass this minute. You might be a desk jockey now but you're still a special agent with the FBI and you're in my goddamn division. You don't get out of shape and you don't get out of practice, have you got that?"

Matt's jaw tightened. "Do I have a choice?"

McCall said evenly, "Yeah. But I don't think you'll like what it is."

Then he softened a little. "Look, Matt, I've done what I can for you and I've done it for as long as I could, you know that. But we need you on this and you damn well know that, too. Nobody expected you to hide behind that teacher's lectern forever."

"I did," Matt replied, and got to his feet. He looked McCall in the eye and he took a breath. He said, "I'm not ready for this." Saying those words felt like the hardest thing he had ever done.

McCall answered simply, "I'm sorry."

And Matt knew the hardest thing had not even begun.

Charlie was waiting for him when Matt strode out of the assistant director's office. His jaw was knotted and his eyes were dark, and for a moment she thought he would push past her without speaking. He didn't slow his stride or even look at her as he muttered, "Thanks for being such a goddamned good friend, Charlie. And get the hell out of my way."

She stretched her legs to keep up. "Well pardon the fuck out of me for inconveniencing you. Do you think I begged the A.D. to haul your ass out of mothballs just so I could have the pleasure of your company? You have no idea how much shit is going to fly over this, and most of it's gonna hit me in the face."

"What a pleasure to be around a real lady for a change."

She stopped and caught his arm. "Look Matt, I'm sorry. The local police are going apeshit. We've got two men from every unit working on this around the clock and the son of a bitch is still two steps ahead of us. Tell me you haven't been thinking about this case ever since I brought you the file."

He pulled his arm away, his expression intractable. But there was a flicker of something in his eyes, and that was enough.

She said, "Pack a bag for three days. We have a briefing at Headquarters in an hour, and we leave from there for North Carolina."

*   *   *

On the way to D.C. Charlie got a call on her cellular. Matt watched her face and listened to her silence and when she hung up she said, "We've got two more victims, in a church twenty miles from the last scene, a thirty-year-old mother and her son. The child was only eighteen months old."

She was driving, and she kept her eyes on the road. Matthew was silent for a moment. "This church was off Highway 58, wasn't it?"

"It was someplace called Green Grove, Virginia. Pendleton County."

"Check your map. You'll find it's not too far off State Highway 58. Our man is traveling west to east, and he's got an agenda. The victims are incidental to him, random pattern selection. They just happened to be on his route. The only thing that's important to him is his destination."

"What's that?"

He glanced at her. "We'll know when he gets there."

The briefing room was packed. "Gentlemen," said Charlie as she swept in, "we have a fresh crime scene and a change of itinerary, so we're going to have to cut this briefing short. I believe you all know Special Agent Graham, forensic psychiatrist."

Matt swept an assessive gaze around the room. Since all were graduates of the Academy they would of course recognize him, but Matt knew only a few of them. There were perhaps a dozen investigators and examiners assembled in the small room, and there was a preponderance of gray hair. The most seasoned professionals had been brought in; cases had been reassigned, specialists shuffled to free up maximum mind power and maximum experience. Matt recognized Jim Barber and Harold Long from Hairs and Fibers, Dixie Sims from Materials Analysis, and of course Rob Beam, the unit chief from Investigative Support.

Charlie introduced the rest: Len Cates from Latent Fingerprints; Investigators Brenner, Holly and James; and—a surprise to Matt—Doug Reirson, a young investigator from Headquarters who was already making a name for himself in Violent Crimes.

"Agent Holly will be working with the SAC in Durham, Agent Brenner will be in charge of the Highborn site, and Agent James in Roanoke," Charlie said. "Agent Graham, Agent Reirson, and myself will coordinate the investigation by rotating between the sites. We will be the first response team in case of further developments. For those of you manning the lab back home, we'll do everything we can to make your jobs easier. Give us your input.

"Right now the only thing we know about the suspect is what he's left behind for us to find. And in the way of material evidence, that's not much. In fact the only thing he's left behind is what you all have before you, in the form of the psychological profile drawn up by investigative support. Agent Graham, can you add anything to that?"

Matt bit down on his anger so hard his teeth hurt, then made himself relax. It wasn't Charlie's style to deliberately embarrass or intimidate a colleague, and there was too much at stake to allow egos to come into play. So Matt looked Unit Chief Beam in the eye and said, "We're looking for a man of above average intelligence with some higher education or specialized vocational training, six feet, one-eighty or so. He probably works out, has better than average upper-body strength." Every word he spoke seemed to echo eerily in his head; he thought, *I know this man, I've been here before.* But it was crazy. He forced his mind to focus.

"He's transported at least one of his victims from the primary crime scene to the dump site, so we're looking for a van, not a sedan as was originally profiled, dark blue, black, or green with dark upholstery that doesn't show stains. We're talking about a fairly new model—he can afford it or it's a company vehicle, but it's going to have high mileage. He is somewhat familiar with the area; he didn't come upon that church in Roanoke by accident. I'd say he travels in his job, and his territory is the North Carolina/Virginia/South Carolina/Tennessee region."

He could have stopped there. That was enough. But he was in it now. He had to go on. "This is a man with a mission, gentlemen," he said quietly. "He's got a purpose, a destination, and a reason. That makes him dangerous enough. But there's more." He took a breath, swept the group with his eyes. "I don't think he's working alone."

Thirteen

There were a half-dozen copies of *Newsweek* on Ben's desk, all featuring the same cover: the famous photograph of Ellen on the bridge, arms uplifted and weeping, gray border, black lettering headlining: "America's Failing Infrastructure." Ben was reading one of the magazines and he looked up, abashed, when George walked in.

"How much would you charge me for an autographed copy?" he said.

Ben grinned and tossed the magazine aside. "Seeing as how your autograph appears on my paycheck, I could probably cut you a deal."

George picked up a copy and sank easily into the chair across from Ben, flipping the pages. "It only goes to show a little bit of notoriety is not necessarily a bad thing. Has your mom seen this?"

"Are you kidding? Who do you think Fed-Exed me all these copies?"

George found the page he was searching for and held it up. "Nice photo of you. Good interview, too."

"Glad you approve." Ben leaned back and waited.

George said, "I guess you've figured out I've been assigned the task of mentor, counselor, and personal confidante to get you through this thing. How'm I doing so far?''

"Pretty lousy."

"I believe in a hands-off approach. Seriously, how are you doing?"

"Fine."

"Then I'm done." But he made no move to leave. "You've handled yourself well through the whole thing, Ben," he said. "I don't know what must be going on inside your head, but you seem to be keeping it all in balance. God knows your patient list has more than doubled, which we certainly appreciate, but you haven't let celebrity interfere with your work. It can't be easy, being thrust into the spotlight like this at your age."

"For something I don't deserve, you mean?" Ben's wry tone was mitigated by a shrug. "I caught on to that pretty quick. When I go on talk shows and get written up in national publications I want it to be because I've discovered the cure for cancer or delivered viable sextuplets in a cab or something, not because I was in the right place at the right time doing what any decent citizen would do. The whole thing was starting to get a little embarrassing, if you want to know the truth. I'm glad it's dying down."

George looked at him thoughtfully for a moment, then gave a muffled sigh and a shake of his head. "You *are* young. But if you can keep your head when all those about you are losing theirs, more power to you, I say. If you need anything, even if it's just to talk, ask, okay?"

Ben grinned. "You're starting to make it sound as though I'm a valuable part of this organization."

"Hasn't anyone mentioned that lately?"

"Once or twice, maybe."

"Then I'll have to speak to the partners. A memo went out that each one of us was to make you feel valuable at least twice a day."

Ben's private line rang, and he excused himself to answer it. It was Ellen, and he was surprised. She had never called him at the office before.

"Ellen! Is anything wrong?"

"No, not at all. I didn't expect to get you. I was just going to leave a message with your secretary."

"Well, you're lucky, then, or I am. What's up?" Ben was acutely aware of George, pretending not to overhear. He felt a little awkward.

"It's silly, really. Do you remember when you suggested I should go back to my hometown and talk to that reporter?"

Ben wanted to tell her how glad he was that she felt she could call him even with something silly, and if George hadn't been there that was exactly what he would have said. Instead he stuck to the subject. "Still having trouble with the birth certificate?"

"It's a long story, one of those misunderstandings that just won't go away. Anyway, Diane had the same idea you did—that I might have more luck if I went there in person—and I was wondering if you'd like to drive over with me on Saturday. It's a long trip," she apologized, "and short notice, I know. But we could take the dogs, and maybe have a picnic or something, It's beautiful country."

Ben said, "I'd like to. Let me see what I can do about my schedule." He wondered whether, if George had not been so conspicuously trying to be inconspicuous, he would have suggested they stay overnight to break up the trip. If it had been another woman he might have. Would Ellen misunderstand? Would *he* misunderstand? He hadn't felt this unsure of himself since tenth grade and he wondered whether that was a good sign or a bad one. "Let me call you back at home."

"Thanks." There was a hesitance as though she wanted to say more. But she added only, "And thanks for taking my call. I know you have patients to see."

"Always a pleasure, you know that." The phrase sounded glib the minute it was out and he wished he could take it back. He tried to ease it with, "I'll talk to you later."

"Sure thing. Bye, Ben."

George dropped any pretense of not eavesdropping. "Ellen Cox?" he said. "Are you still seeing her?"

"Now and then." Ben was uncomfortable. He hadn't realized until now that this was something he had kept almost deliberately from his colleagues. So much about his and Ellen's common life was so very public, he had felt compelled to keep this part of it for himself. Or perhaps he was simply uneasy about the reaction he would get if anyone else knew, and the reaction he had worried about was more or less what he saw on George's face now.

"Well, that's a little strange, isn't it?" the other man demanded frankly. Then, in a halfhearted attempt at levity he added, "I mean, seems like a lot of trouble to go to just to get a date."

Ben held his gaze mildly. "Oh, I don't know. I've performed many more remarkable acts of heroism to impress the opposite sex in my day. I used to ride my bike standing on my hands in front of Marcia Wheeler's house every day when I was ten."

George said, "I know it's none of my business."

Ben wanted to agree with him, but he knew the other man meant well. He said slowly, "Something like this . . . the whole bridge thing, I mean . . . it changes you in ways that aren't easy to explain. Not that I put myself in the same category with the survivors, or the families of the victims, but just having been there seems to separate me in some way from the rest of the world." He shrugged little. "It's good to be with someone who understands that. Not only understands it but feels the same way, even more so. We both know the dangers of reading more into this than there is, but . . ." And he grinned a little self-consciously. "I like her. She's interesting. And she's cute, don't you think so?"

Once again George gave a shake of his head that was half amused, half exasperated. "Remind me not to waste my time worrying about you, will you?"

"Does that mean you're resigning your position as my mentor?"

"It means I never met a man who needed one less. Let me know if you develop a drug habit or start showing signs of clinical depression. Otherwise, carry on."

Ben stopped him as he reached the door. "Say, if you meant it when you asked if there was anything I needed . . ."

George glanced back.

"What about trading off with somebody for the Saturday shift? I know I just had last weekend, but

I covered all the married guys' shifts during the holidays."

George thought about it for a minute. "All right, see Marcie about who's available. But don't make a habit of it."

Ben called Ellen's school and left a message confirming the date for Saturday.

Fourteen

It was a four-hour drive from D.C. to Pendleton County, Virginia, the scene of the latest obscenity, which was four hours too long to trust such fragile evidence to inexperienced rural law officers. They took a military helicopter.

As soon as the briefing broke up, Doug Rierson approached Matthew Graham and offered his hand. "It's an honor to be working with you, sir," he said. "I'm an admirer."

Graham's pale gray eyes had skimmed across his face without welcome or acknowledgment and he moved on without accepting Rierson's hand. One of the other agents gave him a sympathetic shrug that seemed to indicate such behavior was par for the course from Graham, but it bothered him.

Once on board the helicopter Graham settled down in the copilot's seat and opened his briefcase. The fact that he did not put on his earphones effectively excluded both Doug and Charlie, who were sitting in back. It also made it possible for them to hold a conversation without Graham's overhearing.

When they were airborne, Doug spoke into his

mouthpiece. "So what's the deal?" He nodded toward Graham, whose back was to them.

Charlie followed his gaze. "It's the way he works." But she looked troubled, and Doug thought it had to do with more than the case, though that was enough.

He said, "Look, if there's a problem I think I have a right to know."

She shook her head. "No problem. Not for anyone but him, that is. He works cases like these by total immersion. He won't let himself get distracted." Her lips tightened briefly and she added, "It's going to get worse before it gets better. Just give him space, and don't take anything personally."

Doug chose his next words carefully. "I heard he had a breakdown."

Charlie's eyes sharpened. "Where did you hear that?"

"It's not true, then?"

"No. It's not true." But she looked away when she said it.

Rierson gave her a moment. Then he said, "Look, I know he's a friend of yours. Hell, the man's practically a legend and I'm not trying to stir anything up. But it's all over headquarters how you went to bat with the AD to have him assigned to this case and how he's not exactly grateful to you for it. If there's shit going on that has nothing to do with this case, that's fine. But I know you don't expect any of us to be tiptoeing around somebody else's feelings when we've got a job to do."

The look Charlie gave him was long and cool. "There's no shit going on," she said. "As for what I expect—I'll let you know, and when I do you won't have any doubts about it. Was there anything else, Special Agent Rierson?"

Rierson took a moment to reassess her position and to steady his own. Then he said. "Yes. One more thing. I want to know whether we're looking for one suspect or two, and how the hell he decided the perpetrator isn't working alone."

"I guess," Charlie replied steadily, "we'll just have to wait and ask him that, now won't we?"

They arrived on the site a little after noon, slightly more than five hours after the pastor had made his grisly discovery. The entire church and half the parking lot had been roped off with crime scene tape and the sheriff assured them the area had been secured. He did admit, however, to photographing the scene, and to allowing the coroner in for a preliminary look at the bodies. Charlie and Doug looked at each other, but said nothing about the trace evidence that might have been destroyed with those two routine actions.

The three agents went inside to look at the bodies, Followed by a cadre of officers and a pall of horror. Matt stayed inside the longest, gazing at the bodies, standing where the killer had stood, tracing the route the killer had taken, looking at what the killer had seen. When he came outside, Rierson was talking to the coroner, who was anxious to take the bodies away, and Charlie was having it out with the sheriff.

"The first thing you should've done," she was saying in short, clipped tones, "was seal the area. Lay down a roll of butcher's paper over the carpet where people absolutely have to have access—Jesus, there's no telling what's been trampled in over the scene. Anything we collect now is going to be useless. Just useless. And what about the primary crime scene? The woman was killed in the woods, right, and brought back here? I hope you didn't just leave the site unguarded."

Sheriff Lelan Camp drawled, "No, ma'am. I surely didn't do that." But his eyes were narrowed and his color was a dull and angry red, and it didn't take an expert in body language to sense the resistance.

Charlie, as usual, was coming on too strong without even realizing what she was doing or that there might be a more effective way of accomplishing her goal. For a black woman in a rural southern town, particularly one representing the FBI to a small-town sheriff, almost anything would be more effective than a display of power.

Matt inserted himself into the conversation with a light touch on Charlie's arm and an apologetic smile to the sheriff. "The important thing to remember here, Sheriff," he said, "is that we're here to offer whatever support we can. We know these are your people, and you're bound to know more about what went on here than we do. But it sure would help us out if you'd let Miss Fontana here ask a few questions, and ask your boys to cooperate with her, too."

He felt Charlie stiffen with every word he spoke, and he thought she'd jump out of her skin when he called her "Miss." He went on, deliberately injecting the faintest patronizing note into his tone, "Charlie, why don't you start by talking to the reverend? And Sheriff, if I could borrow one of your men I'd like to do a drive-through of the area, try to recreate the crime in my mind."

The small lines of anger and tension around the

sheriff's eyes started to ease somewhat as he turned to call over a deputy, and Charlie and Matt walked a few steps away.

"Don't you ever do that to me again," she said, low and hard under her breath.

Matt retorted, "If you start acting like an experienced investigator instead of a rookie just out of the Academy, I won't."

She turned to him, dark eyes flaming. "You undermined my authority and made me look like a fool in front of the local authorities. If this is your way of getting back at me for bringing you in, I wish you'd left it back at Quantico. All you've succeeded in doing is making everyone's job a lot harder."

"Damn it, Charlie—"

But she walked away, leaving him frustrated and silent and wondering why he felt compelled to explain himself to her in the first place. The job wasn't off to a very prestigious start, and the worst was yet to come.

Those unfamiliar with the process of criminal profiling often found it spooky, mystical, even miraculous. More than once Matthew had been accused of owing his success more to psychic power than to logic, and he could not be one hundred percent sure those accusations were wrong. He could tell that the Pendleton County police officer who had been assigned to escort him through the crime scene was already wondering whether the Church Pew psychopath was the only nut involved in this case.

He pulled the car over to the side of a narrow two-lane road where a dirt track led into the woods. "We figure this is where he killed the mother," said the deputy. "Tire tracks going about fifty feet up that road match Mrs. Kellerman's car, and there were splashes of blood from where he must've transferred her to the backseat so he could take the wheel."

Matthew said in a flat, polite monotone, "Thank you, Deputy Ramey. Please don't speak to me again." He heard the report and knew the basics of the crime, but from this point on it was essential that his own perceptions not be tinted by other people's opinions.

He got out of the car and walked up the dirt track. The evidence gathering was complete and the scene had been released, which was to his disadvantage. To his advantage was that in such a remote area the scene had probably not been contaminated by too many others; it was likely that, except for police, the killer was the last person to stand here.

Matthew imagined the day ending, deep dusk settling in. The killer would have been in the backseat holding his weapon on the driver. He had spent some time exploring the area, and he knew about this road, knew he was unlikely to be interrupted for the few minutes it would take to complete his business. He commanded her to drive here. She would have been pleading for the life of her child, who was strapped in his carseat beside her in front. She would have agreed to anything if only he would spare the baby. He would have assured her that no harm was going to come to the child if she did as she was told. She would have done anything. She would have desperately tried to form an escape plan, but with the baby there was nothing she could do. She couldn't crash the car without risking the child, she couldn't leap out and run for help, leaving the baby behind. Her eyes might have darted desperately to the baby, who, sensing his mother's distress, was probably crying by now. Would the crying enrage her attacker? Would he try to silence the baby with his knife? Perhaps her hand reached over, patting the baby, trying to soothe it; perhaps she even tried to fumble with the clasp on the seat restraint, grasping at the one faint, futile chance she might have had to snatch the baby and run when the car stopped. But it takes two hands to unfasten the seatbelt, and she couldn't even free her baby to hold him one last time.

She was trapped, facing rape and probably worse, and helpless to do anything to save her baby or herself.

Knowing this, the killer had cut her throat the moment the car stopped. She couldn't have run away, she couldn't have summoned help, she couldn't have fought back. Yet he wasted no time fondling her, tormenting her, raping her. He simply killed her, quickly, silently, and efficiently, as had been his intention all along.

He had placed a plastic bag over her head to keep the blood from soaking into the upholstery of the car, but some had been smeared on the surrounding foliage as he dragged her out of the front seat and placed her in back. Then he walked down to the stream that he had also discovered when he scouted the area earlier, and washed the blood off his waterproof jacket and rubber boots, rinsed off his gloved hands. Blood would have splashed his face, so he cupped handfuls of the icy water to his face and hair, slicking it back with his fingers. When he returned to the car, he was clean. Being clean was important to him.

The baby was still crying, so he had rummaged through the diaper bag on the front seat and found a bottle of juice, which he uncapped and gave to the child. He was still wearing gloves then, so no fingerprints were visible, but there were traces of blood on the bottle. He replaced the cap carefully in the diaper bag, and drove back to the church.

It was around six-thirty then, and the last of the day-care workers had left at six. In small towns like this, six to seven was still considered the family hour, and no activities were scheduled at the church before seven-thirty. He had plenty of time.

The sanctuary was unlocked, as it always was. He had parked close to the front door, in the pastor's reserved spot, and walked inside. There were six decorative sconces on the walls, each holding four tapers. He lit them all. Then he returned to the car and removed the body of the woman. He didn't want to get blood on the carpet, so he left the bag tightly around her upper torso until she was positioned exactly where she belonged. Sixth row left, forty-two inches from the aisle. *Exactly where she belonged.* He had known that without mistake or hesitation.

Blood pooled from the plastic bag and soaked the cushioned seat around her. That didn't bother him; it was part of the effect. He removed the bag. Her jacket. He didn't like it. He took it off, wadding it up in the bag. And the hair was all wrong. He released it from it chiffon bow and combed it with bloody gloved fingers down around her face. There. That was better. He stepped back to admire his work, leaving a smeared toe imprint of a Sears Workman heavy-duty rubber boot, size eleven and a half, in the carpet aisle. It was faint, and he might not have seen it in the candlelight, but he had. He had bent down, touched the imprint with a gloved finger, then decided it didn't matter. It bothered his sense of the aesthetic, that was all.

He went back outside. It was dark, but the parking lot was lit by the amber glow of overhead street lights. Anyone passing by on the side street could have glanced over and seen him. But he wasn't afraid of the light. He wasn't afraid of the dark, either. He wasn't afraid of anything. He was protected.

The baby had dropped his bottle and was crying. The crying didn't bother him; it didn't enrage him or inflame him, but it was inconvenient. A crying baby could attract attention, and he didn't want to deal with that. So he took out his scalpel, the same one he had used to kill the mother, and then . . . then something had gone wrong. A hesitation here, a confusion. Something had happened. He had braced his hand on the car, leaving a faint smear in the road dust. He had turned around, backed up. He had started to close the car door. Then he had reached into the diaper bag and taken out a diaper. No more hesitation. Swiftly, cleanly, he cut the baby's throat. The child never felt anything.

He used the diaper like a bandage to absorb the blood and carried the baby inside, arranging it carefully, precisely on its mother's lap. He had had some trouble getting the lifeless bodies to remain upright in the pose he wanted, but he was patient. He had time. As a finishing touch he had placed in the baby's hands a fuzzy, jointed-limbed teddy bear that he had brought with him. He had tied the child's hands together with the green plaid ribbon from the bear's neck so it would look as though the child were holding the toy.

He was finished.

He disposed of the bag and the bloodied garments in a dumpster behind the church. He used the men's room downstairs to wash the remnants of the child's blood from his hands, scalpel, and jacket. Once outside he had removed the gloves and tucked them with the scalpel into the zippered pocket of his jacket. He had then walked the six miles back to the shopping center, where his car was parked.

Matthew was back at the church, steeped in the dark soup of twisted purpose that was the residue of evil, and he was not entirely sure how he had gotten there. He blinked his eyes a couple of times to let the images of Linda Kellerman and her eighteen-month-old son Jess dissolve and give way to present day. Yellow police tape, overhead florescents, burned-down candles. A wide blackish stain on the beige pew cushion forty-two inches from the center aisle, sixth row left.

He turned and walked down the aisle, back into the parking lot.

Charlie was interviewing the sheriff's deputy who had been first on the scene, and she had softened her technique considerably. Reirson was talking to the sheriff. Each looked up when he approached. There were more than a dozen other local police officers, all looking as grim and angry as the brutality of the crime warranted, all of them waiting, more or less, for what he had to say. The silence of accusation and expectation was deafening.

He thought, *This was one of theirs. They knew this woman, this child. Somebody lived next door to her. Somebody attended her wedding. Somebody delivered her baby and now somebody's got to tell her husband, her mother.* This town would never be the same. The caul of innocence that surrounded life in a small town had been shredded, allowing evil to seep through, and its stain was black and eradicable. No one would ever feel safe here again. No one would ever say, *It can't happen to me.* It could happen to anyone.

The power the killer held over the minds and the hearts of an entire society sickened and infuriated Matt.

He walked over to the sheriff, who awaited him with a half-suspicious, half-fearful look far back in his eyes. "Sheriff," Matt said quietly, "you're not going to catch this man."

Into the shocked, sharp silence that seemed to stab him from a dozen angry eyes, he went on gently, "I know it's hard, something like this happening on your watch, but if you're looking for the satisfaction of bringing him in you might as well go home. The killer has been out of your jurisdiction for almost thirteen hours now. The best you can do is give us what help you can and let us go from there."

He looked at Rierson. "Check out the nearest shopping center; you'll find a dark-colored van was parked there most of the afternoon yesterday. See if any of the stores sell that bear, but it's my guess he brought it with him."

Reirson said, "What about the plates?"

"He wouldn't have missed an opportunity like yesterday to switch plates with another vehicle in the parking lot," Matt agreed, "but he's smart enough to have stuck to the same make and color if he could."

Charlie said, "Sheriff, you need to start running the tags on every van in your jurisdiction. I know it's going to be a slow process, but our people will help you narrow the field was much as they can."

To Matt's satisfaction, after only the briefest hesitation the sheriff gave a short, acquiescent nod. "We'll pull double shifts until it's done."

To Charlie, Matt added, "We need to get a bulletin out with a description of the van. The driver is five-eleven, one hundred seventy-five pounds, muscular arms and shoulders, thirty-eight to forty-five years old. He's wearing a dark-colored nylon windbreaker with a waterproof finish and zippered pockets. In the back of the van you'll find a toolbox or a briefcase with a supply of plastic garbage bags and disposable surgical gloves, also a supply of stainless-steel surgical scalpel blades. His name is something from the Old Testament—Noah or Abraham or Ezekiel, something along those lines, and it's probably an alias.

"He'll be staying in chain motels and paying cash. Don't bother checking the dives, he's too fastidious for any place that isn't spotlessly clean. The longer this goes on, the less often he'll stop to sleep. He'll never stay overnight in the direct vicinity of a crime. He's smart, above average I.Q., pleasant looking, and friendly. He's casually but nicely dressed, dark clothes. Nothing about him will arouse suspicion in anyone he deals with."

Charlie looked up from her notes. "Is he traveling alone?"

"I don't know yet."

Reirson spoke up. "Now wait a minute. Earlier you said there were two suspects. Have you changed your mind?"

Matthew tried to cut him off with a sharp glance, but too late. Already shock was stirring through his audience. The sheriff demanded, "What the hell is that? Are you saying there's more than one of these maniacs loose out there?"

Matt replied calmly, "We're considering the possibility that the killer may be working with someone else. Whether or not that party is actually traveling with him or is directly involved in the crimes at all isn't clear yet."

A grumbling of questions and protests began and Charlie said, possibly a little more sharply than she should have, "We're trying to keep this information from the press, gentlemen. Your cooperation will be appreciated." And the look she gave Reirson could have killed.

Matt put in firmly, "The Raleigh field office already has a profile of the man we're looking for—a level-headed citizen, member of the church, works in a hospital or medical supply house, possibly as a security guard. He makes good money, ex-military. And this is important. *He is not a criminal.*"

He had succeeded in distracting the officers from their outrage. The skepticism and amazement he had seen in their eyes earlier was turning into derision. Only Charlie's gaze remained steady and intent on his. Matt went on before anyone could interrupt his train of thought, "He doesn't think like a criminal, act like a criminal, or associate with criminals. You're not going to catch him shoplifting or speeding or buying drugs. He's a man with an agenda, a job to do, and he's going to do it in the most effective, most efficient way possible."

Someone spoke up angrily, "And his job is to murder innocent women and babies?"

Matt shook his head. "Not just women, not just children. And he doesn't look at it as murder. To him it's more like—sacrifice."

Someone said, "You mean like devil worship?"

"No, there's no sign of satanism at all. In fact I'd said his religious background has its roots in traditional Christianity."

Charlie looked at Matt, then swept around the group, sensing more hostility than credulity. She gave Matt a chance to say something more, but when he did not she took a breath and said, "I think what Agent Graham is trying to say, gentlemen, is that this is very much a work in progress, for us as well as him. So far, he's just a little better at doing his job than we are at doing ours. Let's see what we can do to change that equation, shall we?"

They accepted a ride back to town with one of the deputies, and there an agent from the nearest field office had a car waiting for them. The remaining sites would be surveyed by more conventional—and less expensive—means of transportation.

The silence among the federal agents was palpable on that ride to town, and it wasn't until they were alone and standing outside the car that Charlie said to Reirson, "*Never* challenge a fellow investigator in front of local law enforcement, have you got that? And where the hell did you get the idea it was okay to volunteer information you got at an official briefing? Jesus Christ, doesn't your brain have any control over your mouth? You could be seriously reprimanded for this."

Reirson said stiffly, "I screwed up. I'm sorry." The way he spoke indicated he had known what was coming, had considered his options, and had decided an apology was the least unpleasant of them.

Charlie slapped the keys into his hand. "You're driving."

Rierson got behind the wheel and Matt started to walk around the car.

"And you." Her fingers closed on Matt's arm, holding him back. Her tone lowered a fraction, but the anger burned even colder. "I don't give a shit how good your intentions are, don't you ever treat me like that again. Not in private, not back at headquarters, and for damn sure not in front of a bunch of rednecked white cops."

Matt looked at her for a moment, trying to force down his own irritation. "I didn't mean to hurt your feelings, Agent Fontana."

She released his arm with a snap and half turned, but not before the faint flicker of vulnerability crossed her fine-boned features. Her voice was slightly subdued as she answered. "It's just that I've been taking that kind of crap from men my whole life. I didn't expect it from you."

Matt didn't know what to say. He genuinely hadn't meant to hurt her, and he found himself irrationally annoyed at her for allowing this to happen. "It's the case," he said. "We're all under more stress than we realize, I guess."

She barely glanced at him as she pushed past. "You're the psychiatrist. You should have figured that out sooner, shouldn't you?"

Charlie took the backseat, where she kicked off her shoes and used her cell phone to call headquarters. Matt put on his sunglasses and leaned his head back, closing his eyes and trying not to see the faces of that mother and child. The child. It must have been hard, doing the child. Suddenly he realized what the blood-soaked cloth diaper had been used for, before it had been used to stop the blood from dripping. He had put it over the baby's face, to cover the eyes. He might not have been able to finish it otherwise.

He's not doing this for pleasure, Matthew thought. *He has a conscience. He's doing this because he has to.*

Reirson spoke, interrupting his thoughts. "Why churches?" he said. "Aside from the obvious, I mean."

Matt opened his eyes, refusing to be annoyed. There was too much tension in this car as it was, and he was going to be living with these people for the next three days. At least. "What's the obvious?"

"They're never locked, easy to get to, but usually set back from the main traffic areas, especially in small towns. Poor security lighting. And at most churches, a car in the parking lot even at odd hours wouldn't attract much attention, or even someone moving around inside. That's the nature of their business. And as public buildings, they're hard to collect evidence from. Any fingerprints, hairs, or fibers we find could have come from any of several hundred people, and even if they could be traced to the suspect he could claim a legitimate reason for being there."

Matt nodded. "But none of that is why he's using churches. He's not worried about avoiding detection or about convenience. The church is a symbol to him. It sanctifies his act. That's why those cops back there were so wrong trying to make this into an act of satanism. Satanists, even pseudo-satanists, are defiling a holy place. This guy is seeking a benediction from it."

"Why no Catholic churches? Seems to me they would be a prime target—not to mention an easy source of candles. So far, he's been bringing his own."

Matt shook his head impatiently. "It's just logistics. He's traveling through rural Virginia, not exactly a haven of Catholicism. Also, Catholic churches are occupied more often and for longer hours than Protestant ones." And the thought came unbidden to his head: *But he has used Catholic churches before. In another time, when he was another person* . . . Irritably he pushed the thought down.

Reirson said, choosing his words with obvious care, "I took your course on profiling the ritual killer. You probably don't remember me."

"I get a lot of students," Matt replied noncommittally, although the truth was he did remember Reirson. He kept track of all the Academy graduates, particularly when they went out of their way to make their careers noticeable.

"I was impressed as hell. But I've got to tell you, I don't get how you came up with the two-killer theory."

Matt said, "Then I guess I wasn't a very good teacher."

Reirson cut his eyes to him, but he refused to commit himself further.

From the backseat Charlie finished her call and disconnected. Matt took a breath. "Look," he said. "What you've got to understand about this guy—and it is one guy, the same guy, doing the actual killing so far—is that for most of his life he's followed a steady, predictable pattern. Then something happened to interrupt that pattern, and it was something big. Now he has a new agenda, a new scenario to play out, and he's not going to stop until it's done. There's something else you should know. He's not afraid of you. He's not afraid of being caught, of going to jail, of dying, of anything. He believes he's under some kind of protection. If apprehended, he should never be cornered, particularly if any chance exists for a hostage situation to develop. Remember, the most dangerous man in the world is one who believes he's right and who has no fear."

A brief silence followed his speech, and he could sense Charlie's attention was on him as well as Reirson's. Then Reirson said, "You keep talking about an agenda, implying we won't know what it is until he's done. Any idea when that might be?"

Matthew hesitated only a moment before replying. "May first."

SATURDAY, APRIL 26

Fifteen

Ellen said, "I feel really stupid, making you drive all the way out here on your day off."

"Yeah, it's a real hardship spending the afternoon with a pretty girl in some of the most beautiful countryside God ever created. But you did buy me lunch, so I guess I can't complain."

Ellen laughed. The spring day couldn't have been more perfect, nor the company more ideal. They had bundled the two dogs in the back of Ben's jeep and set off for West Virginia shortly after ten, stopping at a wooded Victorian inn for lunch and a glass of chilled Mondavi chardonnay. She felt pretty in a pink shirt and khaki walking shorts, and she could tell Ben thought so too—even if he had not said it. Ben told stories that made her laugh, and after lunch they walked the dogs beside a creek that ran behind the inn in sun-dappled eddies and still pools toward a small, slick-rocked waterfall. If Ellen could have forgotten, even for a moment, the purpose of the outing, it would have been among the best days of her life.

Ten minutes earlier they had taken the turnoff to Wintersville, West Virginia. According to the map, they had less than thirty miles to go.

"Do you have any friends or relatives who still live here?" Ben asked. "Anyone you want to look up?"

Ellen cast him a grateful look. He had never once questioned her sanity, which was more than she could say for herself. He had just assumed that she was right and the reporter and the Colquitt County Hall of Records was wrong. She could not remember if she had ever known anyone who had more faith in her than she did herself, and she could not imagine why that should be so.

She said, "We moved to Norfolk when I was twelve years old. That's a long time ago. I can't even remember the names of my friends from seventh grade, can you?"

"Roger Milcot and Harry Barnes," he replied promptly. "We built a smoke bomb and put it under the principal's chair. Unfortunately, it misfired and caught the chair on fire—not while the principal was in it, luckily for us. They're in prison now," he added, "which leaves me as Henderson Middle School's proudest achievement."

She laughed again, but the sound was less genuine than it had been moments before. Anxiety was building in her chest with each mile closer they drew to her hometown. She said abruptly, "Do you still have bad dreams about what happened on the bridge?"

His glance was concerned, although he tried to disguise it. "Not so much anymore. But I wasn't the one who was trapped eighty feet above water for eight hours."

"Water," she murmured. "The dripping I hear—it has to represent water. But the faces, Ben, the people on the bridge . . . they're so clear I could pick them out of a lineup. And they're haunting me. I just can't seem to let go of them.''

Ben said slowly, "I've been thinking about that. The faces in your dream, they can't be from the bridge. Aside from me, the only people you saw on the bridge were the two rescue workers who got you out, and the paramedics in the ambulance. I saw dozens, maybe even hundreds of people that day. But you were trapped in your car facing eternity, so to speak, and you didn't see anything—or anyone— who didn't come to you. So the faces have got to be composites. Symbolic of something.''

She shook her head adamantly. "They're real. They're so real I almost know their names. The fat man with the gold cross on a necklace, the woman with the salt-and-pepper hair and glasses on a chain, the blond boy with the sharp nose, the brunette in the red shirt—they're all so *clear*. How could I make up such details?''

"You probably didn't," acceded Ben. "These may very well be real people—people you've seen in the movies or on television, or in a shopping mall or on the street. The subconscious mind is an amazing thing, and it can reproduce images with uncanny accuracy when it wants to. I'm just saying none of these people were on the bridge, so whatever you're dreaming about probably doesn't have a lot to do with the latest trauma in your life.''

"What else could it be?''

"Psychiatry isn't my strong suit,'' he said, and he glanced at her again, as though trying to determine whether she'd take his next suggestion as an insult. "But if you'd like, I have a colleague . . .''

She shook her head tiredly. "Not yet, okay? I'd like to think I have the emotional stability to get through this on my own . . . although it doesn't look as though I do, does it?"

"A few bad dreams . . ."

"And this whole obsession with my hometown. Just think, if I hadn't become a national celebrity by almost falling off a bridge I might have gone my whole life thinking I actually knew where I had grown up. Life is strange, huh?"

"Come on, I told you before there could be a million explanations for that. The only way you can know for sure is to get a certified copy of your birth certificate."

"What if I can't?"

"Well there could be a few possible explanations for that, too. Believe me, I've filled out some birth certificates in my time. Mistakes happen."

She smiled at him. "You're a really nice guy, Ben."

"So I hear."

"Thanks for—you know, for being with me through this."

"That's what I'm here for."

This time she hesitated a moment longer. "Are you getting tired of it yet?"

"What?"

"Me. The problems. The whole never-ending nightmare that started with the bridge and keeps unrolling like a bad film."

He reached over and lay his hand lightly atop hers on the seat. "It's not a nightmare," he said quietly. "And no, I'm not tired of it."

Then he said. "This is it. Look familiar?"

Ellen felt her heart speed as she saw the sign, a weathered arch with peeling black paint: Welcome to Wintersville. She turned her head to read the opposite side "Leaving Wintersville—Drive Safely!" She hoped it was not just her imagination, it probably *was* her imagination, but it did look familiar somehow—the sign, the road, the curve of the land. She said, "I think so. It's hard to tell. There should be a crossroad coming up—turn left."

To her enormous relief, there was a crossroad, and when Ben turned left the road led them through a small downtown area. Ellen noticed the offices of the *Herald*, a department store, an appliance store, the brick courthouse. The dogs, realizing they had reached their destination, or perhaps simply noticing the change of speed, were alert in the backseat, their excited breathing loud and warm on the back of Ellen's neck.

She said, "I think I remember this." But she sounded even more uncertain than she felt. "Maybe there used to be a soda fountain there on that corner, or a drugstore where Mother would take me for grilled-cheese sandwiches, and I think I remember buying shoes there . . . only it's a flower shop now."

"Maybe we should try to find a map," Ben suggested.

"No. No, let me try this. Let's drive around a little first. Turn right at the stop sign—oh, they've put in a light. Turn right. I'm pretty sure my street is down that way, and the park that circled the lake is right in front of it. There's a church on the corner."

But the street wasn't there. Neither was the church or the lake or the park. Ben drove patiently through every street that crossed the town while Ellen, in increasing frustration, failed to recognize a single landmark. Finally he stopped at the Chamber of Commerce, and came back a few moments later with a map. They spread it open on the seat between them.

There was no lake. There was no park. There was no street by the name of Jericho, and there was, as Mike Bethune, the *Herald* reporter, had indicated, no Nathaniel Hawthorne Elementary School.

"Do you think I could be remembering someone else's childhood?" Ellen joked weakly, but her hands were a little unsteady as she refolded the map.

Ben's expression was thoughtful. "I would suggest you rethink any plan of talking to that reporter. I don't think anything you could say is likely to look very good in print."

Ellen released a long breath. "I'm glad I didn't tell him I was coming."

Ben started the engine again. "It's a shame it's Saturday," he said as he pulled out of the parking lot. "We could have checked the county records if the courthouse had been open."

"Yeah." Ellen looked out the window, concentrating on trying to find something—anything—she recognized. "Poor planning on my part."

"Was it?"

Ellen turned to him. "What do you mean?"

The line of Ben's jaw tightened briefly with frustration or reluctance, then he said, "Ellen, you knew the county offices would be closed today. You could have called that reporter and asked him to do some research for you, but you didn't. You didn't even tell him you were coming. I think you knew what you were going to find when you got here."

She stared at him. "You think I'm making this whole thing up? Why in the world would I do that?"

Ben gave an impatient shake of his head. "No, I don't think you're making it up, not on purpose anyway. Just listen; bear with me for a minute. Does any of this look familiar to you?"

"Yes, I told you. Some of it. It looks *familiar*—I think I've been here before—but it's not home. The things I remember just aren't here."

"What about the churches?"

"What?"

He was stopped at a stop sign. Directly opposite was a big stone church with a sign that said "First Methodist." A half a block to the south was a brick building with a steeple and a sign welcoming visitors to the First Baptist Church of Wintersville. Both were located on what was appropriately called Church Street.

Ben said, "You've mentioned the church you went to as a child more than once to me. It must have a strong association for you. Do either of these look like the church you remember?"

Ellen shook her head without hesitation. "Mine was smaller, a white clapboard building with a steeple and big oak trees around it. It had five long wooden steps to a little porch outside the front door. Inside it was dark and smelled like furniture polish. We sat on the fifth row from the back on the right side. It always reminded me of the Church in the Wildwood."

Ben stared at her for a moment. "Well," he said. "I don't know why you're doubting your memory."

The car behind him tapped its horn and Ben crossed the intersection. Ellen frowned. "That's funny. I can remember every detail about that place—except of course, where it is."

"When do you first remember telling someone you were from Wintersville?"

"Good heavens, I don't know." She thought a moment. "High school, I guess. Yes, it was high school, because I remember having my records transferred from Wintersville. Everyone else had gone to junior high together and I was the new kid in town."

"What do you remember about junior high?"

"I don't know what you mean. It was junior high. Geography, history, math."

"Do you remember any of your friends? Your teachers?"

The question made her uncomfortable for some reason. "Do you?"

"Ellen, you just described for me in perfect detail a church you haven't been inside for close to twenty years, but you can't remember your best friend in junior high. You can remember things that happened when you were four years old but not when you were eleven."

Ellen swallowed hard on a suddenly dry throat. "That's—weird."

"Do you want to know what I think?"

"No," Ellen said slowly, rubbing her arms. "I don't think I do. But you'd better tell me anyway."

"I think you probably *did* live here at one time. I think you went to junior high here and maybe even elementary school. But something is causing you to block the memory of the time you lived here, and substitute memories of a happier place, probably from earlier in your childhood."

"I don't understand."

"The things you remember—the park, the lake, the church—they're real memories, from a place you actually lived. But it wasn't here. Because you have no memory of living here, you had to fill in the blanks somehow and your mind just naturally substituted images of that earlier place for this one."

"But why would I do that? Why would I forget a whole town, several years out of my life?"

Ben hesitated. "Trauma could do it."

"Like an accident?"

"Or a psychological trauma."

She stared at him. "Do you mean child abuse?" She gave a short angry shake of her head. "You've been watching too many talk shows."

"Look, I'm not going to speculate, and it'll take someone with more time and qualifications than I have to trace down the answers. But that's my theory."

Ellen turned toward the window again, mostly to hide the sudden tears that stung her eyes from his view. In a moment she said, her tone muffled, "I'm sorry Ben. I didn't mean to be short with you. I appreciate everything you've done, and I know you didn't have to but—it's all a bit much."

"Please stop thanking me." Ben's voice was tinged with exasperation. "I volunteered for this mission, remember? I'm involved. I'm interested. Besides . . ."

He glanced at her, and gentled his tone with a coaxing smile. "I kind of like you."

Ellen closed her eyes briefly, trying to force the tension from her shoulders. "You know you're too nice for your own good, don't you?"

"I'm not trying to be nice," he answered. "I'm just trying to be . . ." He groped for the word. "Real."

Ellen opened her eyes and smiled at him. She knew without even thinking about it exactly what he meant. Since the bridge, reality had been defined in different terms for her as well. She also knew that it was that—the fact that she understood without asking—that made him want to be involved in her problems, just as it made her want to depend on him for help.

She said with a small sigh, "Well, I hope you know what you're getting into, Ben Bradshaw. Because this is about as real as it gets."

Sixteen

Matt found Charlie in the hotel bar. "Reirson wanted to know if you wanted to get something to eat." He took the stool beside her.

She shook her head without looking up. "After what we saw today? How can either one of you think about eating?"

"I was wondering if you'd noticed. You were pretty tough out there."

"I threw up twice before we left that church. I couldn't let any of those assholes know."

Matt lifted a finger at the bartender. "Scotch, neat."

Now she looked at him. "You're drinking?"

"Why not? I'm not in a program."

"It's just been a long time since I've seen you drink."

"Yeah, well it's been a long time since I had a day like this, too."

He got his drink and touched her shoulder, indicating a booth toward the back.

"You're not eating?"

"There's a lot of nutrition in peanuts."

They settled into the booth and sipped their drinks in silence for awhile. The Interstate Holiday Inn was probably not the hottest spot in the Raleigh-Durham area on a Saturday night, but it was moderately crowded. The clutter provided a comfortable cover for conversation, or for the lack thereof.

"Durham," Matt said eventually, looking around. "I was here in eighty-two. It hasn't changed much."

"The hotel or the city?"

"Both."

"I apologize for jumping your ass this afternoon. Reirson, too, although he deserved it more than you did."

"Tell me about him."

"He's okay. Little bit of a brown-nose, but hell, we all were when we started."

"I wasn't."

"You didn't have to be." She took another sip of her drink and then looked down at the glass. "Do you know what this case could mean to me? I know it sounds shitty to put it like that."

"You've had big cases before."

She shook her head. "Not like this. Nobody's had a case like this."

"Thank God."

She looked at him. "They gave it to me because of you."

"They gave it to you because they knew you could handle it." Matt's voice was sharp.

"That," she agreed, "and I'm the only agent left who can work with you."

They just looked at each other for a moment. Then Matt said, lifting his glass to her, "To a hell of a team."

She smiled faintly. "You got that right."

Matt's phone rang. At first he was surprised because he wasn't expecting anyone, and he answered it automatically. He felt something start to shrink inside him and wither away into a cold hard knot the moment he heard her voice.

"Hey, Captain, you must be out partying. Your voice mail has been picking up at home and at work so I thought I'd try your cellular. What's up?"

"I'm on a case, Polly," he said. Matt's tone was flat and emotionless, discouraging further conversation. "I'll have to call you back."

She didn't give him a chance to disconnect. "What do you mean, a case? I thought—"

"This is not a good time." Firmer now, colder. He could feel Charlie's eyes on him and he was irritated.

"Don't do this to me." Polly's voice lowered with determination. "Don't push me away, not now. I can help you through this—"

"No. You can't." Then, relenting fractionally, trying to force gentleness into his tone, he added, "We have an appointment Richmond airport, two-fifteen on May first. I won't miss it, that's a promise. I'll talk to you then."

"You need me, damn it!"

He disconnected.

Without looking up, he dialed Headquarters. "This is Graham. I'm turning off my phone. If you need to reach me, coordinate through Agent Fontana." He disconnected, turned the phone off, and pocketed it.

Charlie said, "Jesus, Matt."

"Don't start with me, Charlie."

Charlie was silent for a moment, obviously choosing her words. "Did you ever think that compartmentalizing your life like this might not be the best thing for the relationship?"

"You're not my therapist," he said sharply. He cut his eyes away, searching for composure. "I just can't have both of them in my head at the same time."

He could sense she wanted to say more, but restrained herself. The silence had an edge to it until she changed the subject. "So. It's a copycat, after all."

Matt hesitated. "It looks like it."

Charlie picked up on his uncertainty immediately, and answered with a sharp frown. "What do you mean, it looks like it?"

"There are similarities, but it doesn't track like a typical copycat. Hell, Charlie, you don't need me to tell you that. The Mayday Killer is killing the same woman over and over again, always on the anniversary of an event with some tremendous significance to him. This guy—same technique, maybe even same motivations, but different victims."

Charlie said, "What do you mean, same motivations?"

But Matt shook his head. "I'm not prepared to commit myself further."

Charlie's hand tightened around her glass and she leaned forward fiercely. "Damn it, Matt, save the party line for Washington! This is me you're talking to, and for God's sake, if you know anything—"

"I'd tell you, damn it! This is a little more than the Charlie Fontana show, or hadn't you noticed?" He took a breath. "Get me an anniversary date search. Go back twenty-five—no, thirty—years. Maybe something will ring a bell."

Charlie said stiffly, "Anything else?"

Matt said, struggling with the words, "Charlie, look. I told you I wasn't comfortable coming back. Give me some time, okay? What I'm thinking . . . if I'm wrong, it's going to mean more than my career or yours. Just give me some time."

And Charlie answered, "As far as I'm concerned you've got until next Christmas. I just hope Churchpew gets the same message. And maybe, if we're lucky, no more babies will die in the meantime."

Matt looked at her steadily, but said nothing.

Charlie lifted her glass, drank from it. "You're calling him upper middle class, salesman type, right? I got a map from Triple-A, tracing the route down 58 and the stops he's likely to make. What do you think about putting agents in place at churches in the vicinity of his next likely stops?"

Matt shook his head. "These are crimes of opportunity. You can stake out every church you think he's likely to hit, and he'll hit the one you're not watching. Or he'll take his victim from one area and dump him in the next unguarded church. He's not stupid. And he's not ready to be caught."

Charlie said, "Shit." She lifted the glass again. "I'm placing agents anyway."

"You have to," Matt agreed.

Matt saw Charlie's eyes focus over his shoulder and he looked around as Reirson approached their table.

"Good news," he said without preamble. "A security camera at the pawnshop across the street from the shopping center where our suspect parked his van caught him on tape switching plates. Only the hands and arms were in the frame, so no possible I.D., but we've got an APB out now for the new plates."

Matt shook his head. "He will have switched again by now."

Reirson slid into the chair between Matt and Charlie. "I thought you said this guy wasn't a criminal, implying lack of criminal mentality. Now you've got him acting like a professional."

Matt replied, "He's not a criminal. But he's getting outside advice. What about the original plate? Was the camera able to capture that?"

"That's the bad news. He kept his original plate, and the camera only got a partial. Three digits. We sent the tape to Documents for analysis."

Charlie said, "Meantime, I'll alert the local police to search parking lots of the chain motels along the route for the van."

Reirson said, "I'll phone it in to headquarters, if you like."

"Thanks."

Then he looked from Matt to Charlie and back again, quickly, in an almost furtive gesture. He said, "I've got to know. What makes you think he's getting advice? How do you know he's working with someone else?"

Matt said, "There was a good set of footprints in the second murder, in the mud outside the abandoned church. If you study the crime scene photos you'll see the suspect kept a measured stride for approximately eighteen paces, carrying the body into the church. Then he stopped and turned, and stood there for some period of time, as if talking to someone. He did that again inside the church, as the mud pattern shows, before he placed the body."

"There have to be a dozen other explanations for the pattern of those footprints," Reirson objected. "A hundred reasons why he would stop and turn around."

"While he's carrying a body that's already twelve hours old, trying not to spill congealed blood all over everything?"

"Maybe he heard something," Reirson argued. "A car or a snapping branch—"

"Then you pause, check it out. No more than thirty seconds. Evidence shows the suspect stood there a good three to four minutes, shifting his weight, talking. And since there's no evidence of another murder or abduction, we've got to assume that whoever he stopped to talk to knew him, and approved of what he was doing. Perhaps he even advised him. He did the same thing at the Kellerman murders. Before he killed the baby, he hesitated, turned around, moved in a way that wasn't consistent with a man alone, concentrating on a mission."

Reirson looked at him for a moment. "That's it? That's what you're basing your conclusion on?"

"No. That's not all." But he wasn't ready to talk about the rest of it. He wasn't sure he wanted to even think about it, because it was becoming harder and harder to draw the line between intuition and hard evidence, particularly when the intuition was so outrageous as to be unbelievable, even for him. Particularly when so much was at stake if he was wrong.

Reirson said, "There was no evidence of a second set of footprints at the scene—either scene."

"There might have been," Charlie reminded him sharply, "if the scene hadn't been contaminated before we got there."

Matt refused to show his gratitude for her support—and therefore his own lack of confidence—by glancing at her.

Reirson was silent for a moment. Then he said to Matt, "I remember from your course you used to say that this wasn't an exact science."

"I'm glad you remembered."

"Have you ever been wrong?"

Matt replied, "I'm wrong at least once a day every single day of my life." He lifted his glass and drank. "The best I can hope for is I'm not wrong about this."

SUNDAY, APRIL 27

Seventeen

They were calling him the Church Pew Killer. Daniel watched the news on television in the Motel Six in which he'd passed a dreamless night and he was aware that this new notoriety would complicate matters for him for a while. It worried him a little.

Ariel grinned at him, sensing his uneasiness. "You're famous," he said.

"The police are going to be looking for me now," Daniel said unhappily.

"Since when does anything the police do concern us?" Ariel answered impatiently. "They've been looking for you for years."

That made Daniel uncomfortable. "That was another life. I don't like to talk about that."

"Of course you don't." Ariel's expression was gentle and sympathetic. "You were lost then. You didn't even know what you were looking for."

Daniel said slowly, and with a touch of wonder as gradual understanding dawned, "I think I was looking for you."

Ariel smiled, and laid his hand gently on Daniel's arm. "I think you were, too."

*   *   *

In the dark early morning he began driving, heading toward the ocean through rambling back roads bordered by pretty springtime meadows. This was horse country, gentle and rolling, and it reminded him of home. Not long after dawn he came upon a small brick church of the kind he liked best: simple, unadorned, isolated. The white sign out front said "Rock Springs Baptist Church, Established 1922." There was a gravel parking lot and a cemetery with old-fashioned marble monuments and markers out back. He felt calm and strong when he parked the car and got out into the pale morning sunshine.

A twelve-year-old boy was in the back of the van, his head wrapped in a plastic garbage bag to keep the blood from leaking through the floorboard. Although he had hated to keep the body overnight— it seemed disrespectful somehow—he should have known there was a reason. This perfect child, this perfect little church—there was always a reason.

If he had not believed in miracles, Daniel would have been amazed at how sweetly the souls surrendered themselves to him, how perfectly they presented themselves to him. Oh, sometimes he had to settle for an approximation or arrange a prop, but the essence was there. The symbol, the purpose. Eleven people, plus one. The holy number.

He opened the console and took out a handful of votive candles. The problem with Protestant churches, particularly Baptist ones, was that they rarely displayed altar candles. The church inside was as simple and unadorned as he had hoped: a dozen pews on either side, a choir loft, a podium, and a small baptistery. He set up the candles lining the aisle and lit them. He returned for the body and placed it precisely where it belonged, on the sixth row from the back, three spaces from the aisle. He stepped back and the picture he saw was a beautiful sight to behold.

He removed his protective gloves, folded them carefully into a small neat square that fit into his jacket pocket, and reluctantly turned to go. He heard the doors to the vestibule open as he was turning, and a square of light flooded up the aisle. A man in a plaid shirt and jeans stood there, blinking uncertainly in the dimness. Not the minister. Perhaps a janitor, or church member here on unknown business.

This was unexpected. His heart began to pound.

Ariel, standing a little behind Daniel, whispered, "Don't panic. You can handle this."

The man said, "Can I help you with something?"

He saw the candles and they clearly made him uneasy, but he had not yet seen the boy, who was not tall enough to be visible above the top of the pew, particularly slumped as he was. *You can handle this.* Daniel smiled and kept coming toward him at an easy stride. "No thanks," he said, "I was just leaving."

"Hey, wait a minute. Did you put those candles there? What were you—"

"Fear no evil," Ariel whispered. "You have the power."

Daniel walked past him and the man had to turn to follow him with his eyes. In mid-turn, Daniel grasped the man's hair, jerked his neck back, and slit his throat. It was messy, and there was a struggle.

He didn't die at once. Daniel resented that, but he tried not to let it take the power of the event.

When it was finished he stood over the body, breathing hard, trying not to panic. "This wasn't supposed to happen," he said, closing his fists. The raggedness of his breathing made his voice sound shaky. "Why didn't you warn me? This wasn't supposed to happen!"

Ariel stepped carefully around the body, surveying it with a pleased, calm expression on his face. "Of course it was," he replied.

"How can you say that? Look at this mess!"

"You see a mess," Ariel countered reasonably, "I see something more significant. Look at him, Daniel," he commanded. "Really *look* at him. He's perfect."

Daniel turned his eyes back to man and then he saw it. The age, the size, even the plaid shirt . . . perfect. It was as though he had been sent here to this place, at this time, to fill his place on the aisle seat, next to the boy.

Daniel raised his gaze to Ariel in awe. "How could you have known?" His voice was barely above a whisper. "Who *are* you?"

Ariel just smiled. "Haven't you figured that out yet? I'm your guardian angel."

The community of Rock Springs, Virginia was served by a twelve-man sheriff's department whose workload of about two major crimes a year did not justify sophisticated crime-scene equipment. But the department, like every other one in the tristate area, had received the FBI bulletin, and it was specific: the involvement of the local police departments was to be limited to immediate notification of the FBI, and securing the crime scene. No one, not even law officers, was to be allowed on the scene until the FBI arrived. For Sheriff Don Pats this was a difficult directive to obey; the murdered man was his brother-in-law.

Nonetheless, when he received the hysterical call from Midi Leisom, who cleaned the church once a week, there was no doubt in his mind as to what they were dealing with. He called the FBI. Their crime scene van was on the site twenty minutes after his own people were. Pats had done nothing in that interval except determine the identity of the deceased—one known, one unknown—and interview the witness. He had followed procedure exactly.

Matthew and Charlie arrived just as the forensics team was finishing its initial sweep. There were traces of blood in the baptistery. A bloodied trash bag was found in an outdoor trashcan with a tight-fitting lid. The candles had been brought to the site. A crime scene vacuuming would prove futile as over two hundred people had passed through it since the last cleaning. Similarly, fingerprints, even if they could be found, would be impossible to isolate.

"Son of a bitch is clever," muttered Charlie. "Rural churches are never locked, crime scene is impossible to isolate, small towns, inexperienced police force . . ."

"That has nothing to do with it," Matt said. He stood with his hands in his pockets, in the aisle across from the bodies, well back from the area of investigation. "The churches are chosen by circumstance; he doesn't choose them. They remind him of something, probably the church where he grew up. He's a preacher's boy, small southern town, and he's creating a diorama for his daddy."

He nodded toward the bodies. "The child he brought all the way from Ringgold, wrapped in a plastic bag in the back of his van. He was looking for a church, that's all. The candles you'll probably find he bought at WalMart back in Durham; he's been carrying those around too. He set up the candles first, wearing gloves and his waterproof boots and jacket. Then he went out and got the child. He arranged the body, disposed of the trashbag, rinsed the blood off his gloves and jacket in the baptistery. He could have used a water fountain or a sink, but there's a definite significance in the phrase 'washed in the blood' for him. He was getting ready to leave when the second victim came in and surprised him. But even though he hadn't planned this, he was able to make it fit into his plan."

He turned to Charlie. "Look for fingerprints on the adult body, possibly on the back of the pew where the body is placed." He took a breath and released it. "There's your hard evidence, ladies and gentlemen. Now all we need is a suspect."

MONDAY, APRIL 28

Eighteen

What Ellen found most astonishing was the fact that life went on as normal. She dealt with calls from the garage that was repairing the broken axle on her car, all the time wondering if she would ever have the courage to drive it again. She drove her rental car back and forth to work, going five miles out of her way to avoid passing the detour around the Bay Bridge, which offered too clear a view of the construction that was going on there as engineers and DOT people tried to put their piece of the world back together again. She was aware of a definite tightening in her stomach every time she drove onto a bridge and she avoided looking down at the water. But those were minor inconveniences, barely worth mentioning in a life that in all other respects proceeded without interruption. Without interruption, that was, except for the nightmares, and except for an occasional strange tinge of disassociation, as though she were in fact two people: the one who had lived before the accident, watching curiously from the far side of the bridge while the present Ellen, who had been born of trauma and terror, suspended over water on a bright spring morning, went on about her business.

She tried to put the entire trip to Wintersville out of her mind. There was obviously a mistake somewhere, and what difference could it make to her now what that mistake was? Ben wanted to pursue the mystery; Ellen found it embarrassing and distressing and she wasn't even sure she wanted to know the answer anymore.

Most of the time, particularly when she was immersed in the controlled chaos of her classroom, Ellen could pretend everything was just as it should be. Only at night, when she was in the grip of the dreams, was she helpless to keep the horror at bay. At least that was how it had been until now.

It began so simply. As part of the "Nature and Me" unit Ellen taught every spring, the children were asked to bring in something from the natural world that affected their lives and to give a report on it to the class. There were four reports left, and Ellen had carefully scheduled these for a day when her teaching assistant, Karen Ann, would be there. The class was always particularly excitable on show-and-tell days.

Lili Marshal brought her seashell collection and gave a two-paragraph report on the ocean that looked suspiciously as though it had been copied directly from a computer-loaded encyclopedia. But she signed it very nicely, even the difficult words, so Ellen had no choice but to grade her highly. Jimmy Bishop brought in a frog, which kept the classroom in upheaval for a good ten minutes. Rachel Morris, whose mother was an ecologist, brought in a beautiful little terrarium and left no doubt that she, too, had had a certain amount of hands-on help from her parents in preparing her report.

After the frog incident, Ellen was better prepared to deal with the last presentation: Philip Hendricks, who had received special permission to bring in the pet rabbit he had gotten for Easter. The rabbit had been nibbling on lettuce and carrots in a wire carrier all morning, and Ellen had promised the children that when Philip finished his report the rabbit could be taken out of its cage and passed around for everyone to pet, but only if they remained seated and quiet, so as not to startle the animal.

Philip, shifting from one foot to the other, did a brief and rather awkward report on what Mr. Wiggly liked to eat, where he lived, when he slept. He was obviously anxious, as the rest of the children were, to take the rabbit out and show it off. Ellen signed her permission for him to do so.

Philip was a somber, thin-faced ten-year-old with straight dark hair that fell forward over his left eyebrow and olive skin. But when he turned from the wire cage, holding the rabbit in his hands up to her, suddenly he was a different boy. His hair was red and curly, his face freckled, his eyes green. And he was covered with blood.

At first she didn't realize what it was, the spreading red stain that crept from the neck of his tee shirt and darkened his clothing, dribbling down his arms and over his hands and soaking the fur of the limp, mangled rabbit he held up to her. That was when she knew. *He had killed the rabbit.*

And then Diane was saying, "The rabbit's okay,

sweetie, and so is Philip. You just sit still and relax for me."

It was as seamless as that.

The school nurse was bending over her, unwrapping a blood pressure cuff from around her arm. She was in the infirmary, and a jolt of panic went through when she realized that. She pushed away from the sofa on which she was sitting. "The children! I can't—"

"The children are just fine," Diane assured her. "Karen Ann is with them, remember?"

Ellen looked from Diane to the nurse in growing alarm. "What happened? Did I faint?"

The nurse asked, "What's the last thing you remember, honey?"

Ellen repressed a shudder. "Philip—and the rabbit, covered in blood. The poor thing was dead! God, I should have watched it more closely. Only . . ." And now she caught her breath, remembering. "Only it wasn't Philip, was it? It was another little boy . . ."

Diane and the nurse exchanged a meaningful look.

She tried to shake away the remnants of confusion. "I must have fainted. Those poor children, they must be terrified. I have to get back, and let them see I'm okay."

The nurse put a restraining hand on her arm, and then Diane said gently, "Sweetie pie, you didn't faint. You just wandered in to my office and sat down. That was over an hour ago, and you haven't said a word since."

The noon news was on in the doctor's lounge where Ben was scribbling out orders for his four hospitalized patients. The twin headlines competed for attention, as they had done for over a week: blame-casting for the Virginia Beach bridge disaster, and the continuing saga of the Church Pew Killer's gruesome spree across the state.

"This is the most publicity this state has received at one time since 1776," commented Maureen Lister, glancing at the television on her way to the vending machine. "Do you think there's such a thing as state karma?"

"How about synchronicity?" suggested the surgical resident, crushing his soda can into the trash on the way out.

Maureen answered, "I think you've got your disciplines mixed up, young man. I'm glad you're not on my service."

The resident grinned. "Me, too. I hear tell you're one tough old broad."

And he disappeared before she could do more than mutter, "Impudent scamp."

Maureen, a consulting psychiatrist, was not technically on staff at Doctor's Memorial at all, which was one reason the resident felt free to tease her. The other reason was that she had the reputation, deservedly so, of being the most compassionate doctor in the three-hospital area, and always went out of her way to make young staff members feel comfortable.

"When are they ever going to get something besides junk food in this machine?" she grumbled, plunking quarters into the slot.

"Where were you when we took the vote?" Ben said. "French fries won over fresh fruit two to one."

"And people wonder why I look like this." She

gestured futilely at the forty extra pounds concealed by an oversized silk shirt and wide flowered skirt, then selected a package of chocolate chip cookies and came over to him. "Speaking of the famous and near-famous . . . how're you doin', kid?"

"Okay." Ben nodded toward the television, where the newscaster was reporting the details of the sixth and seventh victims of the Church Pew Killer, who had been found before Sunday services in a church in a town called Rock Springs, Virginia, about thirty miles from Portsmouth. "What's your theory?"

Maureen lifted an eyebrow as she tore into the package. "That is what we call in the business an abrupt change of subject." Then she shrugged. "Honey, they pay experts a whole lot more than I'll ever make to theorize on that kind of thing. I heard yesterday the FBI's brought criminologists out of retirement to profile this guy."

"I mean, this obsession with churches—kind of a weird twist, isn't it?"

"Like slaughtering children isn't?"

"They're not all children."

"True." She bit into a cookie. "That'll probably make him harder to catch. Most offenders follow a fairly predictable pattern when they choose their victims. This one seems to have forgotten to read the rule book. As for the church connection, it's not really all that weird, relatively speaking. More damage is done to the psyche in the places we should be safest—the playground, the church, the bedroom, the parent's arms—than in the world's most violent battlefields."

Despite himself, Ben was intrigued. "So you think

the killer is getting revenge for some kind of trauma that happened to him in a church when he was a kid."

Maureen took out another cookie and made a face. "I think," she answered, "that it's obscene to put chocolate chip cookies in a vending machine where there's no milk."

"Have my coffee. I haven't touched it."

"Thanks."

Ben turned back to his charts for a few minutes. Then he said, "The reason I was thinking about it, I guess, is that I have a fr—" He changed that immediately to "patient" but he did not deceive himself into thinking that Maureen, a trained listener, had not noticed the slip. "I have a patient," he repeated firmly, "who seems to be suffering from a kind of selective amnesia that I think is related to a childhood trauma. In this case, the only thing she can remember about a certain period in her childhood is a church."

"That is interesting," agreed Maureen, her tone still conversational. "I think we forget sometimes how these primal matters of faith and ritual affect us all. We think we're so sophisticated, so liberated from the superstitions of our ancestors, but we're all just frightened cavemen at the core."

Ben put down his pen. He said, "Rabbits are symbolic of sexuality, aren't they? In dream interpretation?"

"They can be, among other things." She was guarded, as was only appropriate.

"My patient," Ben said, "in addition to having lost what appears to be several years of her early childhood, has recurring nightmares about dead rabbits. I suspect sexual abuse, possibly as early as age six. Am I completely off the track?"

"You know I can't give an informed opinion without seeing the patient," she answered. "That's one possibility, certainly. I take it this amnesia isn't directly related to whatever you're seeing her for, and that she's not in therapy now?"

Ben was beginning to feel awkward. "I've suggested counseling. I didn't really realize how serious the problem was until just recently. She's been under a lot of stress lately and I don't think she's ready to admit the memory loss could be related."

"But you obviously think she's approaching a crisis point or you wouldn't have mentioned it to me."

Ben hesitated, then nodded. "I think it's serious. But I'm on shaky ground here, for a lot of reasons. I'm not sure what my next step should be."

Maureen smiled. "I can clear any morning this week for you. Or I'll see her after hours. You're a good doctor, Ben. We need more like you."

Ben sighed. "Thanks. But I don't think it's going to be that easy."

His pager beeped, and he saw the number of his office illuminated in the display. He excused himself to call in, and Maureen settled back to finish her cookies and his coffee with a celebrity interview via satellite from the local news station.

The receptionist had an emergency message to call Diane Virion at the Branson Academy. Ben's pulse was racing with alarm as he did so, and he couldn't shake the feeling that he had somehow precipitated a crisis by anticipating one. The dread of disaster that had settled in his stomach eased only slightly as he listened to what Diane had to say. He thanked her for calling him, assured her he would take care of things, and then hung up the phone.

His expression was grim as he turned to Maureen. "How about tomorrow?" he said.

Ellen was making an ice cream sundae, heavy on the caramel sauce, when she saw Ben's car pull into the driveway. If he hadn't spotted her through the kitchen window and waved, she might not have answered the door.

He came in with a bag of Chinese take-out and the aroma of sesame oil, spotted the sundae glass piled with ice cream, and lifted an eyebrow. "And all I brought was Mongolian beef and almond chicken."

Ellen closed the door behind him and returned to the counter, where she topped the whipped cream and put it away. "Diane shouldn't have called you."

"That's right. You should have."

She turned and lifted the sundae glass to him, forcing a bright smile. "No need. As you can see I'm perfectly fine and about to commit dietary excess. Care to join me?"

But even to her own ear her voice sounded shrill and the gentle sympathy in Ben's eyes made her want to cry. She turned abruptly to search for a spoon, but found she had suddenly lost her appetite. She put the glass on the counter top. "So," she said dispiritedly, "what's your diagnosis?"

"I'm not here in a professional capacity." He began to unpack the containers of take-out food. "Tonight I'm playing the role of the supportive friend."

"And tomorrow?"

He met her gaze. "Tomorrow we go see a colleague of mine who can help you get through this."

Ellen set her teeth and drew in a sharp breath. "Forgive me for not being more excited, but this is the first time I've had a boyfriend decide I was crazy before the three-week mark. It's a first."

He smiled. "Is that what I am? Your boyfriend?"

Color came unbidden to her cheeks. "Great. Now I'm humiliated *and* crazy."

"Don't be humiliated," he said, "I kind of like the idea. And you're not crazy. I think what happened to you is what we call a fugue state. It's an extreme reaction to stress or trauma, of which you've had plenty the past couple of weeks. But it should be treated."

Ellen dropped her eyes. "Diane doesn't want me back at school for a couple of weeks. I don't blame her. God, what if I'd hurt one of the children?"

Ben touched her arm. "You wouldn't have done that."

But she shook her head fiercely, drawing away. "You don't know that. You don't know what I'm capable of."

She hugged her arms and walked into the living room. The television was tuned to the evening news, volume low. "Come on, Ben, something's wrong, you know it is. You've probably always known it. I'm the one who was trying to pretend. First the nightmares, then I can't even remember where I was born, now this . . ."

"All of those things are perfectly explainable. You survived something not three people in a million have ever done. Not only that, you had your life turned upside down because of it. A little psychological trauma is the least of your problems, and it's all fixable, I promise."

He put his hands on her shoulders gently, trying to reassure her, and felt the sudden stiffening there. She was no longer listening to him. Her attention was riveted on the television, where two photographs were flashed upon the screen.

"Another gruesome development in the so-called Church Pew Slayings today," the newscaster was saying. "Twelve-year-old Bobby Randolph, who disappeared yesterday from his Ringgold home, was found brutally slain in a Rock Springs, Virginia church. With him was the body of William Saulter, a forty-five-year-old layman from the church . . ."

Ellen said hoarsely, "That's him. That's the boy I saw this afternoon. The boy with blood all over him."

Ben looked at her curiously. Her face was stone white, her eyes huge and dark and fixed upon the screen. "Oh my God," she whispered. "That man. He's the man from my dream! I know them both!" She turned on Ben, her expression wild. "Dead people!" she cried. "I've been dreaming about dead people!"

Nineteen

None of them had really expected to be home in three days, least of all Matt. He wasn't surprised to find himself in a two-star motel in Fairfield, Virginia—twenty-five miles away from the Rock Springs site but the location of the nearest motel—but he wasn't happy either. At least, Reirson had been heard to comment with a certain wry savagery, the killer seemed to be leading them closer to Washington, with its functioning showers and twentieth-century crime scene technology. Matt didn't think so.

He didn't think the nation's capital was anywhere near the top of the killer's list of priorities.

They had two rooms, with the connecting door propped open between them. A fax machine and two temporary lines were set up in Charlie's room; the room whose malfunctioning shower Matt shared with Rierson was the repository of partially eaten meals, a coffee pot, and walls covered with gruesome color crime scene photos. Visitors, whether they were delivery boys or police officers, did not stay long in this room.

Earlier in the day Matt had received the FedEx package he had requested from headquarters: a plasticized storyboard mock up of the interior of a composite church, with different colored silhouettes to represent the victims. He had asked for a dozen silhouettes; he hoped he didn't need that many.

Matt had placed seven of the silhouettes in the positions in which they had been found on the pews. He had been studying the picture that was formed for so long his eyes burned.

Charlie came in with a sheet torn from the fax machine. "Okay, here's the first installment. *A* through *G* on your anniversary date search going back thirty years, including airplane crashes, train wrecks, natural disasters, and shootouts in McDonald's. Do you have any idea how much shit happened on May first over the past thirty years?"

Matt said, still staring at the mock up, "I think we can narrow it to events involving seven or more people."

"Now you tell me." She tossed the paper on his desk. "And I have one for you. What makes you think this copycat knows, or cares, anything about what happened on May first?"

He didn't answer, and she sat on the edge of his desk, fixing her gaze on the board in front of them. She lowered her voice a little. "Just talk to me, Matt. Tell me what you're thinking."

Matt took off his glasses, and pinched the bridge of his nose. "It's not a copycat," he said. It was as simple as that. "It's Mayday."

She didn't react. He suspected she had guessed his train of thought days ago. Her voice was even as she answered, "That's not likely, Matt. Everything we've ever learned about criminal behavior tells us that a

203

serial killer doesn't just change his behavior in the middle of the stream like this."

"He hasn't changed his behavior. He's still using the same M.O.—the knife, the wrapping in plastic, the vicinity of churches, even the water is still there. Everything is just in a slightly different context."

"Not to mention the victims, for God's sake. This guy is a spree killer, not a classic serial personality, and he's choosing his victims at random."

"Not entirely at random," Matt said. "He's playing out a scenario, and it's the same one he's been playing out for the past fifteen years. He's just using a different cast of characters this time, that's all."

"May I make a suggestion?"

Reirson had been leaning against the connecting doorway for the last part of the conversation, listening so quietly that Charlie and Matt barely noticed him. When he spoke up they looked at him.

He nodded toward the board. "Look what he's doing. Whoever he is, he's filling up a church, one by one. Maybe we should concentrate the anniversary date search around disasters in churches."

Charlie's features sharpened. "Wait. Wasn't there a church bombing back in sixty-seven, sixty-nine?"

Matt was guarded. "There have been a lot of church bombings in the past thirty years, Charlie."

"No, this one was big—thirty or forty people were killed. And—Jesus! It was in North Carolina."

"I remember reading about that," Reirson said. "It was at Christmastime, wasn't it? Some kind of civil rights case?"

Charlie got up. "I'm calling it in."

Matt said. "It doesn't fit the profile."

And Charlie retorted on her way out, "Doesn't matter."

Reirson came into the room. "Look," he said. "Don't take this the wrong way, but *does* it matter? If it's Mayday or Churchpew, and the profiles are the same, what difference does it make?"

Matt turned back to the board. His expression was intent on the photographs. "Look at the positioning of the bodies," he said. "So precise, so exact. There's a pattern there; I just can't see it. What is he trying to create?"

Reirson said, "If it means anything, I had the same thought. That it might be Mayday, resurrected or reformed somehow. I think Fontana did, too. We were just waiting for someone to say it, because you have to say it out loud to shoot it down."

Matt said, "For fifteen years he's been killing the same woman over and over. Now he's suddenly changed his M.O. Now it's more than one person he has to kill, but not just any person. He's choosing each one carefully for certain characteristics—physical characteristics, most likely—and he's giving them a part to play in his own doomsday scenario. I think he's trying to recreate an event from his childhood, giving himself the control this time over a tragedy he couldn't control before. We already know at least seven people were involved in this event, whatever it was, and something that big would have made the papers. I'm thinking a fire or an airplane crash or a train wreck. Fire because—"

"Because most serial killers have an early history of pyromania," Reirson supplied for him. "He might have accidentally started a fire that killed someone close to him—or maybe intentionally set the fire but someone died he didn't intend."

"Maybe a lot of people. The religious connotation indicates a great deal of guilt." Matt looked up at Reirson. "I'm not ruling out an actual event in a church," he explained. "But I'm not limiting the possibilities, either."

Matt went on, "This is it for him, his swan song. Whatever the stressor was this time, it was big, and he's on a suicide mission. He doesn't care if he gets caught anymore, partly because he doesn't believe we *can* catch him, and partly because he knows that on May first—four days from now—it's going to be over. All these years, he's been so careful. But now he's got a deadline, he can afford to take chances he didn't before."

"Are you saying he wants to get caught?"

"No. I'm saying we're not going to catch him—not yet, anyway. Knowing who he is won't bring us any closer to stopping him. We've got to figure out what he wants."

He turned his frowning gaze away from the board and onto Reirson. "That's why it matters," he told him simply. "Because if it's Mayday, we already know what he wants."

"What's that?"

Matt answered, "The red-haired girl."

The woman's name was Kelly. He knew that because of the badge she wore on her green and white waitress uniform. He had struck up a conversation with her at the roadside diner, during the course of which he learned that she drove a ten-year-old blue

Honda that was always breaking down. He tipped generously so that she would remember him, then went outside and casually loosened the battery connector wire. Then he simply waited for her to get off work.

He had no trouble getting her to accept a ride, although she undoubtably knew better. He had that kind of face, and he further disarmed her by apologizing for not being able to take her all the way home and offering to take her instead to the nearest service station, where she could get help. That last had been Ariel's idea, and it worked.

He took her to the church he had spotted earlier, a charming stone-faced structure at the intersection of two quiet rural roads. She made a fuss and screamed and tried to get away; she even scratched him on the wrist trying to wrestle the door open, but in the end she went as peacefully as the others.

He removed her nametag and tossed it aside. He tied back her streaked blond hair with a rubber band and pushed her arms into the sleeves of a navy blue sweater. He arranged her in her proper place inside the church, and she was perfect.

Yet he felt empty.

"I need to see her," he said aloud to Ariel. "I need to see Ellen."

It was a long time before Ariel replied. But when he spoke, the words were the most soothing Daniel had ever heard. "I think that can be arranged," he said.

Ellen said, "You're probably right. It has to be my imagination."

But her voice was stiff, and Ben could tell she was far from convinced. "I think," he said carefully, "that the stories of these murders have been all over the news this week. It wouldn't take much of an imagination to confuse images from one disaster with another, and that's probably what's happened in your dreams."

She nodded. "Besides, these pictures . . ." She gestured to the newspapers he had bought and spread out over the dining room table. Between them, they provided photographs of the seven victims of the Church Pew Killer. "They're not the faces from my dreams. Except for the little boy." Her voice caught there, and she cleared her throat. "There's really not much of a similarity at all. In my dream there was a fat man with a gold cross, and a woman in a red shirt, and a dark-haired woman with a baby—"

Ben said, "What?"

"A woman with dark hair, holding a baby in her lap. The baby has a teddy bear, one of those fuzzy ones with jointed arms and legs."

Ben's face was carefully neutral as he searched through the papers, and finally found a photograph. "Like this?"

Ellen started to shake her head, then hesitated. "The woman—that face isn't the same. But the baby . . . they kind of all look alike, don't they?" Then she shuddered. "God, what kind of monster could do this to a baby?"

Ben said gently, "Ellen, you've got to see what you're doing. You're hearing about these murders, and you're putting your own faces on them. Why you're doing that is something only you know, and

I think Dr. Lister can help you find out. Meantime, maybe it would make you feel better to write down the details of your dreams—everything that you remember—and compare them to the stories about these killings. God knows, this—" he made a distasteful gesture toward the papers—"is enough to give anyone nightmares."

She smiled wanly. "Maybe I'll do that." Then she hesitated. "Are you tired of me yet?"

"Are you kidding? Things are just getting interesting."

But when he reached for her hand she stood up and walked away. "So what time is the eminent Dr. Lister expecting me?"

"I'll pick you up about ten."

"You don't have to do that."

"I want to."

"Really, Ben." Her tone was firm, perhaps a little too firm. "I'm not an invalid. I'd rather drive myself."

"Okay. But you know the only reason I wanted to go was so that I could get all the gossip on the way home."

Her lips tightened in a rueful smile. "You're too good to be true, you know that? I wish you'd known me before I was crazy."

He stood, took both her hands in his, and kissed her lips lightly. "You probably wouldn't have given me a second glance then. Are you going to be okay? Do you want me to stay?"

She shook her head. "Go feed the dogs before they eat your sofa. I'm fine." And when he looked doubtful she added, squeezing his hands, "Really."

In a moment he smiled and nodded and kissed her again. It was a nice kiss, but tempered by uncertainty. Ellen hated the fact that the residue of disaster—the very thing that had brought them together—was now keeping them apart.

Still, she was glad when he was gone. She sat down at the table and began writing down what she remembered of her dreams. She worked feverishly until midnight, obsessed with the task, and finally fell into an exhausted sleep where, mercifully, no nightmares awaited her.

TUESDAY, APRIL 30

Twenty

Maureen Lister was nothing like Ellen had expected. She was plump and middle aged, with chin-length salt-and-pepper hair. She wore a dirndl cotton skirt in a flowered print and a cardigan sweater, and glasses on a pearl-studded chain. She looked like someone's favorite aunt.

Her office was as cozy and casual as a parlor, with chintz furnishings and a display of miniature teapots in a corner cupboard. They chatted about the collection for a while, then Maureen invited her to be seated. Ellen sat on a comfortable, dark blue flowered sofa, and Maureen brought her a cup of coffee before taking her own seat in a wing chair adjacent.

Ellen said, "It was good of you to see me on such short notice. I feel a little awkward."

Maureen smiled. "Most people do, at first."

"I should know better." She tried to force lightness into her tone. "I'm an educator."

Maureen put on her glasses. "Tell me what happened yesterday."

Ellen described the episode as best she could. "Of course," she finished, "Philip hadn't really hurt the rabbit at all. It was perfectly okay and so was he. I guess—I hallucinated the whole thing. And then, when I got home . . . this is too weird." Ellen put down the coffee cup and passed a not quite steady hand over her hair. "When I got home there was a picture on the news of that child who was killed by the Church Pew Killer—and *that* was the boy I saw in my hallucination. He was dead, but I didn't know it when I saw him with the rabbit."

"Has anything like this ever happened to you before?"

"A hallucination?" She shook her head. "No. But the dreams—I've been having these awful dreams about people I don't know, people whose faces are so clear I can't get them out of my mind even when I'm awake. Last night I realized that these people are dead, too. They're all victims of the Church Pew Killer."

Her voice had grown tight and a little breathless. She had to stop and regain her composure. "Here, I wrote down the dreams, everything I could remember." She took out the paper and handed it to Maureen. "There are eleven distinct faces I remember from my dreams. Six of them have one or more things in common with one of the Church Pew victims—a physical characteristic or a general description or a piece of jewelry. At first I didn't believe it." Her voice was growing breathless again. "I thought there were only one or two. But when I started writing them down, and then looking up descriptions of the victims in the last week's newspapers, it was incredible. The photographs didn't always match, but the descriptions did."

The other woman studied the list for a while.

"These are incredibly vivid descriptions," she said in a moment, and passed the paper back to Ellen. "I want you to keep this, and continue to add to it as you have more dreams. Are there ever any rabbits in these dreams?"

Ellen was a little confused by the change of subject. "Well, yes. But—"

"What do rabbits mean to you? Just off the top of your head."

"Well—Easter? Springtime?" She turned her palms up helplessly. "I never really thought about it."

"Let's go through the dreams, step by step. Are they always the same?"

Ellen said that they were, and described the candlelit cave, the sound of dripping water, the people all lined up as though sitting on a bus—the clothing they wore, the color of their hair, and how one would occasionally assume more prominence in her dream than the others—then how the dream would dissolve into herself looking down at the bloody rabbits in her lap.

"How old are you in the dream?"

Ellen hesitated. She had never thought about that before. "No age, really. Wait—I don't know. Maybe young. I seem to be looking up at everything."

Maureen said, "Could this place in your dream be a church?"

Ellen stared at her. Her chest felt tight, although whether the sensation was from excitement or dread, she didn't know. "Why—I never thought about it. Maybe."

Maureen consulted her notes. "Candlelight, dimness, people sitting in rows as you described, even water—those are all things found in a church, aren't they?"

"Well, yes, I suppose. But—"

"Are you a churchgoer now?"

"No. As a matter of fact, not since I was eight or nine. I remember having a big fight with my mother about it, and we never went again. But how can any of this explain why I'm having dreams about people who are going to be murdered by a serial killer?"

Maureen clipped her gold Cross pen to the steno pad in her lap and took off her glasses, letting them dangle from the chain around her neck. Ellen stared at the glasses for a moment. Something about them— or perhaps it was simply the gesture—seemed oddly familiar somehow, but then she let it go.

"I don't think you are dreaming about people who are going to be murdered," Maureen explained with a kind matter-of-factness that made Ellen feel more reassured than foolish. "I think you're incorporating the news stories about the murders into your dreams. You said the faces in your dreams didn't match the photographs of the murder victims, didn't you?"

A little reluctantly, Ellen nodded. "But I really haven't been following the murders that closely. I'm not even sure I heard about every one of them. Some of them took place while I was in the hospital and— well, I had other things to worry about."

"Your conscious mind may not have registered it, but your subconscious surely did," Maureen responded. "It's been impossible to have been any-where in the state of Virginia—or in the nation, for that matter—over the past week without having heard or read something about each and every one of the murders as they happened. In fact, I'd guess that the fact that you weren't paying close attention would account for why your dream people differ somewhat from the real victims."

"But what about yesterday? The police didn't even discover the body until after I had seen the face of that little boy in my—hallucination."

"Did you really see him?" suggested Maureen. "Or did you just rewrite the memory after you saw the victim's picture on television?"

Ellen was silent for a moment. When she spoke again she was subdued. "Nothing like this has ever happened to me before."

"You've never been trapped in a car on a broken bridge eighty feet above water before either, I'll bet," Maureen pointed out with smile. "Sometimes the mind reacts to a sudden trauma like that by associating it with other traumas in life, as though a gate had been opened and all our buried fears and insecurities come flooding through. In your case, maybe what the gateway is opening onto is a lost memory."

Ellen frowned a little. "Like the lost memory of my childhood?"

"Perhaps."

"But I don't understand what the Church Pew killings have to do with anything. I mean, these are horrible crimes, but they don't affect me in any way personally. And as I said, I haven't been paying any particular attention to the progress of the case."

"Maybe it's nothing more than the name," suggested Maureen, "that triggered an association in your memory. Ellen, could something traumatic have happened to you in a church when you were a child? Something you've now blocked out?"

Again that tightening in her chest, an anticipation or a recoiling, but try as she might she could not put a memory to the feeling. "I don't know," she admitted. "It doesn't seem likely. I had such a Norman Rockwell childhood . . ." And then she faltered. "Or at least I thought I had. Now it turns out I can't even remember where I grew up, much less what really happened there."

Maureen said, "There are several possible explanations for that, one of which, of course, is that the mind substituted these memories of a perfect childhood for memories it finds not quite so acceptable."

"Ben thinks it was abuse of some kind," Ellen said. "And you don't?"

Ellen shook her head. "I know it could be just denial, and how can I say what didn't happen when I can't remember what *did*, but—no. It just doesn't feel true to me."

Maureen smiled. "You should always listen to what feels true. We're going to get to the bottom of this, Ellen. I'd like to see you next Tuesday afternoon for a regular session, but in the meantime there's something very simple you can do to put your mind at ease about your memory loss."

Ellen felt cautious hope unfurl. "What's that?"

"Do you have any living relatives?"

"Aunt Gencie, my mother's sister. She's in a nursing home, but she's still sharp as a tack."

"Then go see her," suggested Maureen. "Ask *her* where you grew up, and what happened during those years that are hazy for you."

It was such an obvious solution that Ellen couldn't understand why she hadn't thought of it before. Unless Maureen was right and she didn't *want* to remember the truth. She said hesitantly, "There's just one problem. I would have been to see Aunt Gencie before now—I know she's been worried about me—but the nursing home is in Williamsburg."

For a moment Maureen looked blank, and then she understood. "And that's one long bridge from here to there," she said.

Ellen swallowed, started to speak, then nodded.

Maureen leaned forward and put a sympathetic hand over Ellen's. "It's time to cross that bridge, Ellen," she said. "Only—don't do it alone."

From the church parking lot across the street Daniel watched Ellen come out of the building, get into her car, and drive away. Her hair had a golden tint in the sunlight, and the way it bounced with her steps and was ruffled by the breeze made his breath catch in his throat. He didn't expected this. He hadn't expected how he would feel when he actually saw her, alive and real and ready for him. The beauty of it brought tears to his eyes.

He had traded the blue van for a red one as soon as he had reached Virginia Beach, so there was no danger of drawing undue attention in the parking lot. He hadn't wanted to, but Ariel insisted, and Ariel was always right about these things. Ariel had also insisted that he buy a van from an individual rather than a dealer, pay cash for it, and leave the blue one in the back of a vast used-car dealer's lot, minus the tags, where it might not be discovered for weeks.

Daniel hadn't like the subterfuge behind any of it, but Ariel was sworn to protect him, and he had to trust that Ariel knew best.

He had followed Ellen from the school, where she had spent less than an hour conversing with the black headmistress and another woman, to this office building that housed medical and law professionals. Now he started the engine and prepared to follow her home, but Ariel put out a hand to stop him.

"I'm going to lose her!" Daniel protested.

"We'll find her again," Ariel said. "I promised you a look, didn't I? You've seen her. Now there's something more important to do."

"There's nothing more important than Ellen," he insisted.

"It's not time for her yet." Ariel's voice was sharp, but his expression became gentle as he turned his eyes toward the building Ellen had just left.

Daniel followed his gaze and saw a plump, gray-haired woman standing on the steps. She checked her watch, tugged at the cardigan around her shoulders, and went down the steps toward the pharmacy next door.

"Someone else is waiting for you," Ariel said, "and she's just perfect."

In a moment, Daniel understood. He turned off the engine and settled back to wait.

Twenty-One

"It doesn't make sense." Charlie pushed around a forkful of cold scrambled eggs and stared morosely down at her plate. "We've had almost one killing every day for the past six days and now suddenly nothing. Has he met his quota? Is it over?"

Matt shook his head. "No. We just haven't found the body yet."

"It's like waiting for the other shoe to drop."

They were in a pancake house across the street from the motel. Since it was almost noon the breakfast crowd had thinned, and they had the place almost to themselves. Both had ordered large platters of pancakes, eggs, and ham for their first non-takeout meal in over seventy hours, and both platters were barely touched.

Matt could not remember the last time he had slept. His eyelids felt like sandpaper, his muscles stiff with fatigue, and even his voice was growing hoarse. These symptoms of incipient exhaustion only irritated him, because he wasn't ready to give up the fight yet. He couldn't stop the racing of his mind, the frantic, pulse-pounding effort to try to make sense of the evidence that seemed to be painting him a portrait of the killer as clear as a photograph. Why couldn't he see it?

Matthew passed a hand over his eyes. "Maybe I'm wrong. Maybe he's stopped. Maybe he's been in an accident or been picked up for some other crime. Maybe he's dead. It happens. But if something doesn't break pretty soon I don't see that there's much more I can do here. I need to get home. I have things to do."

She smiled faintly. "And promises to keep."

His gaze was unapologetic. "To myself, and to her."

"You can't walk away from this Matt, you know that. And if you're right about Mayday, it'll all be over in a couple of days. You'll be home in plenty of time."

Matt said, "I'm right. And it might be over for him by May first, but for us the work will just be starting. I don't think we're going to catch this one, Charlie."

Charlie was silent for a moment. "Okay, so there doesn't appear to be much of a chance of a connection to my 1969 church bombing idea. Which you knew all along."

He shrugged. "It was a black church. These victims are all white, and serial killers don't cross racial lines."

"Yeah, well, there are a lot of things serial killers don't do that this one seems to have no problem with. But I'm not willing to give up the church bombing idea altogether—bombing, fire, something catastrophic. I asked them to narrow the anniversary date search to those criteria, but so far nothing. Did anything strike a chord with your list?"

Matt had been up most of the night researching the facts behind promising-sounding headlines from May first going back thirty years. Now he shook his head. "Not yet. But something's there. I know it."

She said, glancing down at her plate, "I didn't mention your theory about Mayday to anybody at Headquarters. I wanted to give you a chance to re-think it."

He didn't answer.

"Matt, if you're wrong—"

"If I'm wrong we'll have the entire state of Virginia looking for a man who matches the wrong description while the real suspect calmly walks past us to kill again and again. Do you think I haven't thought of that?"

She started to reply, then her expression changed as the door to the restaurant opened. Matt glanced around to see Reirson approaching.

"Anything?" Charlie demanded as he reached them.

He shook his head. "Except . . ." He took a folded slip of paper from his pocket and sat down, offering it to Matt. "There was a call for you, forwarded from headquarters. Someone named Polly."

Matt had started to take the message; when he heard the name he picked up his coffee cup instead. His jaw tightened infinitesimally.

Reirson looked uncomfortable as he glanced down at the message slip. "Um, she said you might do that. She said I should read it to you." A faint dull flush circled his collar as he unfolded the paper and glanced at Matt apologetically. "She made me promise."

Charlie grinned. "She's a charmer."

But Matt didn't look at him.

"It says . . ." Reirson cleared his throat. "It says, 'Captain. I'm not giving up on you. Love, Polly.' "

This time when he offered the note, Matt took it and, without glancing at it, folded it into his pocket.

Charlie said, "Why does she call you that?"

Matthew finished his coffee. "What?"

"Captain."

He looked for a moment as though he wouldn't answer, then apparently changed his mind. "You ever see *Dead Poets Society*?"

Charlie shook her head.

"Robin Williams played a teacher, and he had a line where he quoted this poem."

"Oh, sure," Reirson put in, "Walt Whitman. 'O Captain, my Captain, our fearful trip is done/The ship has weather'd every rack, the prize we sought is won.' About Abraham Lincoln. No offense, but I don't see the connection."

The look Matt gave him could have been reprimand for his intrusion or simple impatience with his youth—and expertise. He said, "Anyway, Robin Williams said something to the effect of 'Don't call me sir, call me captain' and she latched on to that for some reason. Maybe to embarrass me. Maybe it was because that was the first movie we watched all the way through together, where I didn't have to get up in the middle to answer a call or go out on a case." He shrugged. "Inside jokes aren't supposed to make sense, I guess."

But Charlie's smile was indulgent enough to make him think she understood anyway. Then she said, pushing a soggy corner of a pancake around on her plate, "Polly has red hair, doesn't she?"

He tensed. "Don't start getting psychological on me, Charlie."

"I shouldn't have to, should I?" she returned evenly.

The atmosphere between them was thick and edged, and when the waitress stopped by Reirson took the opportunity to break the silence by ordering coffee. When she was gone he said to Matt, "So how sure are you about the Mayday connection, anyway?"

Only a slight tightening of the lines around his mouth betrayed Matt's annoyance. He replied, "As sure as I've ever been. Which is to say, not very sure at all."

When the waitress returned Matt held out his cup for a refill. "As I was just explaining to your esteemed colleague here—" the glance he gave Charlie was faintly dry—"that's one of the hazards of the profession. It's an inexact science with no room for error, and every time I'm right I'm just as surprised as I was the first time—and just as sorry. Because getting it right means I know way more than any normal man should ever know about how a monster thinks. If it were up to me, I'd rather not know any more about the way this one thinks, or anything else about him."

Reirson opened a plastic container of milk and emptied it into his coffee. "Is that why you quit? You knew too much?"

Charlie looked startled at the question and even more surprised at Matt's easy reaction to it.

"Did I quit?" Matt replied. "Then this must be just a recurring nightmare. Thank God, I thought I was actually stupid enough to be out in the field again."

"They say it was because you were shot."

"That's not reason enough?"

"For some, maybe."

"Those who can, do, Agent Reirson, haven't you ever heard that? Those who can't, teach."

"I heard you've always been pretty good at both."

Matt looked at Charlie, absently stirring his coffee. She pushed a forkful of cold pancakes into her mouth and kept her features unrevealing. Then Matt seemed to come to a decision, and glanced back at Reirson.

"Did you ever hear of Leon Farmer? Kidnapped little girls from hotel lobbies around the South during the late eighties. You would have been about twelve then."

Reirson gave a half smile. "Not quite that young."

"We found four bodies; we think the total may be as high as eight." He sipped his coffee. "Farmer committed the crimes over a period of three years and in five states, so it took a while for a pattern to develop. In 1989 he lost his job as a pharmaceutical rep—the very job that had allowed him to get away with the murders all those years—and his wife divorced him. We later learned that she suspected him of something 'weird,' as she put it, but that's often the case. People close to the perpetrators usually have some idea about what's going on, even though they deny it to themselves. Anyway, that's when he screwed up, and took two of his victims from the same state and within a month of each other. Laurie Ann May disappeared from a Jacksonville, Florida

Holiday Inn on July twelfth. Her body was found two weeks later in the Ocala National Forest. She had been tortured and raped and strangled with a two-foot cord.

"That next week Kathy Barnes, a nine-year-old girl from Washington State who was vacationing with her folks, went down to the video arcade room at their hotel in St. Augustine, Florida. She was last seen talking to a man in Bermuda shorts and a tropical shirt—which proved to be a false lead, by the way. The man was an off-duty hotel employee and local police wasted almost twenty-four hours with him before calling us for a profile.

"We knew the killer kept his victims alive for a time for sexual purposes, so there was a good chance Kathy was still alive. We profiled him out by age, occupation, the usual stuff, and began to trace back the other murders until, by process of elimination, we found the common name on the guest list of every hotel in which a murder had taken place— except, of course, the last one, which was within thirty miles of Farmer's home address. The SAC sent a team in to storm his home address but I didn't think he was keeping the girl there. These kinds of personalities don't like to mix their two lives—the family man and the predator—and even though he was living alone now he had fallen into an established habit of keeping the girls away from his home and I doubted he would break that pattern now. I should have made a stronger case; it might have made a difference. But I didn't, and the team went to the wrong place.

"Farmer wasn't there, of course, and neither was

the girl. Nor was there any sign that she had ever been there, or Laurie Ann May either. And while the team was out there blowing their warrant I was still working on the profile. And that's when I found out that Farmer's ex-brother-in-law had a cabin on the edge of the Ocala National Forest.

"I left word with the office and took off out there. No backup, no authority, nothing. It was a hunch, and I guess there was a part of me that didn't expect it to pay off. But I had to check it out, and the clock was ticking down for that little girl.

"I got there about dark, and the cabin was empty. I was more than a little relieved over that, I can tell you. Maybe a little too relieved because I almost walked out before I noticed the pink ponytail band on the floor. Kathy Barnes had been wearing pink shorts when she disappeared, and though her mother didn't say anything about hair ribbons, all the pictures showed her with a long pony tail. That's when I started looking closer.

"Anyway, to make a long story short, the cabin was built on a concrete block foundation, and there was a trap door in the back of a closet that led underneath the house to a crawl space about three feet high, dirt floor, dark as pitch. He had fenced off a section with kennel wire and penny nails and that was where he was keeping her, gagged and tied and wearing nothing but her underpants. She was covered with insect bites, as well as bruises and burns, and I guess being locked up in the dirt and the dark like that was just about as bad as anything else he'd done to her, maybe worse.

"All I could see was her eyes, and they were so

terrified, so big and scared. I knew she thought I had come to hurt her, and why shouldn't she? I had a gun, and I was shining the flashlight at her so she couldn't see me. I tried to tell her I was a good guy, I was like the calvary, I was her guardian angel and I wouldn't let anything else bad happen to her. After a while she almost looked as though she believed me. Guardian angel.

"But I couldn't get the wire open, not without tools. He must have figured on being gone a long time to nail her in like that, but I didn't know what a long time was to him, or how long he'd been gone. For all I knew, remember, the team had captured him at his home. At any rate, I had to get her out of there. I told her I had to leave, to find tools to get her out with, but she didn't understand that. All she knew was that I was leaving her there. She started to cry, and I could hear her trying to scream beneath the gag, but she had screamed so much over the past couple of days that she didn't have much voice left. It sounded like the mewing of a kitten. 'I'm your guardian angel,' I told her. 'I'll be back. I won't let anything happen to you.' And I left her there, crying in the dark with the bugs and the snakes.

"When I came out of the cabin, Farmer shot me with a deer rifle from the bushes where he'd hidden when he came up and saw my car. I never went back for Kathy Barnes."

"But it was a solve," Charlie said quietly into the long chill silence that followed. "The police set up an all-points for his car, road blocked the area leading from the cabin, and picked him up within the hour with Kathy Barnes in the trunk, still alive. You got to your radio, didn't you?"

"It was a solve," Matt answered, "a conviction on four counts once he told us where the other bodies were. The victim was taken alive. But she spent the next two years in and out of mental hospitals, and finally succeeded in killing herself in 1993 at age thirteen."

No one knew what to say. Silverware clinked in the background, the door opened and closed as another customer entered. Someone turned on a radio in the kitchen, and its tinny sound was like the droning of an insect far away.

Matt put down his coffee cup. "I'm going back to the motel and pack. There's nothing more I can do here."

Charlie watched him go, sipping her coffee.

Reirson said, "Quite a story."

"He left out a few parts."

"I sensed that."

She hesitated, then shrugged. "It's not a secret. He was in the hospital for six months. His wife left him, took their kid. It happens a lot, the strain just gets to be too much for them, you know? And Matt, the way he works—he closes everybody out except the monsters. It's a hard way to live.

"A few months later," she went on, "his wife was killed. You probably heard about it. The killer had apparently been stalking her for some time, stabbed her twenty-seven times in the laundry room of her apartment building."

Reirson's cup hit the saucer with a dull click. "That was *him*?"

Charlie nodded. "He doesn't talk about it, we don't talk about it. But he blames himself. Maybe something worse than blame, I don't know. You've got to see the irony—you spend your life trying to save other people from violent deaths and the one person you can't save is your own family member. Well, hell. You can imagine."

She finished off her coffee. "Anyway, that's pretty much it. There was a court battle over the kid, and Matt lost custody to the grandparents. That was when he asked for the desk job, something about it looking better to the judge, but that was just an excuse."

"But we got the guy, right?" Reirson said.

"Oh, yeah, we got him. But it didn't bring his wife back, his family. And that was the thing, see. Getting him didn't make any difference. It started with that little girl in the dark basement, and it ended with his own wife, and what it taught him was that getting them doesn't make a difference. Let's face it, we're just the clean-up crew. Somebody's got to die before we even have a job."

"Maybe," agreed Reirson. "But if we do our job we can keep more people from dying."

"Yeah, and most of us know that. But Matt—he just stopped believing that. Or caring about it." She put down her coffee cup and looked at her watch. "Look, I'm going to—"

Her phone rang, and she answered it. Reirson watched her changing expression and he was on his feet almost before she had disconnected.

"Let's go," she said, sliding out of the booth. "The other shoe just dropped."

Twenty-Two

Ellen had promised to let Ben know how the session with Maureen went, so she stopped by his office on her way home. Traffic was still difficult to negotiate due to all the detours while the bridge was under construction, and Ellen wasn't particularly comfortable driving. After the early-morning trip to school, where she handed over her lesson plans to the substitute and made formal arrangements, with great reluctance, to take the rest of the semester off, and then back to Maureen's downtown office and across to Ben's beachside clinic, she was exhausted.

Ben must have read that on her face, because concern crossed his as he entered his office and closed the door. "Was it bad?" he asked, coming over to her. "I told you I should have gone with you. Did one of the girls offer you something to drink? Coffee? Coke?"

Ellen had to smile. "I hate men who refer to their female employees as girls. And yes, they were very nice. Tripping all over themselves. They think I'm a celebrity."

"Not at all." He appeared to relax, and sat on the

corner of his desk, close to her. "They just know I like you, and I, of course, *am* a celebrity."

"You look different in your white coat," she told him.

"Sexy?"

"Kind of nerdy."

He grimaced. "Just the look I was going for."

Ellen laughed. "Your friend Maureen was very nice. I'm going to continue with her."

"Good." He scrutinized her face. "But?"

Ellen hesitated. "She pretty much had the same theory you did about the dreams, and the Church Pew killings—that I was superimposing the real victims onto what I *thought* I remembered from my dreams. But that's not right, Ben," she said firmly. "I know it only makes me sound crazier to argue with two professionals who agree on a diagnosis, but you're both wrong."

She could sense Ben sliding into his professional demeanor, and she tried not to resent it. "What makes you say that?"

"I took your advice," she said, "and wrote down my dreams." She pulled out the paper and handed it to him. "Maureen didn't seem very impressed. But if you'll look closely you'll see details I couldn't possibly have gotten from the newscasts—like the shape of their faces and the color of their shoes. And if I were dreaming about people I've seen on television or in the newspapers, why wouldn't the descriptions be exact, instead of similar? Do you understand what I mean? Why wouldn't I dream of an exact replica of the victim instead of just certain characteristics— just enough characteristics to recognize the person by?" She shook her head. "I don't know what the answer is, but I know I'm not transferring, or whatever you call it, or mixing up memories in my head. There's got to be another explanation."

Ben looked up from the list and started to offer the logical explanation—the only explanation, in his opinion, once again—then changed his mind. He said, "Your theory is that every one on this list was a victim of the Church Pew Killer, right?"

A little hesitantly, she nodded.

"You realize there are twelve people here, and only seven victims of the Church Pew Killer."

"I think—" she cleared her throat—"I think some of the bodies haven't been found yet. Or—the murders haven't happened yet."

And at his faint but unmistakable frown she threw up her hands and said, "I know, I know how it sounds. And I'm *not* saying I'm clairvoyant or that I have any kind of special insight into the killer's mind, but, Ben, I had dreamed about *all* of these people before the first one of them died. Don't you see? I even told you about some of them, I'm sure I did."

Ben tried to remember whether or not she had in fact described any of the people in her dreams to him before they became supposed victims of a killer. Maybe she had, but the descriptions hadn't been distinct enough to cause him to make the association, or even remember them.

He said, "What if I could prove to you that you were wrong about the people on this list?"

"What do you mean?"

He looked down at the list. "Okay, what if there

was no fat man with a gold cross? Or no brunette with a ponytail?"

She shook her head. "Mr. Bleckly, the second victim, was quite a bit overweight from his picture, and bald, too, just like in my dream. And the first victim was a brunette with a ponytail."

"But what if she wasn't wearing her hair in a ponytail when she died? What if she'd had her hair cut? What if Mr. Bleckly wasn't wearing a gold cross? Don't you see how fragile your evidence of an association is? If I could prove to you that any part of the description you're basing your theory on is wrong, would it be easier for you to accept that there might not be any connection at all?"

She looked doubtful. "It's an awfully big coincidence, Ben."

"Maybe not as big as you think." He placed the paper atop a pile of charts on his desk.

Ellen said, "I have a favor to ask. Or I probably should say, another favor. Maureen suggested I go see my Aunt Gencie and ask *her* about my childhood. Pretty obvious, huh?"

"I can't believe I didn't think of it. What's the favor?"

"Will you drive me?" She looked uncertain. "It's across the Bridge-Tunnel. It might not be any easier for you than for me. Maybe I shouldn't have asked."

He smiled. "How about tomorrow?"

She smiled as she got to her feet. "How about I make you dinner afterward?"

"You've got a deal."

He walked her to the door, and before he opened it she turned and kissed him. He looked surprised and pleased, and his tone had a husky-soft quality to it when he spoke. "Nice," he said. "Should I even ask what that was for?"

"I happen to like the nerdy look," she answered, and touched his face before she left. "See you tomorrow."

The first thing Daniel did was call the school and ask for Ellen. He was bitterly hurt and disappointed to learn she wasn't in, and that she was not, in fact, expected in for a week at least. He felt betrayed, but then it occurred to him this might simply be a test of faith.

After a time he took his toolbox from the car and went inside. There were no security measures at Branson Academy; if there had been he would have dealt with them. As it was, he simply walked into the cool corridor that smelled of library paste and construction paper, past a bulletin board display of Easter bunnies and spring daffodils, and followed the signs to the office.

To the right was a half-open frosted door that read Diane Virion, Headmistress. Inside he could see a black woman in a turquoise top and a canary yellow gauze scarf working at a computer terminal. Directly ahead of him was a hinged counter, and behind it a bank of file cabinets and a computer workstation. A slight, rather plain brunette turned from her terminal when he entered.

"May I help you?"

He held up a flat black metal tool case with a look of apology. "You reported some problems with your computer? I know I'm a little late but I got held up with the detour, the bridge and everything."

She frowned. "I didn't report anything."

He placed the toolcase on the counter and took out a sheet of paper. "Branson Academy, right? 313 Oak Wilde Avenue? The invoice reference is Diane."

"Ms. Virion?" She looked uncertain. "I can't think why she would be involved in something like that."

"Perhaps she was interested in our free upgrade," he supplied helpfully.

She got up from her chair. "I'd better check. You're—?"

"Professional Business Services," he said. "Do you mind if I have a look at your peripherals while I wait? Wow, that's an antique, isn't it? I promise I won't touch anything."

He gave her his most winning smile. She said, still looking uncertain, "I'll be right back."

He took that as a yes and lifted the counter when she went into the office. With only part of his attention on her movements he went straight to the file cabinet and pulled open the drawer labeled employee records. The folder on Ellen Cox was the second one. Her address and phone number were printed on the tab for quick reference. The entire operation took him less than ten seconds, and he felt like a world-class spy. He had never tried anything like that before, much less gotten away with it. The sensation was exhilarating.

The receptionist came out of the office, pulling the frosted door closed behind her. It was then that Daniel realized the significance of the hand movements he had caught with his peripheral vision, and realized he had not heard any conversation. The head-mistress was deaf.

The receptionist said, "I'm sorry, there must be a mistake. We're not having any trouble and Diane said she didn't order service."

He scowled as though deeply concerned. "Man, I'm going to be in so much trouble if I screwed this up. Listen, I'm sorry I bothered you. I'll have to call my supervisor and straighten this out."

She looked sympathetic. "Do you want to use my phone?"

He smiled and lifted a hand, starting for the door. "Thanks, I'll use the car phone. Sorry to bother you."

But as he left he turned back and looked at her, and he felt a sudden stab of excitement, of certainty. Of course. The symmetry was perfect. He had come here for a purpose, but he had more than one mission.

When Matthew dreamed the images were so hideous he was glad to be interrupted; absurdly, almost pathetically grateful to wake. He dreamed of monsters forcing him to consume human arms and legs; of being chained to a wall in a dank gray dungeon to the steady drip of water while someone slowly peeled away his skin, strip by strip, exposing the raw, oozing flesh beneath; of a young girl, a different one every time, who ran down a dark, narrow maze, sobbing and whimpering with terror, while he called out for her to stop: *Don't run, don't run, I'm here to help you! I'm your angel, your guardian angel; I won't let anything happen to you!* But every time he drew close she would turn a corner and plunge deeper into the maze. Sometimes the dream ended when he caught her, and she turned on him with a garishly twisted face on a little girl's body, hissing like a lizard, and plunged her fingers deep into his eye sockets, plucking out the eyeballs like grapes from the vine. Sometimes he looked into her eyes and saw his own features there, dark and distorted, just before he twisted her head off her body and tossed it aside.

This time it was different. This time the girl had red hair, and the maze was lit with candles, and he gradually came to realize they were in a church. The walls of the church were lined with photographs, and he didn't want to look at the photographs because he knew what he would see there. But she kept pleading with him, *Look, look, it's so clear if only you would see! We're all going to die in here if you don't look!* He tried to look at the photographs, but his vision was blurry. He lifted his hands to rub his eyes and his hands came away bloody and sticky with goo.

And that was when he awoke with a gasp that sounded more like a muffled cry and someone's hand on his shoulder. He had fallen asleep in the car with crime-scene photos spilling from his fingers; that much he knew immediately. A woman named Kelly Cameron was waiting for him in a church somewhere—*where?*—and he couldn't even stay awake long enough to see her. Now Charlie was saying something to him, but he didn't know what it was.

"Twelve," he said abruptly.

Reirson was driving; Matt had the back to himself. Charlie was leaning over the passenger seat to shake

Matt awake; now she released his shoulder and stared at him. "What?"

"There are going to be twelve victims," he said.

"How can you possibly know that?"

He shook his head abruptly, pinching the bridge of his nose to chase away the last of the sleep haze. "Nothing. I don't know. Something I dreamed." He looked down at the photographs scattered over the car floor, searching for the memory, searching for the clue. "It's gone."

"Matt," she said, "I just got off the phone with headquarters. Documents was able to enhance that license plate on the van to a readable four numbers. That narrowed it down to thirty-two suspects in the Raleigh-Durham area. Eliminating unmarried women and—" there was only the slightest hesitation over the next words—"others who didn't fit your profile, they started going through military records for fingerprints. They got a hit on the third try. His name is Daniel Nichols, a computer consultant from Durham specializing in medical programs. Local agents are on their way to his apartment now."

Matt was instantly awake. "Get me there."

"A helicopter is standing by. Reirson and I will take the Cameron investigation, and then will be coordinating out of the Norfolk field office. Matt, the guy enlisted in Norfolk. Navy, just like—" the hesitance was barely noticeable—"just like you said. Could he be going home?"

"That's not home for him. But there may be something there he wants. He's in a hurry now, and he's going to be taking chances, getting careless. He's counting down in hours, and he's got a quota to fill. This may be your chance."

Reirson glanced over his shoulder. "Twelve," he said. "That's a holy number, isn't it?"

Matt meet Charlie's eyes. "Yeah," he said.

Daniel thought it would be difficult this time, without Ariel standing by, looking over his shoulder, waiting in the shadows, always approving. But he had done so well in the deaf woman's office, he was filled with confidence. One more. The last one. Then there would be just him and Ellen, the way it should have always been.

He could feel his angel's presence, though. He felt it the minute he looked back and realized the woman in the red sweater was his last offering. He felt it when he drove around the campus and realized there was a small chapel on the premises. And why not? It was a private school, established by the Methodist Church and maintained by grants and contributions; that much he read in the brochure while waiting for the children to leave their classrooms and the parking lot to empty of staff cars.

The parking lot was almost empty when she came out, the woman in the red sweater. He called out that a child had been hurt, and she ran with him toward the chapel. The candles were already burning, and she died silently. He placed her on the sixth row left, and in his mind he saw them together again—the boy, the father, the mother. Perfect.

Almost.

He washed the blood from his hands in the small

alcove behind the altar. His back was to the door when he heard it open. Someone called out, "Helen? Are you in here?"

His heart started to thud.

It was the black woman he had seen earlier. A surge of anger and frustration rushed through him and he blamed Ariel for not being here, he blamed himself for not being more careful, he thought *I'll have to kill her and this ruins everything, everything.*

There was only one way out, and that was past her. There was no way to get to the door without being seen or heard. He had no choice. His hand closed on the scalpel in his jacket pocket. This ruined *everything.* How could this have happened? When it was all so perfect, how could this have happened?

And then he remembered. He remembered just about the time she moved midway down the aisle, her horrified gaze moving as in slow motion from the flickering bank of candles to the blood on the carpet, to the sixth row, center, and the body that had once housed her secretary. She was deaf. She couldn't hear anything.

Fear no evil.

Daniel moved quickly behind her and toward the door. By the time her first hoarse choked gasps for breath had turned to screams, he was gone.

Twenty-Three

Ben saw his last patient at six-thirty which, considering the way his schedule had been going lately, was pretty good. He ate half a sandwich left over from an interrupted lunch while scribbling notes on charts at his desk, but every time he looked up that yellow sheet of paper was there. Ellen's list. He wondered if he was doing the right thing, interfering. He had referred Ellen to Maureen; shouldn't he leave her care to her? Where did the bounds of friendship end and the encroachment onto professional judgement begin?

He looked at his watch again. It was possible Maureen was still in her office, and if not he could leave a message with her service. He could at least thank her for seeing Ellen, and perhaps, if he could find a delicate way of doing it, ask her opinion on just how much interference was too much.

The telephone rang six times, and he was prepared for it to switch over to the answering service. Instead, a rather choked-sounding voice answered with a stammered, "Yes? I mean—hello?"

Ben frowned a little at the telephone. "I was dialing Dr. Lister's office."

"Oh. Yes. Yes, this is it."

The frown deepened. "This is Dr. Ben Bradshaw. Is she in?"

There was a very long silence. Ben became aware of voices in the background, and other noises he couldn't identify. "Dr. Bradshaw." The voice came again, strained and high, and he recognized the element in it he could not quite identify earlier. Tears. "Haven't you heard? There's been—something terrible has happened. Dr. Lister is dead."

The apartment was nothing like Matthew expected, and everything that it should have been. It was always like that. He walked in expecting a chamber of horrors and, except for very rare cases, he discovered the house next door.

This one represented the abode of a moderate to moderately high-income single man who had some measure of disposable income. The stereo was expensive and the C.D. collection extensive. There was a twenty-seven-inch television set and a sleek VCR. The furniture was leather, the carpet Berber. The apartment, big and airy with skylights and pale ash paneling and a view of an adjacent lake, went for twelve hundred a month. He lived well, this Daniel Nichols, computer consultant.

The preliminary evidence collection was complete by the time Matthew arrived, but the agents had been instructed to remove nothing, disturb nothing. The SAC from the Raleigh field office began reading off his laundry list as soon as Matt was inside the door. "Daniel Nichols, no middle name, age forty-two, private computer consultant specializing in hospital systems. He got his training courtesy of Uncle Sam through the United States Navy, where he enlisted at age eighteen, honorably discharged in 1991. His Navy career revolved mostly around security, although he served a brief stint as a medic in his 1982–85 enlistment. During his last tour he worked security for Bethesda Naval Hospital and he was interviewed, along with every one else in his unit, in connection with the 1990 murder of Sheryl Lynn Cates, who was found floating in the Potomac May third, her throat cut. Excuse me, Dr. Graham, am I boring you?"

While he listened to the report, Matthew had been moving about the apartment; now he dragged his attention with some difficulty from a seascape print over the mocha leather sofa. "What? No. Sorry. I was just thinking—I have that same print at home."

He turned abruptly to an elaborate computer workstation on the west wall. "Have you broken his files?"

"We'll send the hard drive to the lab for examination, but so far nothing out of the ordinary. He had eight or ten local accounts, another half-dozen in Virginia and Tennesee. They paid well, as you can see. One of his accounts was Community Medical, where Judy McFarlane, the first victim, worked. No doubt they knew each other. He has some pretty elaborate equipment over there, but nothing that bizarre for a computer buff, I guess. One thing I thought you'd find particularly interesting."

He gestured Matthew over to the desk, where another agent removed a manila folder from a glassine envelope. The folder contained what appeared to be computer-enhanced photographs.

"It's an aging program," explained SA Riker. "Some call it 'morphing.' The computer works with an existing photograph and alters it according to a given set of data, in this case aging. Cosmetologists and plastic surgeons use it, as well as law-enforcement agencies, to track missing children or extrapolate an I.D. from a partial description. Nichols probably got hold of the original software in the Navy—some of the early renderings are pretty crude, you'll see—but he's been using the latest, up-to-date technology for the past few years."

Charlie said, "Any idea where he got the original photo?"

Riker shook his head. "No sign of it."

With gloved hands, Matthew examined the photographs, one by one. They were all of the same girl, beginning from about age twelve to the last one, aged to show a woman in her early thirties. Matthew knew without being told the girl had red hair, and though the early aging was somewhat rough, sophisticated technology had shown a remarkably natural and detailed development for the past fifteen years.

He went back to the first photograph. The grainy texture suggested it had been extracted from a book or a newspaper, and even he could tell that it had been altered in some way. Her features had been changed, or perhaps just touched up, in the way a professional photographer might airbrush blemishes or turn an obstreperous child's scowl into something more appealing for the family portrait. The alterations were obvious even to the naked eye because of the change in the density of the pixels at points around the eyes and mouth, for which early computer programs were not yet refined enough to compensate. What was he trying to hide? Bruises? Scars? A professional back at Sci-Crime would have to look at it to determine. But why alter the original just to feed it back into the aging program? Would the computer automatically compensate for non-permanent blemishes in subsequent reproductions?

He said, "He would have had to have photographs of her parents to do this."

The other agent looked at him without comprehension and Matt explained himself impatiently, "These aging programs aren't magic. You've got to have pictures of the child, and pictures of the parents to approximate the characteristics of aging. Find the pictures of the parents. And find out how the hell he got them."

He flipped over to the last photograph, the one most recently aged. He held it up to Riker. "Does anything about this look familiar to you?"

Ricker studied it carefully. "Hard to say. Maybe. She's a pretty girl. Not gorgeous but . . . yeah. You do kind of think you've seen her before. Actress? Maybe he's playing out some kind of fantasy on the computer?"

Matthew returned the sheet to the stack. Something else bothered him about the pictures. The pose was awkward. The girl was in partial profile to the camera, her face tilted up as though searching the sky for something, her lips parted. Her hair, in the original photograph, was curly and mussed, although various hairstyles were developed as she aged. The original, it was obvious, had not been a posed photograph, which meant that even if it was from a newspaper, as he suspected, it had been an action shot, not a supplied photograph from her family. That could only mean that the child upon whom Nichols had fixated had been *part* of a breaking news story, not peripheral to it.

He said, returning the papers to their envelopes, "I'm taking these with me. I have an idea."

Ben knew he had to tell Ellen before she heard it on the news. Maureen had walked down to the drugstore for a sandwich right after Ellen's session, and she hadn't come back. Because the office had closed for lunch for an hour, no one missed her until one o'clock. But it wasn't until she missed her two o'clock appointment entirely that the alarm was sounded.

The police arrived at three-thirty. At five-fifteen Maureen's body was discovered in the church across the street.

Someone in the drugstore had seen her talking to a man on the street when she left, but that was not unusual for Maureen. Someone else described a red van that had been parked behind the church until noon. There were no other leads.

Ellen was silent for so long that Ben thought she had dropped the phone. Then there came the sound of a soft, choked gasp, like a stifled sob, and she said, "The glasses! I should have known—I *did* know! Oh, God, Ben, look at my list! A gray-haired woman with glasses!"

At first he didn't know what she meant, and then a chill came over him that was even deeper than the one he had felt when Maureen's secretary, stammering and shaking, interrupting herself once or twice to answer a question from the police, had told him the news of her death.

He made his voice very calm. "Ellen, a lot of women wear glasses and have gray hair."

He could her breathing. "I feel like it's my fault. I was there and then—it's as though I brought a curse to her! I told her my dreams and then she became *part* of my dreams, a player in the nightmare she was supposed to cure!"

Ben said, "I'm coming over."

"No." There was a muffling sound, and Ben knew it was her hand covering the receiver so he couldn't hear her unsteady breathing as she tried to bring herself under control. "No." When she came back her voice was a little stronger, although still husky. "Don't. I'm feeling—a little out of control right now and pretty vulnerable. I don't think it's a good idea for you to be here."

He tried to make himself smile. "I promise I won't take advantage of you."

"But I might take advantage of you." She drew a long, almost steady breath. "Oh, Ben, I'm so sorry. I know she was a friend of yours."

"She was a friend to everyone," Ben said quietly. "To me no more than anyone else. It just seems so unreal."

"Will you want to see the family or . . ." Her voice faltered.

"No, I wasn't that close. I think the best thing to do is to go ahead with what she suggested, and go to Williamsburg tomorrow. If you're up to it, that is."

Ellen was silent for a moment, and then she agreed, "I think it's more important now than ever."

He didn't hang up the phone until she sounded more like herself, and he was persuaded she would be all right for the night. Then he couldn't help himself. He turned to the list. He spent a long time staring at it. *Brunette with pony tail and white shirt . . . Mother and child with teddy bear . . . fat man with gold cross . . . man in plaid shirt . . . boy in red and white polo . . . gray-haired woman with glasses on a chain . . .*

He put the list aside, took out the telephone book, and looked up a number. He spent a long time staring at that. Then he lifted the receiver.

"Jesus, I can't believe I'm doing this," he said softly, and dialed.

Jacob Reinhart was the sharpest analyst in the Special Photo unit, which meant he was also the busiest. Matt got him out of bed when he arrived in Washington, and although he cursed and grumbled about it for a good five minutes on the phone, he met Matt at the lab inside the hour. Once at his workstation, curiosity overcame his irritation, however, and he flipped through the pages Matt gave him with interest. "These are computer-generated images," he said, "not photographs. What's the deal?"

"But they were generated from a photograph, right? And not just a photograph, but I have a hunch it was a newspaper or magazine photograph."

Reinhart went through the pages again, studying more closely. "Yeah. The original's been cleaned up quite a bit as we go on."

"I want you to take it back down to the original photograph," Matt said.

"Oh yeah, sure, Doc, piece of cake," was his mild reply. Then he looked up at him. "You are kidding, right?"

Matt took out his phone and began to dial. "How long will it take?"

"Between ten minutes and forever. And that's if I can get hold of the right software."

"Better get started, then." Matt walked away as the line on the other end of the connection began to ring. "I don't know if we've got ten minutes."

Charlie answered the phone.

"Sorry, I know it's late," he said.

"Where the hell are you?" she demanded. "I've been trying to reach you for hours. Turn on your goddamn phone!"

"I'm in D.C. I think I have a lead on what—or who—Nichols is after. The Cameron woman—she didn't have red hair, did she?"

"No, blond. And, Matt, there've been two more. One was in Portsmouth, a sixty year old ex-Navy chief. The other was a psychiatrist in Virginia Beach, fifty-four years old, in broad daylight, for God's sake, fifty feet from her office. That brings the total to ten."

"Witnesses?"

"Pretty sketchy, so far. We think he might be driving a red or maroon van now, no clue on the license plate. It looks like he lured her into the empty church on some pretense or another—hell, asking her to check the ladies' room for his missing daughter, or help him carry in a box of church bulletins, I don't know, it's ridiculously easy to do. Why aren't people more careful? Haven't they caught on yet? Jesus, there's some maniac out there killing people in churches and what does this bright, educated, successful middle-aged woman do but go off with a perfect stranger to a fucking church!"

She caught an angry breath, and was silent. Matt understood her frustration and her anger, and he gave it the respect it deserved.

In a moment she went on, "It was the police who found her, about three hours after she was reported missing, so in that way this case could be a break for us. He's got to still be in the area."

Matt said, "What about Kelly Cameron?"

"There are some breaks there. We got a physical description of a man she was talking to earlier, and it matches Nichols. Her car was found disabled in the parking lot, a slipped battery wire. This fellow has a regular arsenal of tricks. It looks like she went with him willingly, too, and he drove her to a church about five miles away. He killed her in the parking lot outside the church."

"He didn't want to get blood in the van," Matt said. "He was getting ready to dispose of it and he didn't want to be hampered by a big clean-up job. Send her clothes to the lab," he suggested. "I'm willing to bet she put up a fight before he got her out of the car, and there may be traces of his blood mixed with hers on her clothes. Tell the coroner to look for nonmatching blood, too, and check under her nails."

"Done. Are you on your way down here?"

"I've got to see this through. I'll be there as soon as I can. You're right, he's still in the area, and he's going to stay until he finishes what he has to do.

There'll be another murder, but not tonight. Before, he was using the dark to avoid detection, but now the agenda has become more important than his own safety. He's looking for something specific now, and he's running out of time."

Charlie said, "Look, I hate to bring it up, but Polly called earlier. She's worried about you. You should call her back."

"No."

"Matt, for the love of—"

"She knows the only reason I'd call her in the middle of a case is to cancel our plans. I'm not doing that."

There was a moment's pause. "Maybe you should consider the possibility—"

"Not an option," he said tersely.

In a moment Charlie said, "We can blanket the Tidewater area with pictures of Nichols by morning. His name and description will be on every broadcast—"

"Don't," Matt said, and even as he spoke his chest tightened. If he was wrong, he might blow their only chance to catch the killer. But he didn't think he was wrong. "It won't do any good and it might do a lot of harm. We're dealing with a man balancing on the edge of a delicate fantasy here and if you do anything to push him over he may just end up in a church tower with a high-powered rifle. We don't want to do anything to give ourselves even less control over him than we have now."

"For Christ's sakes, Matt, how could we possibly have less control than we have now?"

"At least now we can predict what he's going to

do. This guy . . .'' A flash of the computer-aged girl went through his head. "It's like he's morphing, adapting to the circumstances as he has to. First he behaved as a classic serial killer, then he took on elements of ritualism and the mania of spree killer. I don't want to see what he's going to turn into next, and if we change the playing field we're going to find out.''

She was silent for a moment. "This isn't going to sit well with the local police—or Headquarters, either. I can buy you a day or two at most.''

Matt said, "If we haven't caught him by then, it won't matter.''

WEDNESDAY, APRIL 30

Twenty-Four

10:30A.M.

The residential care home was just outside of Williamsburg, an hour and a half drive from Ellen's house. Ellen knew she could have never made the drive over the Bridge-Tunnel by herself. Simply admitting that made her feel somewhat better, and she was immensely grateful for Ben's quiet understanding and support.

He kept up an easy stream of conversation across the bridge, and Ellen didn't remember what he said; she was sure he didn't expect her to. When it was over and they were safe on solid ground again Ellen said, only a little shakily, "I think Maureen would be proud of me."

That was the first time she had mentioned the psychiatrist, and Ben had been kind enough—or professional enough—not to inquire. Now he said, "Did it go okay with her, then? You're not mad at me for recommending therapy?"

She laughed a little, though it wasn't a particularly mirthful sound. "How could I be mad at you for pointing out the obvious?" Then she said, "I liked her. She wasn't like I expected. She thought . . ." Ellen hesitated, feeling odd to be discussing this woman, this dead woman whom she had barely known but who had touched her life in an important way, so dispassionately. "She thought we could get to the bottom of this."

Ben said, "You don't have to tell me. I don't expect you to."

Her smile was genuine as she looked at him. "You're a good friend, Ben."

"Now, I'm not sure I like that. The last I heard, I was the boyfriend. I think you are mad at me."

She scooted across the seat and pressed her head briefly against his shoulder, but she didn't say anything. He seemed to understand, and made no comment when she moved away and began to point out familiar scenery along the way.

They arrived at Clara Barton Convalescent Center a little past eleven in the morning. It was a sprawling, red brick structure with well tended and landscaped grounds and a graceful Greek Revival exterior. Ellen explained that the facility catered to all levels of need, from those who required full time nursing care to those who merely needed someone to look in on them once in a while and prepare an occasional meal.

"Aunt Gencie is what they consider intermediate care," Ellen explained as they walked up the pansy-lined path toward the central courtyard at the side of the building. "She's in a wheelchair because it's more comfortable for her, and the stroke affected her speech center, but for the most part she's independent. She calls this her 'retirement cottage.' " Ellen smiled fondly as she said it, and she added in the same noncommittal tone. "Maureen thought there may be some *reason* I don't remember where I grew up, and that the reason might have something to do with what happened there. Aunt Gencie is the last person who might know what it was." And she shrugged a little self-consciously. "It can't hurt to ask, I guess."

Ben noticed immediately that she had said *what* happened there, as though it were an established fact, not what *might* have happened. It was a small slip, and one of which she was apparently unaware, but he thought it was significant anyway. He put his hand protectively on her elbow as they entered the building, for no reason at all.

The designers had gone to a great deal of trouble to make this part of the building look more like an apartment building than a care facility. The unit numbers on the high-gloss exterior doors were brass, and there were individual mail slots. Inside, the room was bright and airy, with a small kitchenette and a colorful chintz seating group, a television, filled bookshelves, and french doors with a view of the courtyard. The doorways were wide and the countertops low for easy wheelchair access, the carpet low pile. There were emergency call buttons strategically located, but otherwise the unit resembled nothing so much as a homey, well cared for apartment.

Gencie Kellog was a slender woman with thick, wavy silver hair now drawn into a loose chignon, and quick blue eyes. It did not take much imagination to know she had been a beauty in her time. Her left hand was weak, and the stroke had left a slight downward pull to the left side of her mouth, but it was hardly noticeable when one looked into her smile. Ben thought it spoke volumes on the kind of woman she was that, rather than struggle to form inarticulate sounds from her damaged language centers, which was a long, frustrating, and often futile undertaking, Gencie had simply learned to sign, and now carried on bright, articulate conversations at her own pace.

When Ellen introduced him, Gencie's blue eyes twinkled and she signed, "So! Caught yourself a doctor!"

Ellen blushed and quickly sputtered to explain, and Ben laughed. "Don't worry," he told her, "I'm not going to try to get away with that one twice." To Gencie he said, "Not yet, she hasn't."

That made Gencie laugh, and she signed back, "Run harder!"

Ellen pretended to be irritated. "Aunt Gencie, honestly, you're going to have Ben thinking everyone I know has a doctor fixation—or that we're all a bunch of gold diggers."

Gencie opened her arms wide and Ellen embraced her again, even though she had done so at length when she came in. From his vantage point Ben could see the older woman's eyes glisten with tears behind her smile, and when at last she released Ellen she signed, "Worried about you."

Ellen's voice was thick as she answered, "I know."

And that was all that was said about the trauma that had put Ellen's face on front pages across the nation.

Gencie instructed Ellen to make tea and arrange

cookies on a china plate, which was obviously a family heirloom. Ellen did so, and they sat in the sunny living room, drinking tea and having easy inconsequential conversation.

Then Gencie signed, "I know you, baby. Something's on your mind. If you didn't come here to tell me you're getting married—" She cast an amused look at Ben—"then what is it? Something I can help with?"

Ellen glanced at Ben, only because it was good to have someone to turn to, however briefly, for reassurance. And because he understood how much courage what she was about to do required, because she wasn't sure she wanted to know the answers to the questions she had to ask.

She said, "Aunt Gencie, something strange happened to me recently."

The turned-down corner of her mouth made Gencie's smile seem more wry than perhaps she intended, yet there was an obvious effort on her part to lighten the somber expression on Ellen's face. She signed, "Something else?"

To some extent, she succeeded in taking the strain from Ellen's features, although Ellen's smile was weak and faded almost before it was completed. "Yes," she said. "It seems—well, it seems there's no record of my birth in Wintersville. I went back there and the school, the church, the house—everything I remember about growing up there never existed at all. Ben thinks . . ." She glanced at him apologetically. "He thinks I must have the state wrong, or the county, or even the name of the town, but how can a person forget where she grew up? I mean, I lived there until I was twelve years old, for heaven's sake. My whole childhood is in that place. I remember the address of the big white house where we lived, the lilac bush and the wraparound porch. Only there's never been a street by that name there. I remember the lake with the picnic benches and the swans, where Daddy used to take me every afternoon. But there's no lake in Wintersville, never has been. I, um, I've been talking to someone who can help me try to find out why I'm remembering things that never happened, and she suggested I talk to someone who was there when I was a little girl." She forced an uneven smile, but the muscles in her face were stiff. "You're it, Aunt Gencie, the only one who's left. Why am I remembering the wrong town? Why is everything I remember about the place I grew up wrong?"

As Ellen spoke Gencie had gradually turned her face away from her, staring out the window as though seeking answers there. When she looked back at Ellen, there were tears in her eyes. "Because," she signed with a single, shaking hand, "you didn't grow up there."

Ellen frowned a little, afraid she had misinterpreted her aunt's unsteady sign language. "What?"

In reply, Gencie lifted her fingers to her eyes, one at a time, and blotted each one separately. Then she lifted her chin and wheeled her chair across the room. She stopped before a coat closet, backed her chair out of the way, and began to lift herself out of the chair. Ben was on his feet quickly. "Can I help you get something?"

When he reached her she signed, "Box, top shelf." But she did not resume her seat again until the box was in her hands. Ben pushed her chair back to Ellen, who was by this time standing as well, looking at her aunt curiously.

"Aunt Gencie, you shouldn't keep things that high up. You're going to hurt yourself trying to reach them one day."

She made an impatient gesture for Ellen to be seated, and then she spent a long time simply staring at the box in her hand. It was a jewelry box, covered in a faded silk print of blue flowers, latched with a small key that was still in the lock and no doubt more decorative than functional. Gencie signed, without looking at her, "Before Rita died," she said, referring to Ellen's mother, "she gave these to me. I argued with her. I thought you should have had them then. Such secrets, I said, can't be good for the child. But all these years, they had been so careful, and now she thought it was too late." At last she met Ellen's eyes. Her face was wet with tears. "My darling, I am so sorry."

Ellen took the box. Ben came over to watch as she opened it. Inside there were a handful of photographs, a ragged, age-yellowed newspaper clipping that had been crumpled and straightened out again . . . and a birth certificate.

Ellen took the birth certificate out first. It was issued to a woman named Mary Noble for a female child born May 1, 1965. The father's name was Jackson Noble. The child was called Ellen Marie.

Ellen looked up at her aunt, a question on her lips, but Gencie's face was averted, her muscles working in an obvious effort to control tears. Ellen passed over the clipping, which seemed to be a portion of an article on school reapportionment, and picked up the photographs. They were all of the same people: The first was a five-by-seven wedding photograph of a russet-haired man and a pretty woman in a satin and lace wedding dress. She carried a bouquet of orange blossoms and lilies, and he wore a pink rose in his lapel. They were young and smiling and obviously in love. The second was of the same man and woman, each holding a baby. One baby was wrapped in a blue blanket, the other in pink. Twins. The third made Ellen gasp. The man, the woman, and a boy and a girl of about four years old were standing in front of a big white house with a wraparound porch and a lilac bush.

"That's it!" Ellen cried. "That's the house I remember."

She turned the picture over to her aunt. "Who are these people?"

"Your parents," Gencie signed, more or less steadily, "and your brother."

Ellen felt her cheeks go cold. "These aren't my parents," she managed at last. "And I don't have a brother."

The tears began to flow down Gencie's face again; her shoulders shook with silent sobs.

Ben said gently, "Miss Gencie, was Ellen adopted?"

Gencie nodded, and the effort required to do so steadied her somewhat. She signed, "My sister, Rita—grandmother. Maternal."

Ellen managed hoarsely. "My parents, my brother—where are they?"

Gencie made a single slashing motion, but could not finish the sign. Ben supplied quietly, "Dead?"

Again she nodded.

Ellen could not stop staring at the photos. There were others, taken of the same family, and even though Ellen gradually began to recognize herself as she grew older, she could not make herself think of these people as her family. A brother. A curly-haired, freckled-face brother . . . like the child in her vision, with the dead rabbits.

Her fingers felt numb, and it was hard to breathe. She whispered, "How—how can this be? Why didn't they tell me?"

And Ben added, "Is that why there's no record of her birth certificate? Because she was adopted?"

Gencie signed, "Birth name—N-O-B-L-E. Grandparents' name C-O-X."

Ben nodded thoughtfully. Then, "Where were these pictures taken? Where was Ellen born?"

But Gencie started to cry again, covering her face with her one good hand, and would not answer.

Ellen picked up the tattered newspaper clipping and examined it curiously. There was no hint of which newspaper it might have come from, and the article had no interest for her at all. Then Ben said quietly, "Turn it over." '

Ellen turned it over, and felt ice pierce her spine. The caption was, "Child Surv—" The rest was torn off. The photograph was of a little girl—the little girl who once had been *her*—face streaked with tears, hair rumpled, arms uplifted to reach for someone.

"That's where I've seen it before," she whispered. "That's where."

Twenty-Five

Matt was too tired to go home, so after assuring himself that there was nothing he could do to speed Reinhart along, he tried to get a few hours sleep in a nearby hotel. It seemed he had barely closed his eyes when the phone rang.

"We've got it," Reinhart said. "This you'll want to see for yourself."

That was at eleven o'clock in the morning. Matt was back in the Sci-Crime lab by eleven-sixteen.

Reinhart pushed his chair away from the computer screen with a flourish. "Here she is," he said. "The reason it took so long was trying to bring up the text."

Matt stared at the image on the screen. It was of a young girl, five or six years old, with a tear-streaked face and arms upraised. He thought, *I know that child. I know that picture . . .* "What text?"

"You were right, it was a newspaper photograph. And when he clipped the photo to scan it into the computer he was a little sloppy, got part of the caption in with it. Just a fraction of the top part of the letters, so faint you could hardly see it on the later enhancements. But when we magnified this first computer print we could see something was there. It just looked like squiggles and blurs to the naked eye, but the computer was able to reconstruct the letters. This is what it said."

He pushed a button and the screen scrolled down an inch. Beneath the photograph of the weeping child was the caption: Girl Survives Massacre.

"We went through the database and found the story that went with the picture." He pushed another button and the screen divided. "Here it is."

Matt leaned in close. "My God," she said softly. "Of course."

Twenty-Six

1:00 P.M.

"Listen to this," Reirson said, ushering Charlie into the chair in front of a bank of recording and playback equipment. "It came in last night, a routine tip line call."

Charlie put on a headset while Reirson held the earpiece from another against his ear. Cal Morrow, SAC of the Norfolk office, and Special Agent Darnell, who had screened the call, stood by. Reirson pushed the playback button.

The recording began from the moment the call was received by the switchboard. "Um, Yes. I need to speak to someone about the Church Pew killings." The caller was an adult male with a baritone voice accented by a faint Lowcountry drawl, and nervous.

Operator: "Your name and phone number, please."

A long pause.

Operator: "Sir, we need your name and phone number for our records."

Caller: "Maybe this wasn't such a good idea."

Operator: "One moment please. I'll put you through to the task force."

A lot of callers were reluctant to give their names to the FBI and, perhaps understandably, those most reluctant were often in a position to have the most valuable information. As instructed, after a routine attempt to identify the caller, the switchboard put every call through to an agent.

The next voice was that of Agent Darnell. "Special Agent Darnell, can I help you?"

Caller: "Yes. I hope so. This may sound strange, and I don't mean to waste your time, but I was hoping you could give me some information about some of the victims of the Church Pew Killer."

Darnell: "May I ask who I'm speaking with, sir?"

Caller: "This is embarrassing. Do I have to give my name right now?"

Darnell: "It would help, yes, sir."

Caller: "I'd rather not. Couldn't you just check out my information on an informal basis? If it amounts to anything, then I'll be happy to cooperate."

Darnell: "What information is that, sir?"

Caller: "It's more like a question. A couple of questions, really. First, all of the killings have been reported by the media, right? There've only been nine deaths. Not—twelve?"

Charlie's eyes widened as she looked up at Reirson. His expression was grim. "Only nine had made it to the press by the time we got this call," he said.

They returned their attention to the tape.

Darnell: "That's correct."

Caller: "And one of the victims, when he was found—was he wearing a gold cross around his neck?"

Charlie stopped the tape, looking at Reirson. "How

the hell did he know what?" Her voice was a little breathless. "We didn't release that."

Reirson nodded. "It gets better."

She started the tape again.

Darnell's voice was phlegmatic. "Why do you ask that, sir?"

Caller: "It's—complicated. There are a couple of other things. Was there a woman with an old-fashioned black purse, the kind with a snap closure?"

"The props!" exclaimed Charlie in a whisper. "He knows about the props!"

Caller: "What about a brunette in a red sweater?"

Reirson shook his head. "He's wrong about that one."

Charlie said, "He could be trying to throw us off."

Darnell: "Sir, I don't have that information on hand. I'll have to clear it through the special agent in charge and call you back. Could I have your number, please?"

Again a long hesitance. "Look, I don't mean to sound paranoid, but there are reasons this could be awkward for me if it turns out to be nothing. Couldn't I call you back?"

Darnell, the consummate investigator, agreed, "You could, but we rotate shifts on phone duty and this is my last one. You'd have to start all over with the next agent you talk to."

A silence. Then: "Okay, how about if I give you my pager number? That way I can call you back the minute I hear from you."

Darnell: "That will be fine, sir."

The call came to an end and Charlie removed her headset. "Good job, Agent Darnell."

Darnell nodded his acknowledgment. "We traced down the pager number," he said. "It's registered to a Dr. Benjamin Bradshaw of Virginia Beach."

"Jesus! How could he not know we'd do that?"

"Maybe he's just playing with us," Reirson said.

"We confirmed with telephone records," put in SAC Morrow, "and the call was made from the telephone of Dr. Benjamin Bradshaw."

"So," mused Charlie, her stomach tightening with excitement, "if he's playing, he's dead serious."

Reirson caught her gaze. "Graham did say there were two of them."

"And this one's a doctor," Charlie added softly. Her breath was so tight in her chest she could barely speak.

"Age twenty-nine," Morrow went on, "been in practice with the Hillsborough Medical Group on the beach for about six months. Father a retired Navy officer, mother a homemaker, both living Suffolk, Virginia. Brother a captain in the Navy, present duty station Guam. About eighty thousand outstanding in student loans but otherwise an upstanding citizen."

"I would say this definitely merits further investigation," Charlie said. "I'd like to start with a few easy questions for the good doctor. If he won't cooperate, I think we have enough here for a limited search warrant. Let's start with his office."

"There's one more thing, Agent Fontana." The slightly dry undertone to Morrow's voice suggested—ever so faintly—that Charlie's female impatience might be getting in the way of her better judgment. Charlie had seen that look a hundred times and had learned not to resent it—almost.

"I said Dr. Bradshaw was an upstanding citizen," Morrow went on, "but I didn't say he was an ordinary one. In fact, you might say he's a little more upstanding than most. Maybe you've read about him in recent weeks in newspapers and national magazines? He's the hero doctor from the Virginia Beach bridge collapse."

For a moment Charlie was nonplussed. She heard Reirson mutter, "Holy shit." A lightning-quick debate went through her head.

She said, moving out of the room, "And I hear Ted Bundy was a real charmer, too. Get me a federal judge on the phone. We need a warrant."

Twenty-Seven

Matt reached Charlie forty-five minutes later. "I have an I.D. on the red-haired woman," he said. "Her name is Ellen Noble." He spelled it. "She's thirty years old and somewhere in the Tidewater area. Check DMV, then birth and marriage records. Put every available man on it."

"I'm in the car; I'll call it in. Do you have a photo?"

"A close approximation. I already faxed it to Norfolk. I can get on a transport to NAS Oceana that leaves in about two minutes. I'll explain it all when I get there."

"Matt, wait. We think we might have a lead on Churchpew. Do you remember you said he was working with somebody, getting advice from somebody—and that that person might not even have been with him at the scene of every crime? Do you agree there's a strong possibility that person might be a doctor? And that one of the reasons Churchpew is here is because *he's* here—his mentor. They're getting ready to link up in person."

"They could have been keeping in touch by telephone," Matt said. "That would explain some of the physical evidence—the change of footprint patterns when he paused to answer his cell phone."

"If we're right, you're not going to believe who this guy is. I've got a search warrant for his office, and I'm on my way there now."

"Don't," Matt advised sharply. "Don't exercise the warrant."

"What, are you crazy? His telephone records will be there—"

"Arresting him is not going to stop the killing!" Matt practically shouted. "For God's sake, Charlie, stop trying to be such a goddamn hero. You don't win this game by scoring the most points. You only win when people stop dying!"

Into her stiff silence, Matt went on quickly, "I'm going to miss my transport. Interview the doctor, make it routine. He'll like the attention, get a charge out of outsmarting the FBI. He'll probably even pretend to cooperate. Whatever you do, don't spook him. He may be our only chance to save Ellen Noble's life. I'll call you back when I'm on the ground."

Tight-lipped, with her eyes straight ahead on the road, Charlie disconnected the call. "Call Norfolk," she told Reirson, who was riding shotgun. "We need to put out an all-points for a woman named Ellen Noble."

"Who is she?" Reirson asked, dialing.

Charlie answered, "The killer's next victim."

Twenty-Eight

"I don't know what you're mad about," Reirson said as they went up the pink marble steps to the portico of what a scrolled sign discretely identified as The Hillsborough Medical Group. "You're the one who told me to keep it low key."

"I'm not mad." Charlie's voice was clipped, her stride long. "I'm just tired of people telling me how to do my job."

"I thought that was why Graham was on board," comment Reirson mildly. "To tell us all how to do the job."

Charlie shot him a sharp look, then jerked open the door.

The waiting room was furnished with a classy Edwardian ambiance; brocaded wing chairs and pale silk sofas with tasseled cushions. The patients were well dressed and mostly middle aged, and there were only one or two unoccupied seats. Charlie rapped lightly on the frosted-glass window that shielded the office staff, ignoring the sign that invited her to "Please Sign In and Have a Seat." A pleasant-looking young woman slid open the window and Charlie held out her badge. "Good afternoon," she said, keeping her voice subdued so as not to alert the patients in the waiting room. "I'm Special Agent Fontana and this is Agent Reirson with the FBI. We'd like to talk to Dr. Benjamin Bradshaw, please."

She saw the familiar fear and curiosity come into the woman's eyes, and in the background several others in the office stopped what they were doing and looked her way. "Um, Dr. Bradshaw isn't in today," the woman replied. "It's his day off. Is there something—?"

Reirson said, "Would tomorrow happen to be his day off, too? May first?"

The woman looked uncomfortable. "Well, yes. But I can take a message, I suppose."

Charlie smiled reassuringly. "We're investigating the death of Dr. Maureen Lister," she explained. "We're trying to interview as many of her colleagues as possible. Do you think one of Dr. Bradshaw's partners would have time to talk to us?"

The woman glanced over her shoulder, visibly relieved. "Yes, it was terrible about Dr. Lister. I'm sure I can catch one of the doctors between patients."

"Do you mind if we wait in Dr. Bradshaw's office?"

The receptionist, who obviously did not feel that her job description extended to protecting her employers from federal agents, was only too happy to show them to the absent Dr. Bradshaw's office, and even obligingly closed the door when she left.

"Smoothly done," commented Reirson, and went immediately for the file cabinet in one corner.

"I've had practice." She sat down behind the desk and slid open the top drawer. "Consider this a covert search. Don't disturb anything. We'll play it Matt's way for now."

"Coincidence that he was off today, just when our man arrives in town? And tomorrow?"

"There's nothing on his desk calendar. Whoa, wait a minute." Her voice grew cautiously speculative as she flipped back a page. Reirson turned from the file cabinet. "Well, look at this. What does that say—Lister? 11:00 A.M. yesterday? Right before she was killed."

"He wasn't on her appointment book."

Charlie thumbed through his "in" basket. Lab report slips, letters neatly opened and clipped to their envelopes, medical journals, insurance forms. She pulled out a sheet of yellow legal paper with handwriting on it. She felt a constriction in her throat as she read it, part with excitement, part with a kind of sick fascination.

There were two columns. In one was a description of twelve victims, using phrases like "Woman with sharp nose, curly brown hair, white sweater" and "Fat man with gold cross on a chain, white shirt, tie." And in the other column were the names of the corresponding victims and the dates and places of their murders. Some of the lines in the second column were empty. Most were filled.

"There it is," Charlie said in a voice that sounded oddly dull and flat. "His laundry list."

The door opened and Charlie slipped the paper into her pocket. Reirson quickly moved in front of the desk to shield her movement from the man who entered, a tall, gray-haired, and imposing-looking gentleman in a white coat and stethoscope. His shrewd eyes went immediately to Charlie at the desk, and it was clear he did not like what he saw.

"I'm Dr. Felton, the senior partner here," he said. "Is there something I can help you with?"

Reirson repeated Charlie's line about investigating the Lister murder, asked a few pertinent questions and got straightforward but unenlightening answers. He went out of his way to make it sound routine. After about five minutes Charlie eased to her feet, and Reirson thanked the doctor for his time.

"Shall I have Dr. Bradshaw call you?" Dr. Felton inquired. There was a certain amount of suspicion in his eyes, although his tone was polite.

"That won't be necessary. I think we have everything we need," Charlie answered.

"Then may I ask why you singled out Ben in particular?" This one was obviously not going to let anything get past him.

"We understood he was consulting with Dr. Lister on a case," Charlie improvised. "His name was on her appointment book."

"Was he?" He thought about it, then shrugged. "Possibly. Maureen was always taking on the new doctors, guiding them through the ropes. She might have thrown some business his way, or vice-versa. But I can't think how that could have any bearing on the horrible way in which she died."

"We never know what's going to have a bearing on it until we ask the right question," Reirson said, and offered his hand. "Thank you for your time, Doctor."

Outside, they took the steps quickly. Reirson said, "It's legal, right?"

"We have a warrant."

"Because it could be major evidence."

Charlie said, "Don't worry. Right now it's enough to get a warrant to search his home. And I have a feeling this is only the beginning."

Twenty-Nine

5:30 P.M.

Ben said, "If I understand all this, the reason you couldn't find your birth certificate is because you were looking under the wrong name. And the reason you have confused memories about Wintersville is because you didn't actually grow up there—you must have moved there after your grandparents adopted you. But we don't know when that was, or where you actually *did* grow up."

"Or why I don't remember any of it." Ellen's voice sounded numb, and she held onto the wooden box in her lap as though it contained precious metals— or a poisonous gas. "How can I not remember my own parents? And—a brother! My God, I had a twin brother! How could I not remember that?"

"I think you do remember," ventured Ben slowly. "The pictures you have in your head—living on Jericho Street, walking to church, going to the lake with your father—I think they're all from the time before you were adopted, just like the big white house with the green porch was."

Her brow furrowed. "But—the man in these picture, the one Aunt Gencie says is my father—he's not the one I remember. I've never seen him before."

"Memory alters as we grow older," Ben explained, "particularly when it's subjected to a variety of stimuli. When I think about my father twenty years ago, I don't see him the way he appears in photographs from that time. What my mind comes up with is a kind of a compromise between the way I see him now and what he must have really looked like. You must have been adopted fairly young—five or six years old, perhaps. You just superimposed your memories from an earlier time on the ones you actually have of family life with your grandparents— maybe as a way of coping with the loss of your family."

"My *grandparents*," Ellen repeated softly, her voice still tinged with disbelief. "But, God, why the secrecy? Why wouldn't they tell me?"

"Attitudes about adoption were different in their generation," offered Ben. "Or maybe they thought, if you were willing to accept them as your mother and father, it was best not to upset you by reminding you of the family you lost. That burying the past was the best way to get on with your life."

"It seems—cruel."

"I'm sure it didn't seem so to them."

"Damn it, if only Gencie could have told us more!" Ellen burst out. "How could she just leave me to speculate about the most important thing in my life?"

Ben didn't answer. Gencie had become so upset that he had finally suggested they leave, and he had made a point to request nursing supervision for the rest of the day. Privately he wondered whether Gencie would ever be able to tell Ellen more than she had already done.

Ellen said in a slightly quieter, though even more strained, tone, "And what about that newspaper photograph? Does it remind you of anything?"

"It's a little weird," he agreed, "that any one person would have her picture in the paper twice in her lifetime—and both times for surviving something."

"What?" she wondered. "What did I survive that time?"

"A car crash?" he suggested.

"Maybe. It makes sense." But she didn't sound very convinced. "Why couldn't Aunt Gencie tell me that, at least?"

"Maybe she doesn't know," Ben suggested gently. "It's not unusual for stroke victims to experience pattern memory loss. Maybe that's why she was so upset—because she doesn't remember."

"Maybe." But she sounded preoccupied, and not particularly agreeable at all. "Ben, I know I promised you dinner—"

"And don't think you can get out of it now. Let's stop and get a nice bottle of wine."

She looked apologetic. "I know you're just trying to distract me—"

"That's exactly what I'm trying to do."

"But it's been a long day, and—"

"And you want to go home and brood over those photographs. Don't, okay? Give yourself some time to put things in perspective."

She looked at him, started to form an objection, and then forced her features to relax. "I guess it would be kind of stupid for me to screw up my present because of something I had no control over in the past."

Ben reached across the seat and took her hand. "Did anyone ever tell you you're a very, very level-headed young woman? And if you ever have any doubts about your sanity again, just ask me, okay?"

"Is twice a day too often?"

But she smiled, and looped her fingers through his, and he held her hand the rest of the way home.

She put the box of photographs on the table and turned on the television. "I'm sorry," she said, "I know it's rude, but it's time for the news and I want to see if there have been any more developments. Not *want* to," she corrected herself, "*have* to."

Ben said, "Ellen, I don't want you to get obsessive about this theory of yours. I double-checked, and there haven't been any reports about a fat man with a necklace or a woman in a red shirt—"

"We don't know what color clothes the victims were wearing," she insisted, "and we don't know about the jewelry, either. The news doesn't report that kind of thing. And even if you're right," Ellen said anxiously, "even if all the others were just images I had heard about and incorporated into my dreams, at least twice I'm certain I knew about the killings before they happened. There was Maureen yesterday, and before that the little boy—"

She broke off, the color draining from her cheeks, and scrambled for the box she had left on the table. She went through the photographs frantically until she came up with the one she wanted, the one showing her brother and herself at about age seven.

"That's him," she whispered. *"That's* the boy I dreamed about. It was my brother, all along." Slowly she lifted stunned dark eyes to Ben. "What does this mean?"

But Ben's expression had altered; his eyes suddenly alert on the television screen behind her. He pointed the remote control to raise the volume.

"Updating our top story at this hour," the anchor was saying, "another victim has succumbed to the Church Pew Slayer this evening. Twenty-eight-year-old Helen Myers, a secretary at Branson Academy in Norfolk, was discovered this afternoon in the small chapel on campus . . ."

Thirty

Matt called Charlie from the Bureau car that was waiting for him when he landed at NAS Oceana in Virginia Beach. She was at the site of the eleventh murder.

"Looks like you were right, Matt," she said. "This is home base. Three killings in the same area inside of twenty-four hours, that's a first. We've got some solid witnesses, it was almost like he didn't care if he got caught. And it can't be just coincidence that this is Bradshaw's home turf."

"What did you get from the interview?"

"He wasn't in. But we found a list on his desk— every victim, described in details, plus a few that haven't happened yet, at least not that we know of. Matt, one of the victims on the list was a brunette wearing a red blouse. Helen Myers was wearing a red blouse."

"Christ," Matt said.

"I've got a team staking out his house. We're waiting for the warrant to come through."

"I want to be there when you talk to him."

"If we get to talk to him. He might not come back there. Are you on your way here?"

"Do this one without me. The database came up with sixteen women of the right age within a thirty-five mile radius of Norfolk named Ellen—it was faster to search first names than last since she might have been married two or three times by now. We've got a team tracking down each one of them but about half aren't home this time of day and they're slowed down by having to check out their places of business. I've got two I want to check out personally, but one's way the hell out in Newport News and it's rush hour. This could take some time, Charlie. Maybe more than we've got."

"No chance of putting her picture on television?"

"Too dangerous. There's a good chance that the killer doesn't know how to find her any more than we do."

"Matt, Bradshaw mentioned twelve victims, too. If that's what they're going for, we're running out of time."

"I know. The stage is set; there's just one piece missing, and tomorrow is the first of May. If we can't find her by midnight, we'll do a media blitz on the morning news, search every car leaving the area, whatever it takes. But until we're forced to do otherwise, the best way to keep her safe is to keep quiet."

"She might not even be here. She might be on vacation or on a business trip or in Europe for the season."

"Then that'll be the best luck she ever had, and I'll close my eyes a happy man tomorrow night."

"Matt," Charlie said, "I want to apologize for giving you flack before. It looks like you're right. Churchpew is just Mayday with a helper."

"You were right about the church," he said. "It wasn't a bombing, but you were right. Do the words Heaven's Hope mean anything to you?"

A soft gasp. "Great Jesus. Of course. And the red-haired woman . . . she's the one who got away."

Matt replied grimly, "So far."

6:30 P.M.

"They say he was right there," Diane said, "in the church, when I—found her. He must have come out of the church when I went in."

She sat very stiffly on a straight-backed petitpoint chair in her Riverside home, her ankles crossed elegantly beneath the flow of her skirt, her hands folded in her lap. Her shoulders were straight, her chin high, her voice calm and even. But her diction was even more precise than usual, each word pronounced with distinct deliberation, a sure sign of stress for those who knew her well. And her color was ashen. For the first time since Ellen had known her, Diane looked old.

"They think he was there earlier," she continued. "He was dressed as a computer repairman. He came to the office. I didn't see him then, but Helen did. She told him we hadn't ordered service, and he left. But he must have—must have waited for her in the parking lot. And I saw him. He was in my office, and I—saw him.''

She stopped for a moment, composing herself, and Ben looked at Ellen. She knew what he was thinking, what all of them were thinking. It could have been Ellen. It could have been Diane. It could have been any one of the children or the parents who crossed that parking lot between four and five, which was when the police said the attack had happened. In broad daylight. In a crowded parking lot. *Where she worked.*

The coincidence, if by any stretch of the imagination it could be called that, was terrifying, sickening.

Diane's daughters, one a history major at the University of Virginia, the other, a social services specialist in Portsmouth, had come immediately. They could be heard now moving around in the kitchen, their voices low and concerned, as they worked on the supper Diane insisted she wouldn't eat. The oldest daughter, Leona, came out with coffee in a pretty china pot and four flowered cups and saucers on a silver tray. ''I know you said you wouldn't stay for supper,'' she said to Ben and Ellen, ''but you're not leaving this house without something in your stomachs. Try some of Carly's cheese pennies. She won a prize for them back before she learned it was politically incorrect to be a good cook.''

Ellen returned Leona's warm smile and thanked her, and accepted the cup of coffee she poured. But she knew she would choke if she tried to eat anything.

Leona bent and kissed her mother's head before returning to the kitchen.

Ben said, "Both of your daughters are beautiful. I know you must be proud."

Diane nodded. "And right now I want to take one under each arm and hug them so hard their faces turn blue, and never let go."

Ellen put her coffee cup down on the table beside her chair without ever tasting it. Her throat felt as though it were filled with dust, and she was surprised she could make any sound at all come out. She said, "Diane, what did he look like?"

"Like—this is what I find so difficult to believe—like an *ordinary* man. Average looking, wearing a dark shirt and black jeans, I think, and some kind of nylon windbreaker jacket. I can't even describe his face, it was so ordinary. He had a nice smile, Ellen, and kind of russet-colored hair, a lot like yours. Nothing about him looked as though he was capable of—doing what they said. That's why I think—well, there's got to be a chance that the police are wrong and it *wasn't* him, right? The person I saw in the office could have simply been an ordinary passerby couldn't he?"

There was such desperation in her eyes that Ellen wanted to reassure her, but she couldn't find her voice soon enough. Ben did it for her.

"There's a good chance," he said. "But the police have to follow every lead."

Diane dropped her eyes. "I don't know why it should matter to me. But it would make me feel less responsible somehow if it didn't turn out to be the right man."

"You're not responsible," Ben said firmly.

Diane's smile was weak. "I know."

Then she turned to Ellen. Her eyes were full of

fear and reluctance, and an awful kind of wonder. "Two of my girls," she said. "Tragedy has had its hands on two of my girls in a single month. How could this happen, honey? How *could* it?"

"Diane, what was Helen wearing today?" The words seemed to burst from Ellen unbidden, as though they had been pressure packed at the back of her mind and could be restrained no longer. The look of confusion on Diane's face told her how inappropriate the question was but she couldn't stop herself. She insisted, voice tightening, "Please, it's important. Do you remember?"

Diane frowned. "Why . . . it was a navy blue skirt, I think, and a red blouse. She always looked so vibrant in red." Her voice choked and she turned away.

Ellen could not look at Ben. Somehow she got to her feet, kissed Diane's cheek, and murmured something about leaving. She heard Ben asking if there was anything he could do. Ben remembered to stop by the kitchen and say good-night to the daughters. Ellen was shaking by the time she got to the car.

There was a light sea mist that danced in the cold orange street light like detritus in a fish bowl. She leaned against the door to steady her legs as Ben unlocked the car, and she felt the sliminess against her fingers, dampening her skirt. She said, "She was wearing a red shirt."

Ben said, "It doesn't mean anything."

"I told you there was a woman with dark hair wearing a red shirt. Helen had dark hair. That's what made me think of it."

"Ellen, a lot of the victims had dark hair."

Her teeth began to chatter, and it was hard to speak.

"I knew her. My God, all this time, I never thought that I would *know* her. The woman in the r-red shirt."

Ben opened the door and she got inside, hugging her arms hard against the sudden chill. He started the engine and turned up the heat, and he didn't speak until they were well into the stream of traffic.

His tone was carefully neutral but Ellen could tell he was as disturbed by the accumulation of events as she was. "Ellen, I don't want you to obsess about this. There's a logical explanation."

"I knew it was going to happen," she said, in a voice barely above a whisper. "I knew, I could have stopped it—"

"You couldn't have stopped it. What you thought you knew—"

"Damn it, Ben, don't tell me I was imagining things! You *know* I didn't make this up, you were there, you heard me tell you there was a woman in a red shirt three days ago! You heard me describe the little boy before it happened, too, and the other woman! What logical explanation can there be?"

Ben was quiet for a moment. Then he said, "I have a more puzzling question, if you can believe that. I'd like to know how it could be that you suddenly start having dreams about these murders, and less than a week later, one of your coworkers, of all the people in the world, becomes the next victim."

Ellen turned slowly in her seat to look at him. Everything inside her was suddenly very still; even the shivering stopped. For a moment it seemed the only thing that moved in the whole world was the pattern of passing lights on Ben's face. She said, "Ben—you don't think I had something to do with it, do you?"

He gave an impatient shake of his head. "How could you? You were with me the entire day, eighty miles away."

She sat back, but her muscles relaxed only slightly. Her stomach was in knots; she felt as though she had been slapped in the face. "But you thought about it. For a minute, you thought about it."

"God, Ellen, I don't know what to think. What do you expect me to think? I meet a beautiful woman— under bizarre circumstances, to say the least—who appears to be suffering from traumatic false memory syndrome and hallucinatory incidents, and suddenly her hallucinations start coming true and people start dying. I didn't bargain for any of this. What the hell do you expect me to think?"

The silence pulsed in the confines of the car. Ellen could see his knuckles, white on the steering wheel, and the set of his jaw and the strain in his shoulder muscles, and she knew she should be hurt, angry, shocked, but she couldn't be. All she could feel was tired.

She looked straight ahead, at the headlights starring and refracting off an imperfect, fog-smeared windshield. Her limbs felt heavy, and so did her voice. The heat that poured from the vents was arid, like the desert. She reached over and switched it off. Now nothing was between Ben and herself but the space of a console and the noise of the road.

She said, with an effort, "I don't know what you're supposed to think. I don't even know what I'm supposed to think. But I've read things . . . and heard things . . ." Her fists tightened in her lap and she could hardly believe the words that came out of her mouth. "About twins. About the strange things that can happen, even when they're separated. And that's what I'm thinking. That I have a twin. And he might still be alive."

7:15 P.M.

Charlie called Matt. "Any luck?"

"None." Matt sounded tired, angry and discouraged. "Of my two most promising leads, one grew up in Canada and was nowhere near Heaven's Hope during the time in question, and the other one is in the Navy and was transferred to California last month. We can hope that's her, but I'm not banking on it."

"You don't suppose, if Nichols can't find her, he might take a substitute?"

"No," said Matt. "He'll find her. He knows she's here; that's why he came here. And if some accident of fate has taken her out of town for few days or gotten her transferred—he'll follow her."

"Where are you?"

"I'm heading back toward Virginia Beach. There's one more Ellen I want to see. She wasn't home earlier and neither were her neighbors."

"The warrant came through for Bradshaw. I'm on my way over there now. I'd rather not do a forcible entry but we can't wait much longer."

"It's almost sunset. The guy might've been out playing golf or boating all day. He doesn't have any idea we're closing in."

"Any suggestions on how to approach him?"

Matt hesitated. "Don't charge the place, Charlie. I'm not a hundred percent sure you're on the right track there. I need to talk to him."

"Your area of expertise is interrogation. Mine is investigation."

"And you never have a moment of self-doubt, do you?"

"At this stage of the game I can't afford to, and neither can you. I've got a dozen agents waiting to go in if he shows up. My strategy is to push him out of his comfort zone. He's a doctor, proud of his position in the community. We go in with a show of force and he's humiliated, shaken, pissed off as hell and maybe not so confident anymore. If that doesn't work we're taking him into custody. We need information and we need it fast. Have you got a better way to do it?"

"Damn it, Charlie, you can't just go in there like—"

"Is it a good strategy or not? That's all I want to know."

"Based on what we know it's a good strategy. But what we know is not a hell of a lot. Wait for me. I can make an on-the-scene assessment."

"I will if I can. But he's not getting away, Matt. I'll do what it takes to make sure of that."

7:30 P.M.

At her door Ben said, "I don't like to leave you like this."

Ellen tried to smile. "You have rounds in the morning. And the dogs."

"No, I mean it." The emotion in his eyes was raw and tormented, but she had not the energy to read beyond the basics. "What I said before—I didn't mean to make you feel bad, or imply . . ." He dropped his eyes, and the hands that appeared to have been about to reach for her. "Jesus, I guess I'm not such a hero after all."

Ellen lifted her hands, and cupped his cheek. "Ben, it's okay. Really. I just—need to be alone for awhile, and think about . . . everything. It's been—a lot, at once."

He gave a wan smile. "Another dinner missed."

"Tomorrow's my birthday," she said. "Maybe I'll let you take me out."

"Not the same. But it's a date, anyway."

His expression was searching. "We should talk. About your theory, about twins. Honey, I don't think it works like that. I don't want you to get involved in a fantasy that's only going to end up hurting you."

Now she did smile, though it was a tired smile, and full of sadness. "You called me honey. I kind of like that."

Now his eyes were sober. "We're not off to a very good start, are we? Relationship-wise, that is."

And Ellen said softly, "No."

After a moment Ben bent down and kissed her lips lightly, tenderly. "You know you can call me, don't you? Any time, for any reason."

She nodded. "I know. I will."

She stood on the porch, and watched until he drove away.

From the shadows underneath the deck on the back of the house, Daniel watched too, and waited, and was silent.

Thirty-One

Charlie called as Matt was turning off the highway for Virginia Beach.

"Dr. Benjamin Bradshaw just pulled into his driveway. Where are you?"

Matt pulled up at the intersection, glancing around for signs. "About eight miles from the beach."

"I can't wait much longer. He might have already spotted one of our vans. If he's at all suspicious—"

"All right," Matt said, and he made the kind of decision he hated—the only one that was possible. "What's the address?"

"1827 Carmine, cross-street Magnolia."

"Give me ten minutes," Matt said, and he turned left instead of right.

Ellen Cox would have to wait.

Ellen sat at the dining room table with the photographs spread about before her. Scenes from her past, memories erased. A birth certificate that symbolized a lie. A newspaper clipping torn from horror. Pieces of a puzzle, scattered to the wind.

Even trying to untangle it made her head ache, and she turned her eyes away tiredly. How could she have forgotten where she grew up? How could she have forgotten an entire *family*? A mother with dark hair and a big smile. A balding father. They were as foreign to her as mannequins cut from a catalogue display, even more so. A brother. A *twin*. Did he look familiar to her? Did she remember that grin, those freckles, that carrot-colored tangle of curly hair? Or was she only projecting her own features on to him, recognizing what she wanted to see there?

She touched the photograph, the most recent one that showed them all standing together in front of a wooden sign beside a wildflower-lined road, the perfect family on vacation. She traced the faces, one at a time, trying to bring them into memory. A mother with dark hair who sometimes like to wear red . . . a father with a ruddy complexion and a summer-weight plaid shirt . . . a red-haired brother in a white shirt who kept pulling at his blue tie.

He had reddish hair, kind of like yours, honey . . .

Ellen sat back, breathing shakily, trying to make sense of it. The woman in the red shirt . . . her *mother*? The man, the boy . . . had she invented this whole elaborate dream scenario to somehow help her cope with their loss? And if it all was no more than an invention of her mind—her childhood mind and her present-day, adult mind—what was the connection with the murders?

She kept thinking about the peculiar connection that had been reported between twins, even when the twins did not know each other. Stories about twins separated at birth, who grew up to major in the same subjects in college, choose the same professions, marry spouses in the same kind of jobs, have their children on the same days, sometimes even share the same dreams. What if her brother wasn't dead? What if she was somehow seeing these horrible things through his eyes?

What if her brother was the killer?

That was the theory she couldn't speak out loud.

8:05 P.M.

Matt hit his brakes at the line of traffic backed up behind the large orange and black detour sign, then slammed his fist against the steering wheel, swearing.

He had forgotten about the bridge.

8:10 P.M.

Charlie looked at her watch. "God damn you, Matt," she muttered.

Reirson was watching the house through binoculars. At dusk, with lamplight illuminating the interior rooms through open windows, the view was perfect. "Okay, decision time," he said, binoculars still to his eyes. "He's picking up his keys, heading for the door.

He could just be going out for dog food. He made a big show about throwing away the empty bag a minute ago. Or he could know we're watching him."

"Shit." Charlie said.

"Front door's opening."

She lifted her radio. "Okay, guys, move in."

Reirson left the car first, weapon drawn. Her phone rang as she was ducking down to follow him. "Traffic," Matt said. "I'm five miles away."

"We'll be inside the house," Charlie said, and disconnected.

Ellen drew a sharp breath and then released it slowly into her templed fingers, squeezing her eyes shut as though to block out possibilities. "Insane, insane . . ." she whispered out loud, and she knew it was. But the worst part was that it made more sense than any other explanation she had been able to come up with.

After a moment she took another deep breath, opened her eyes, and returned her attention to the photographs. She tried to block out speculation by calling forth memories, by trying to place herself inside the picture, by somehow trying to recall where and when it was taken. She looked hard at the photograph, searching for landmarks or clues that would jog her memory. The sign. Most of the letters were blocked by the people standing in front of it, but the "Welcome to" scrolled across the top part of the sign was clearly visible.

She picked up the photograph to examine it more carefully. That was odd. Until now, she had thought the sign marked a tourist spot, a national park or a landmark, and that the four of them must have stopped to pose beside it on their way to somewhere else. But in the distance she could see other things—the shape of intersecting roads, the hazy, vaguely familiar outline of a church steeple. She began to think the sign might belong to a town.

Ellen picked up a pen and pulled a notepad close, scrutinizing the shape of the letters half-hidden by the bodies in the foreground. The first letter, a capital H, was visible beside the woman's arm, and part of what could only be an E. The next visible letter was part of what was probably a W or a V, and another E. The man obscured the next letters, but she could make out most of an O beside the boy, her brother, and part of a B, and another E. When she wrote them all down, leaving the appropriate spaces, she had:

HE WE OBE

She had nothing.

In frustration she turned back to the photograph, bringing it closer, studying it more intensely. Part of the letter before the O was visible, just above the man's shoulder. A straight line—no, two straight lines. Another H?

She wrote it down. HE WEHOBE. Then she marked through the jumble and measured off the appropriate spaces, realizing there was more than one word on the sign. HE WE and the last one, which was complete: HOBE. She looked again at the photograph. Was that a place name? Hobe? Home?

"Hope," said a soft male voice behind her. "The word is 'Hope.'"

Ellen whirled in chair, knocking several of the photographs to the ground. A cry lodged in her chest as she looked into the gentle, smiling face of a tall man with reddish curly hair.

"Hello, angel," he said. "It's time to go home."

Thirty-Two

Matt walked into chaos but it wasn't as bad as he had expected. At least Charlie didn't have the doctor in cuffs, or face down on the floor. But he swore silently when he saw the mess the agents had made of the room: cushions overturned, cabinets and drawers opened and their contents pulled out, books pulled off shelves and left open spined on the floor, papers and magazines everywhere. None of it was necessary, merely a display of power. It was all part of Charlie's strategy, which ruined forever any chance Matt might have had to see how this man lived, and that was crucial to forming his first impression.

His first meeting with a suspect was like his first view of a crime scene: It was a sacred place, filled with a thousand tiny immutable clues. This place had been contaminated beyond repair, this suspect corrupted. Any chance he had of getting a clear and honest impression of the truth was gone, perhaps permanently.

The doctor himself was seated at the dining room

table with Charlie on one side and Reirson on the other, looking furious, anxious, incredulous, and increasingly alarmed as he watched agents in dark jackets with yellow stenciled letters on the backs swarm through his house—none of which was unusual. He kept cutting his eyes toward the back door where a cacophony of sound suggested at least one very large dog who was very upset.

He said, "You people are insane! I don't know what you expect to find here but if this is about that phone call I made—"

"We told you what it's about, Dr. Bradshaw," Charlie interrupted sharply. "It's about your relationship with Daniel Nichols."

"And I told you, I don't know anyone by that name. Is he supposed to be one of my patients?"

"What about Maureen Lister?" put in Reirson. "You knew her, didn't you?"

"Of course I did. She was a consultant on staff at the hospital. Are you treating everyone who knew her like this?"

"Do you have a cellular phone, Dr. Bradshaw?"

"In my car, so I can be reached when I'm on call."

"What about Helen Myers? Did you know her?"

He looked puzzled and upset. "No. Just that she worked at the school, as Diane Virion's secretary."

"So you knew her through Ms. Virion. How long were you at the school this afternoon?"

"I wasn't at the school at all. I was in Williamsburg. Listen, I'm trying to cooperate here, but unless you tell me what's going on I'm going to have to call a lawyer."

Matt took that opportunity to try to salvage what

he could from the situation. The look he gave Charlie was cold, but he tried to keep his tone neutral, even soothing. "Dr. Bradshaw," he said, coming over to him, "I'm Special Agent Graham. You're right, this whole thing started with that phone call you made to the FBI Norfolk office yesterday. Why don't you tell us exactly what prompted you to make it?"

Bradshaw looked at him, seemed to find him the lesser of two evils, and appeared to relax fractionally. At least he made no more immediate mention of lawyers. "I explained that to the agent I talked to."

"Actually, you didn't," Reirson pointed out.

Matt turned to the agents who were tossing the house. "Could you guys give it a break for a minute?" He wanted to gain the doctor's trust, or at least his goodwill. It seemed to work.

Matt took out a notebook and pretended to consult his notes. "It says here you thought you might have some information concerning these Church Pew killings we've been investigating."

Now he looked uncomfortable. "Not information, really, more like questions. I felt a little stupid, actually. But a—patient of mine seems to have become obsessed about the killings."

Matthew noted the slight, almost imperceptible hesitance over the word patient, and he knew it indicated a deception, probably in order to claim patient confidentiality if pressed for a name. Alarm bells began to go off.

Charlie said, "Go on."

Ben glanced at Matthew, who arranged himself beside a bookcase and gave an encouraging smile.

Ben said, a little more carefully now, "It's important that you understand that the whereabouts of this person have been accounted for during each one of the murders, and can in no way be considered a suspect."

Interesting, Matt thought. When he glanced at Charlie he saw the same thing reflected in her eyes.

Bradshaw said with a kind of determined evenness to his tone, "The only reason I bring it up is because I've got to believe that the reason you're here is because the answer to one or more of my questions was yes."

Charlie said, "And I've got to believe you knew that when you called, didn't you, Dr. Bradshaw?"

Matt said, "Your patient, was he hospitalized then?"

Ben looked uneasily at Charlie. "No."

"But you can personally vouch for his whereabouts?"

"Yes."

Reirson got to his feet. "I think we're wasting time here. If he can't give us what we need now, take him in. He can call his lawyer from jail." Obviously, they were well rehearsed.

Bradshaw followed Reirson's movement across the kitchen. "You've got to be kidding. You can't think that I—"

Charlie said, "It's up to you, Dr. Bradshaw. We need to know how you knew the things you did about the Church Pew killings. It's as simple as that. Open a dialogue."

Bradshaw looked at Matt. *How much do you know?* Matt thought. *Guilty or innocent? Talk to me, for God's sake. Talk to me.*

Ben took a breath. "Okay, here's the thing. My patient claims to be having dreams—precognitive dreams, actually—about the murders. In a couple of cases she's actually been able to describe the victims before they were killed, or at least before it was announced in the media."

Matthew noted the feminine pronoun, and so did Charlie.

Charlie said, "Do you think this person is psychic, then?"

Ben shook his head. "I don't know what to think. It would help me to know just how much she *does* know about the victims."

"If your patient has any information that could help us, she should have called us herself."

Ben shook his head. "It wouldn't occur to her to do that."

"But it occurred to you."

Ben said impatiently, "She's in therapy, okay? She doesn't need any more stress."

Matt thought, *He's telling the truth.* In his soul he knew it. But he was so tired. It had been so long since he'd been required to make that kind of gut-level decision. What if he was wrong? What if he'd lost his edge? Maybe Charlie, of the low imagination and high aggression, was right. This was too important to leave to chance. And maybe chance was all he had left.

He said patiently, "Are you going to tell us who your patient is, Dr. Bradshaw?"

"No." Then he hesitated. "Not now. I just wanted some information, okay?"

Charlie smiled faintly. "The F.B.I. isn't in business to give out information, Doctor."

Ben replied evenly, "I am not an idiot, Agent Fontana."

Matt bent to pick up one of the magazines that had been tossed on the floor. It was a *Newsweek*, and he was surprised to realize there were several copies of the same issue. Almost at the same moment he realized what issue it was.

The cover photograph seemed to strobe before his vision like a drumbeat while fragments of the truth like shards of glass bombarded him from every side. The woman on the bridge. Dr. Ben Bradshaw. A girl in a newspaper article. National exposure. Computer-aged photographs. *Girl Survives Massacre.* The woman on the cover, arms uplifted for rescue, tears glittering on her cheeks, wind threading through her red hair . . .

"Charlie," he said hoarsely. He held up the cover for her.

But Charlie didn't immediately understand. It was Reirson who said, "My God. It's her. It's the same as the woman in the computer picture. It's even the same pose."

Reirson bent and snatched up another copy of the magazine, flipped through the pages. "This was— Jesus, this happened April 17. The day before the first murder."

The moment it all came together for Charlie was visible in her face. "*That* was the stressor," she said, her eyes still and dark. "That's how he found her."

"Everyone else in the world knows the details of this story," Matt said slowly, trying not to let the horror overwhelm him. "But we've been so focused on this case we didn't see the one clue we needed."

"It says here she works at Branson Academy," Reirson said excitedly, "where the last victim was found. He came there looking for her."

Ben looked sharply from one to the other. "What are you talking about? Are you saying Ellen is in danger?"

Matt turned on him. "Ellen Noble?"

Ben got slowly to his feet. "How did you know that? How did you know her birth name? She only found out today she was adopted. Her real name is Ellen Cox."

Matt looked at Charlie. "I know the address," he said urgently. "Let's go."

Ben took a step after them, only to find his arms jerked back by two jacketed agents. "Wait!" he demanded. "Is that psychopath after Ellen? Is that what this is about?"

Charlie said to Reirson, "Stay with him."

Ben cried, "Stop him! You've got to stop him! Not Ellen!"

Thirty-Three

Charlie said lowly, "Did I screw up? Was I wrong about Bradshaw? Is he just a nice guy who happened to be caught in a disaster on a bridge that tangled him up in a psychopath's fantasy? Or is he *part* of the fantasy?"

Matt's hands were tight on the steering wheel; headlights flashed by like rapid-fire photographer's bulbs. The speedometer said seventy-five, but it felt as though they were barely moving.

"I don't know," he said tightly. He had wanted to shout at her, *Yes! Yes you were wrong and if I had been here instead of tracking down your mistake Ellen Cox might be safe now!* But he couldn't say that. He couldn't say that because . . . he didn't know.

He made a sharp left against traffic. Horns blared. He slowed fractionally to look for street signs. "Do you remember when I said earlier I was wrong at least once a day? I think everybody should be entitled to that, even you."

He glanced at her. In the street lights he could see that her perfect berry-colored lipstick had worn away

310

in places and the flesh beneath it was ash colored. Her eyes were anxious, the lines around them tight with the effort to disguise it.

Matt said, "I hope this is the time I'm wrong, but Bradshaw said nothing to acquit himself in the interview. His concern for Ellen was genuine, but it could have just been the concern of someone who's lost control of the situation. Maybe Nichols acted without him. Maybe he created a monster. Maybe he's just a nice guy who crossed the wrong bridge."

"For God's sake, Matt, don't give me maybe. I need to know!"

But suddenly all Matt could think about were those who had gotten away. He couldn't afford to be wrong. He was *afraid* to be wrong.

And that was exactly why he'd taken himself out of the field in the first place. That was why he had been afraid to come back.

He saw the street sign and made a right. "Check that clipboard on the console," he said. "Is the address 1837?"

"Yes. That's it on the left."

The lights were on in the modest clapboard bungalow, but nobody answered their knocks or their shouts. Matt noticed the house had a circular driveway, which meant a vehicle could have pulled up behind the house and gone unnoticed for some time. In fact, two cars of federal agents did exactly that seconds after Charlie and Matt left their car in the street. Curtains parted next door and curious neighbors looked out, but no one stirred inside the house.

The door was unlocked. They went in with weapons drawn and stances tense, Charlie and Matt followed by two local agents. Two more agents secured the back entrance. They identified themselves loudly. No one answered. They fanned out, did a sweep. The house felt dead to Matt.

It had happened in the kitchen. She had been sitting at the breakfast nook, where a chair was overturned and the cup of tea was still warm. She had been looking at old photographs, a birth certificate, a newspaper clipping. *The* newspaper clipping. She had a magnifying glass and a notepad. He had been watching her from outside the kitchen window. She wouldn't have noticed him; it was dark and the only light was on her. Besides, she had other things on her mind.

She had been bent over the photograph, concentrating on it, when he came up behind her. He had spoken to her, gotten her attention; he wanted to see the recognition on her face. She had turned, startled. She had started to get up, turned over her chair. Maybe she had even tried to run away, but before she could even scream he had caught her to him, brought his hand up, and stabbed her with a hypodermic filled with a fast-acting sedative.

Matt bent and picked up the spent hypodermic with a handkerchief. He thought, *I should have been here, damn it, I almost was here, I could have saved you . . . Ellen, I could have saved you.* But his face was expressionless as he held the hypodermic out to Charlie, who deposited it in an evidence bag. "We'll need a quick analysis of what was in that. Did you call for a crime-scene unit?"

"On their way." Her voice was subdued. "Is she dead?"

He shook his head. "He won't kill her until tomorrow, and he won't do it here."

"She knows," Charlie said. "Look at this." She pointed to the letters on the notepad.

"Heaven's Hope." Matt looked at her. "That's where he's taken her."

One of the officers stood at the threshold. "A neighbor said they saw a maroon van pull in the driveway earlier and park around back. She didn't see anyone get out and she didn't see the resident leave. But she thinks she might have heard a car door slam about half an hour ago. We're interviewing the other neighbors. The houses are pretty close together here. Someone's got to have seen more."

Charlie said, "Go up and down the street in both directions. See if you can get a make on the van, at least. Meanwhile," she added to Matt, pulling out her phone, "I'll call in an all-points for the maroon van and reissue Nichols's description."

"No hot pursuit," Matt warned. "If he's spotted, he's not to be confronted in any way. He's already on the edge and he thinks he's invincible. Suicide would just be another adventure to him, and he won't care how many he takes with him." He started for the door. "We'll need the cooperation of local authorities in the area to set up surveillance and secure the site. Jesus, I don't even know what county the place is in. We could make it by chopper in an hour or two but I doubt there's anyplace to set down. The forest has bound to have taken over the town by now."

Charlie, matching her long stride to his, was on

the phone. She finished giving orders and disconnected as they reached the front yard, which was now illuminated by the sweep of blue lights and assaulted with the crackle of radios. Officers in blue and agents in black moved across one another's paths while a small group of curious neighbors huddled beneath a streetlight, wide eyed, talking and gesturing.

Charlie said, "What about Bradshaw?"

"Top priority, check his phone records, his travel records, his alibis for the time of every murder—get me something, anything, to prove he's innocent. Meantime, we have to take him with us."

Charlie stopped in midstride. "What?"

"I'll take full responsibility." He reached the car and jerked open the driver side door, his expression grim. "We're out of time and out of options, Charlie. If he is Nichols's mentor, he's our only negotiating point, our only way of getting through to the killer. If he's not—" His throat suddenly, unexpectedly, would not prevent the passage of more words. *I can't afford to lose another one*, he thought very clearly, as though with a sudden illumination. *If I do, it'll destroy me.*

So he wouldn't lose. It was a simple as that.

"If he's not," he managed in a moment, "we've got a hostage situation and we can't have our only chance of saving that woman sitting in a jail three hours away. We don't have time to debate it and we don't have the luxury of going by the book. Nichols already has at least a half hour's head start."

9:30 P.M.

The young agent who had been left in charge of him listened to Ben's answering machine. There was a message from his mother, one from the vet confirming his appointment tomorrow, another from his service, one from Felton making reference to a "disturbing incident" at the office today and asking Ben to call him at home. Ben felt invaded, angry, and terrified—not for himself so much anymore, but for Ellen.

Ben said, "Just tell me what kind of trouble Ellen is in. If I knew what was going on, maybe I could help."

The agent removed the answering machine tape and placed it in an evidence bag.

"Do they think that psychopath is after her? Was it because her picture was on the news? Or because she knew what he was doing?"

The cellular phone in the agent's jacket pocket chirruped, and he answered it.

Ben said tightly, "Okay, goddamnit. If you're going to arrest me you'd better do it now because that's the only way you're going to stop me from going to her."

He swept his jacket off the back of a chair and took out his keys and to his surprise no one made a move to stop him until he reached the door. Then the agent said, "Dr. Bradshaw, wait."

Ben was so surprised to hear himself addressed in a manner that was almost courteous that he stopped, and turned back.

"Ellen Cox has been taken from her home, apparently by force and presumably by the man you know as the Church Pew Killer. If you really want to help, now might be a good time to start cooperating."

Ben felt the blood drain out of his face; he let himself lean against the doorframe for support. "Ellen," he whispered. "My God, no."

9:45 P.M.

Daniel smiled when he saw the line of traffic; the state patrol officers motioning cars to the side of the road, going from driver to driver, checking I.D., shining flashlights inside. It wasn't, after all, as though he hadn't expected it. It wasn't as though he had anything to worry about. Ellen was with him now and nothing could go wrong.

He took his place in line. The speeding of his heart was a pleasant, excited anticipation as he heard the trooper's footsteps approaching. A bright flashlight beam swept the interior of the car, first backseat and then front. Daniel squinted a little as the beam caught his face.

The officer leaned down. "Good evening, sir. We're conducting a search for a fugitive. I need to see your license and registration, please."

Daniel said, "It's a rental. The papers are in the glove box."

The flashlight beam shown in the glove compartment on the passenger side. "Get them out, please."

Daniel opened the compartment and took out the papers, which were in Ariel's name. Ariel had promised to meet them at the church, but he had made all the arrangements for the trip in the meantime. He had assured Daniel there would be no trouble. The driver's license which he had used to rent the car was also in Ariel's name, and it was clipped to the front of the folded rental car papers. The officer took them both and walked away. There was a slight tightening of Daniel's stomach when he walked around to the back of the car, but he knew he was only checking the tag.

In a moment he returned and passed the folded papers, license on top, through the window again. "Thank you, sir. Drive carefully."

Ariel had been right. No trouble at all.

Daniel glanced at the rearview mirror as the flashing blue lights of the roadblock grew smaller behind him, and he smiled. "Ellen," he said, "not much longer now. We're going home."

Ellen, in the trunk of the silver Mercury Cougar, didn't hear, and didn't answer.

9:50 P.M.

Matthew said, "I'd like to talk to Dr. Bradshaw in private, please."

Ben's voice was low and shaking with fury. "God *damn* you people. I already told the other agent I don't know the man you're looking for, I have no way of predicting his actions, I have no idea where he's taken her! That's what taxpayers are paying you for! Why aren't you out there trying to find her instead of wasting your time with me?"

"I assure you we have every resource at the state, federal and local level dedicated to doing just that, Doctor," Matt said. "And you're right—I don't have a lot of time to waste. If we could just step out of the stream of traffic?"

Ben glared at him for a moment, then gestured toward a small room adjacent to the dining area that he used as a study. Matt followed him inside but didn't close the door.

"We've been chasing the man the media calls the Church Pew Killer across the state of Virginia for the past ten days," he said without preamble. "We know his name is Daniel Nichols, a computer technician from Durham, North Carolina, and we know he's a deeply disturbed individual who's been compulsively playing out a trauma from his childhood. We've also come to believe that he's not working alone—that someone, either by telephone or in person, is guiding his steps, feeding his fantasy, pulling the strings, so to speak. Evidence has led us to believe that that second individual could be you."

Ben stared at him. "For God's sake, *why*?"

"It's a long story and as you pointed out, time is short. Off the record, I tend to think you're innocent. That the information you got on the murders came from Ellen's memory of them, and that the fact that you're a doctor and have connections with several principals in this case are just coincidental. But just as strong a case could be made for the fact that you've been using Ellen's memories to feed Nichols's fantasies, directing him to murder, supplying him with weapons and other assistance."

There was a recoiling in Ben's eyes. "You people are sick."

"Perhaps," agreed Matt. "Probably. You can't do this work for very long without becoming just about as twisted as the people you chase. If we've falsely accused you, I'll be glad to support any lawsuit you want to file. But if we're right, and you are involved, I want you to understand this." Matt's eyes hardened. "I've lost eleven victims in ten days. Eleven people have died who shouldn't have died because we got there too late, and I'm not going to lose Ellen Cox. I'll do whatever it takes to make sure of that. Do you understand me?"

Ben was silent for a moment, looking into the other man's eyes. Then he said, "What can I do to help?"

"Here's my dilemma," Matt answered. "If you're an innocent citizen I have no right to ask you to put yourself in danger. If you're an innocent citizen there's no reason for you to do so. But if you're Nichols's coconspirator, it's entirely possible you've created a situation here you don't know how to get out of, and the charges against you would be lighter if you were shown to have cooperated in a hostage rescue. Either way, if I arrest you now, you spend the night in jail, and I need you with me. I need you to volunteer—" he stressed the word slightly "—to come with me, and to talk to Nichols if we get a chance. You're the only one he'll listen to."

"He doesn't even *know* me!" Ben cried, his expression rife with impatience and frustration.

Reirson looked into the room. "We've got local and state boys rolling to seal off the roads leading to the old Heaven's Hope site. The report from that area is that some of the buildings are still standing, possibly even the church. Orders are to keep him away from the church, but only if it can be done without endangering the hostage. No way to get a helicopter in. Agent Fontana's assembling the SWAT team. She put me with you. It's about a two-and-a-half-hour drive from here."

Matt never took his eyes off Ben. "Dr. Bradshaw?"

Ben blew out a long harsh breath and pushed toward the door. "What the hell are we waiting for?"

Thirty-Four

Matt got into the backseat with Ben, but not before he handed over his weapon to Reirson, who was in the front. A man in a state trooper's uniform drove the unit, lights flashing but sirens off. A police-band radio crackled in the background, volume low. Ben pressed his head back against the seat in the dark and thought, *This can't be happening. This can't be really happening.*

Reirson looked over his shoulder. "May first is in two hours. Do you think—?"

Matt shook his head. "I think he'll wait till sunrise. He's trying to recreate the circumstances as closely as possible to the last time. And now that he has what he wanted, he'll want to savor it, like an animal taking the trophy of the hunt back to his den to enjoy it."

Ben winced at the metaphor. *Not happening.* How could this be happening? He said, "What do you mean by recreating events? Where is this place we're going?"

Reirson turned to look at him. "Let me ask you

something, Doctor. If you still maintain you're not involved in this and you're completely innocent of any knowledge of Nichols's activities, why did you agree to come with us?"

Ben met his gaze steadily in the flickering lights from passing cars. "I am involved," he told him. "I'm involved with Ellen Cox. And if you're saying by agreeing to come with you I've implicated myself, I frankly don't give a damn. I've got this hero complex, you see, and if I can do anything to get Ellen away from this maniac I have to try. And I'll tell you the truth, it's starting to look like I'm the only one with that agenda."

Matt said quietly, "I don't think that's a fair assessment, Doctor."

"Then will you tell me what the hell is going on? What is this Heaven's Hope you keep talking about? Why do you think the maniac is taking Ellen there and if you know that, why don't you just stop him?"

Matt said, "I suppose you're too young to remember." He glanced at Reirson. "You, too."

"I'm familiar with the case," Reirson said, although a little stiffly.

Matt said, "The Heaven's Hope Massacre was the most brutal mass murder on American soil in the last half of this century. It took place twenty-five years ago in a remote community called Heaven's Hope, Virginia."

Reirson asked, "Why didn't our anniversary date search pick it up? Surely something that big—"

"No one was ever sure of the exact date it happened. Authorities didn't find the bodies for almost a week; by that time the closest estimate they could make was within three days. The only one who would know the exact date is Nichols."

He turned to Ben. "In 1965, a man called Luther Paradise established a religious community on forty-two acres of land in a remote pocket of the mountains of western Virginia. He was a charismatic, self-proclaimed evangelist, and the brand of gospel he preached was a combination of old-time religion and separatist paranoia. His followers were from all walks of life, a product of the chaos of the sixties, most of them, and whatever it was they sought I guess Paradise gave it to them. There were about forty-five families who settled there, living a semi-communal life, building simple homes, some of them even holding down jobs outside the community. He called the place Heaven's Hope.

"The FBI kept a file on them for a while, but there was nothing very remarkable about them. They were a little weird, but they weren't stockpiling firearms and they paid their taxes, even had a school for the children. They were known as quiet people who never bothered anyone or asked for anything or caused any trouble.

"Five years later, though, Heaven's Hope, instead of growing, was shrinking drastically. That's what happens when one of your fundamental doctrines is keeping away strangers. Some people couldn't stand the isolation and left; others found they weren't able to support their families by living off the land and couldn't afford the commute to work a full-time job. A lot of those who left still believed in Luther and supported his teachings, but some were beginning to find him a little too radical. It seems one of his main tenets was that life on earth was the real hell and only by dying could you find true life. His wife had died during that last year, and at least one person who got out later told us he had always suspected Luther killed her. Everyone agreed that in the last few months he had become obsessed with the glory of dying.

"Anyway, in the end there were less than half a dozen families left—fourteen men, women, and children, including Luther and his son. Luther must have seen his kingdom crumbling around his feet and decided there was only one way to save it. So he called a special prayer meeting one spring morning—May the first—and drugged the communion wine with a heavy barbiturate. Then he calmly went down the rows and cut the throats of every member of the congregation, ending with himself. There were only two survivors."

"Child survivors . . ." Ben whispered through numb lips.

Matt said, "When the police found her she was still hiding under one of the pews, which is, presumably, how she escaped Luther's notice. Her hair and clothes were stiff with congealed blood that had dripped down on her from the victims in the pew above her. She had been locked in that church with those dead bodies for four days."

Ben felt his bile rise and a sweat break out on his upper lip. *My God*, he thought, but couldn't say it. *My God, my God, Ellen . . .*

"I don't think most of the world knew what became of the little girl who survived the Heaven's Hope Massacre. Things were different back then; the media didn't hound people to the ends of the earth like they do now. When I looked it up, I saw she was hospitalized for several weeks in a near-catatonic state. She was released into the care of her grandparents, and they were very protective of her privacy. Apparently they changed her name to theirs—Cox—for just that reason."

"She thought they were her parents," Ben managed finally. "She has—had—no memory of any of it, and they never told her. Her memory seems to have begun somewhere around adolescence, although she's incorporated what must have been parts of her life in that—that place, to create a kind of semifictional childhood for herself. I guess the trauma of the accident on the bridge must have triggered some of the repressed memories, because she started having nightmares, and even waking hallucinations about—dead people."

He looked at Matt. The other man's face had a ghostly quality in the strange flickering light; Ben felt like a ghost himself. "She recognized the resemblance between the people in her dream and the Church Pew Killer's victims, even though the similarities were only superficial to an objective observer. She thought she was seeing the killings before they happened. But she wasn't. She was *remembering* them, wasn't she? This maniac is recreating that massacre of twenty-five years ago, victim by victim—only this time he's not going to miss the little girl hiding under the pew. That's right, isn't it? *Isn't that right?*"

Matt looked at Ben quietly for a long time. "Dr. Bradshaw," he said, "either you're the best actor I've ever seen or I've made a terrible mistake."

"Who was the other survivor?" Ben demanded hoarsely. "Ellen—she just found out today about her family, that she had a twin. She was—she had this weird theory that he was still alive, and she was connected to him somehow. I think she thought the killer—this man you're calling Nichols—was her brother. Is that what it is? Is that why he came for her? Is the Church Pew Killer Ellen's brother?"

The phone rang.

11:45 P.M.

When Ellen opened her eyes she was in a small, dark cave, airless, close. She wanted to run, wanted to fight, but her limbs were like lead, her brain swathed in cotton. She felt herself sinking into the dark.

When she opened her eyes again cool air was blowing across her cheek, but it was still dark inside the cave. A voice floated down to her from far away. "It's okay now, Ellen, we're home. They thought they could stop us, but nobody knows these roads like we do, do they? They don't even know this road is back here. They can't stop us from getting home."

And then she was being lifted, she was floating through the air, stars were tumbling and whirling. She felt earth beneath her feet, cold damp grass, and then the sky tilted wildly and her muscles turned to rubber. She collapsed on the ground in a wretched fit of vomiting.

When the nausea cleared he was kneeling beside her, stroking her hair. "I'm sorry," he said softly. "I'm sorry, angel."

He took her shoulders, helped her to stand up. Her legs were still weak, but her vision was clearer. Her mind felt slow, detached, not quite sure.

She said, "I—know you." Her tongue was thick. She tried to sign the words clumsily, and she didn't know why. She could barely remember how. She felt foolish, helpless, detached.

He smiled and slipped his arm around her shoulders. "Of course you do."

"You—have red hair, too."

He said, "We have to walk a little way, but you can do it. Hold on to me, and we'll be home in no time."

There were trees, and slippery stones, and thorns that snagged her clothes, bushes that slapped her legs when she passed. The pain was always a delayed reaction, a beat or two behind the event. He held her arm, hard, and pulled her upright when she stumbled. Her head spun. Her face felt hot and she broke out in a cold sweat. It seemed a long, long time that they walked.

They came to the bottom of a hill, across a stream. The going was easier. Shapes loomed in the distance. As they came closer she saw houses amid the trees and weeds: here a roof had caved in, here a tree grew through a room, here there was nothing but a chimney. And here a big, sagging porch, and a bush gone out of control. The smell of lilac was overwhelming.

Ellen stopped, pulled away, turned around. "My house!" she whispered.

He tried to catch her arm. "Ellen, come on. They'll see us."

She turned full circle. The house, a gray silhouette in the dark, broken windows like blind eyes, doors sagging open, weeds waist high in the yard. The street—what used to be a street—now barely a dirt track, thick with grass. And across from it, the white clapboard church with its little sheltered stoop and the steeple. "I know this place," she whispered.

And that was when something strange happened. She saw the church, the shadow of a church, with steps that had been rotted through and the steeple that had been blown away by lightening or wind, and gaping windows and missing boards, but she saw the church as it was in her memory, white in the springtime sun with pink azaleas blooming outside the door and soft breezes making the blossoms nod. It was her birthday, that's what it was. Her birthday.

She was six years old. She was arguing with her mother at breakfast because she did not like the dress her mother picked out for her. There were daffodils in a blue jar on the table. She thought she was clever; she deliberately spilled juice on her dress so that she would have to change. Mother told her to hurry, and she and Daddy and Tim walked across the street to church. Ellen didn't hurry. It was her birthday. She primped and twirled before the mirror in the dress she had wanted to wear in the first place, a white dress with bunnies on the skirt, and then she felt very grown up as she walked to church by herself.

She went up the steps, through the open door, trying to sneak in quietly because everyone was praying. It was dim inside, but there were dozens of candles, and it was pretty. Candles, for her birthday. There were her parents, and Tim in his red-and-white-striped polo shirt. There was a brown-haired lady with a baby on her lap. There was her teacher, Mrs. Ledbetter, with her gray hair and her glasses worn from a chain around her neck. There was a fat man with a gold cross necklace, and a blonde-haired young woman and a woman in a white turtleneck sweater. Then there was Brother Paradise, going from person to person and shouting prayers, and she ducked down beneath the pew because she was afraid of Paradise and thought she would be in trouble for being late. There she stayed, making herself small and quiet, waiting for him to go back to the pulpit so that she could sneak out and go to her family's pew. But he never did.

And now she was going up the steps of the church, the grown-up Ellen, the broken steps. Someone's hand hard on her arm, fingers digging into flesh, pulling. She dragged her feet. She didn't want to go. She knew what was inside.

It smelled like night and damp and rot. Something small scurried across the leaf-strewn floorboards. The shadows were deep and terrifying. He said sadly, "Look at this. It's a sacrilege."

He released her arm then, and shrugged out of the backpack he wore. There was a snap, a flash of light that made her eyes hurt. A candle. He lit a candle.

Ellen looked around. Pews were overturned, the pulpit was missing. Cobwebs hung like tattered draperies from the ceiling. Old books—hymnals?—were scattered here and there, their mouse-chewed pages heavy with rot. The pale, flickering light moved, startling bugs and night creatures. Heavy wings fluttered against a wall and were still.

And now he was coming, Brother Paradise, coming in the candlelight. Yea, though I walk through the valley of the Shadow of Death I shall fear no evil . . . That was what he was preaching. He moved from front to back, coming closer and closer to her, and when she peeked up she could see that Ariel was with him. Fear no evil, for thou art with me . . . She knew Ariel and wasn't afraid of him, but she was afraid now, because Ariel was afraid. The older boy was crying, huge, silent terrified tears, and then she saw the knife.

Fear no evil, he said, for thou art with me . . .

Paradise held Ariel's hand on the knife as he went from pew to pew, person to person, chanting a blessing before he drew the blade across their throats. Over and over he assured Ariel that by performing this final service for the sanctified he would truly become an angel of the Lord and reserve his place in heaven. "I will fear no evil," he said, holding Ariel's hand, "for thou art with me." But Ariel was frightened and tried to get away, and when the last throat was cut he broke away and turned the knife on his father. Luther Paradise did not resist and seemed unsurprised, glad to die.

Ellen watched all of it, and when it was over, Ariel saw her. She thought he would come for her, but he seemed confused. He merely wiped the knife on his father's blood-stained robes, placed the weapon gently on the floor, and walked away.

When he was gone Ellen ran to her family's pew and found her mother, brother and father silent and lifeless, bleeding from the wounds to their throats. Sobbing softly she hid beneath the pew again, and blood dripped down through the cracks, splashing the embroidered rabbits on her skirt.

MAY 1, 1997

Thirty-Five

12:35 A.M.

Reirson moved the phone away from his face, turning to look at Matt in the backseat. He had been in constant contact with the team at Heaven's Hope for almost an hour. "They've got him," he said.

Matt leaned forward.

"In the church," Reirson said. "He has the Cox woman with him and she looks okay. The locals don't know how he made it through the roadblocks; must've hiked in."

Matt sank back against the seat. His jaw was set against silent curses.

"Any instructions?"

"Yes," said Matt. "Tell them to do nothing. *Absolutely nothing*. How far away are we?"

Reirson looked at the trooper. "Twenty-five minutes," the driver answered.

"Nothing," Matt repeated.

Daniel set the candle on the raised platform that used to be the altar, and he lit another from the store in his backpack.

"I know you," Ellen said, staring at him.

His hand was tight on her wrist as he dug through his backpack again. "I'm sorry, angel, but I have to tie you up. He said so. I know you wouldn't mean to run away, but you might get scared. I lost you once."

As he spoke, he removed a length of rope from the backpack and looked around for a suitable object to which to secure her. There was a large overturned throne chair to the left of center at the front of the church; Ellen remembered it once had been on the platform where the pulpit stood. Brother Paradise had sat there.

He dragged her over to it, pushed it upright, and brushed the leaves and debris from the seat. He forced her into the chair and tried to stretch her arms backward around its back but the chair was too broad, the armrests too high. Ellen cried out with pain as her shoulders were wrenched; he released her arms and secured the rope around her waist instead, binding her to the chair. Fear pounded through the fuzziness in her head and she said, "What are you going to do to me?"

He stepped back, smiling at her approvingly. "Don't worry. It's not time yet."

Her throat was dry, her lips numb. It was hard to speak. "Who are you?"

"You know me," he reminded her. "Remember when we used to wander those hills behind town? You were always a horrible pest, had to tag along, but you were kind of cute." A strangely frightening, haunted look came over his face. "All that red hair."

Ellen felt tears back up behind her lids. She tried

to fight them back, but it was a losing battle. "You're not him, are you?"

He turned suddenly, as though listening for something, and then he said, "Yes, I know." He looked back at Ellen. "They're watching us, you know, out there in the dark with their night-vision glasses and their high-powered lenses. They're watching us and it's making them crazy because they can't do anything to stop us." Again he looked over his shoulder and smiled. "Can they?"

Ellen closed her eyes and let the hot tears trickle down her cheeks. "You're not him. You're not my brother."

Daniel turned to her, looking puzzled. "Your brother is dead," he said. "You know that."

1:00 A.M.

Access to the abandoned community was via a series of unpaved county roads that wound through the woods in such a random fashion that one was forced to wonder how even the locals could navigate them. The driver was on the radio constantly, getting directions and cursing under his breath. The final stretch was a five-mile length of rutted, overgrown logging road that sent headlights careening off trees and completely prohibited conversation. The car came to an abrupt stop where the road became a parking lot in the woods: state patrol cars, local black-and-whites, unmarked vans and cars lined the forest three deep. The trooper said, "This is it, gentle-men, as close as we can get. The rest of the route is a footpath through the woods. We'll be coming out on top of a ridge, so we're advised to stay low and use penlights to walk by. Otherwise we'll be perfect targets coming out of the woods."

Matt said, "He doesn't have any firearms."

The trooper said, "Yes, sir. But I'd rather not take any chances, if it's all the same to you."

Matt said, "Officer, before you unlock this door, could I borrow your handcuffs?" He glanced at Ben. "I apologize in advance, but there are only so many chances I'm willing to take."

Ben looked at him in disbelief as Matt fastened one loop of the trooper's handcuffs around his own wrist and the other around Ben's. He said in soft disgust as they got out of the car, "Jesus Christ."

Matt pointed his penlight at the ground. "Watch your step."

Ellen thought, *I should be afraid.* She knew he had brought her here to kill her. She knew that having escaped certain death twice in her lifetime her luck had run out, her guardian angel had turned his back. She wanted to be afraid, but all she could feel was an overwhelming sorrow, the dark, heavy weight of grief pushing down on her. Grief for the death of the family she had hardly known, the mother and father who were little more than photographs to her, the twin brother whose smile she could barely remember, the life she might have had with them, the joys she might have known. Grief for the others who had died in this lonely place twenty-five years ago, children who never grew up, the lives that were never lived, and grief for eleven strangers who had died over the past ten days in memoriam to that horror a quarter of a century ago. She grieved for Ben, whom she was leaving behind, for the life that was ending too soon. But mostly she grieved for the two children who had survived that horror all those years ago, the dreams that turned to nightmares, the stolen childhood.

There was a bank of candles on the altar now, but they were small candles and the light they created was more atmospheric than illuminating. He was moving about the church, straightening pews, sweeping away debris with his hands and feet. He worked with a feverish intensity, as though against a deadline.

Ellen said, "How did you find me?"

He smiled. "I have a guardian angel."

"I don't."

He glanced at her, frowning a little. "What are you doing with your hands? Is that sign language? You're not deaf."

Ellen closed her hands into fists to stop them from moving. "No. It's just the way I talk."

"Because it was your brother who was deaf," he continued matter-of-factly, turning back to his work. "Not you. You used to talk with your hands like that to him. But I'm not him. He's dead. I told you that."

The knowledge hit her like a blow to the pit of her stomach, taking her breath away. Her brother. The brother whose life had been taken from her, whose memory had been taken from her, but whose legacy had settled deep into a part of her consciousness and determined the course of her life.

That was when she understood. He wasn't dead. None of them were dead. A part of them lived on and would continue to live as long as she continued to draw breath. Nothing could be stolen from her that she refused to give up.

The grief turned to anger, and that was when everything changed.

1:15 A.M.

Charlie glanced curiously at Ben, then directed Matt's attention to several spots along the opposite rim of the darkened hillside where men with high-powered rifles were positioned, weapons trained on the wreck of a church whose roof and front windows were just visible from where they stood.

"He's got her tied to a chair on the left side of the building," Charlie said. "He's been moving around freely for the past twenty minutes or so. The candlelight is messing with their nightscopes, but there's a good chance of a clear shot if they have to take it."

Matt took the night-vision binoculars Charlie handed him and with his free hand brought them to his eyes. The binoculars worked by magnifying ambient light and focusing it on the subject; the candlelight was just enough to make the picture clear. If it got any brighter, however, the binoculars would lose focus and become useless, as would the infrared and thermal scopes the markmen were using. In a moment he lowered them. "He's setting the scene," he said.

"What about spotlights, loud music, something to take the situation out of his control?"

Matt shook his head. "It could be dangerous to disrupt the fantasy like that. We'll use it if we have to, but first I'd like to try to manipulate his fantasy. What kind of weapons have you been able to determine he has?"

"We don't know what's in that backpack. Could be an arsenal, could be a bomb. Or nothing more than a scalpel."

"For Ellen Cox, that's enough."

"For God's sake," Ben said tightly, "will you listen to yourselves? He's holding her prisoner, he's got a scalpel, he could use it at any time! You've got twenty armed men on this ridge that I can see. Why don't you just go down there and get her?"

Matt glanced at him, then at Charlie. "Anything on his background and alibis?"

"Reirson's coordinating with the Norfolk office. Nothing yet."

Matt looked back toward the church. "Can we get any closer?"

"Not and maintain a clear shot in case of trouble."

"There's your answer, Dr. Bradshaw. It would take us thirty seconds to get down the hill, at least. It will take him less than one second to cut Ellen's throat. We may get our man, but we'll lose the hostage. Not an option."

Ben released a tense, unsteady breath. "No. My God, she must be scared to death. With all that's happened to her, why this, too? For God's sake, you've got to do something.''

Matt raised the binoculars again. He studied the scene below for a moment and then he said, ''Have you tried to get a telephone in?''

''We were waiting for you.''

''Let me have the megaphone.''

In a moment Matthew's electronically magnified voice rang through the night. ''Daniel. Daniel, we know you're in the church, and we know you have Ellen with you. We just want to talk to you. We're going to send a telephone down to you. You don't have to come outside to get it. We'll leave it at the door.''

He had hardly finished speaking when a voice echoed upward, hoarse and a little wild. ''Infidels! Stay away from us! Leave us alone!''

Matthew lowered the megaphone, glanced at Charlie. ''I didn't think so,'' he murmured. He turned to Ben. ''All right, Dr. Bradshaw. Now we get to see whose side you're on.''

He lifted the megaphone again. ''Daniel. I have someone here who wants to talk to you.''

He held Ben's eyes as he offered the megaphone to him. Ben hesitated, looking at the instrument.

Charlie put up a blocking hand. ''Think about this, Matt. You don't know what he'll say.''

''It doesn't matter. I just want Daniel to hear his voice.''

''He could tell him to kill her!''

''I don't think he'll do that.'' Matt's gaze didn't waver. ''Will you, Doctor?''

Ben slowly reached out his hand and took the megaphone. ''How do you turn it on?''

342

Matthew showed him the switch. Ben lifted the instrument to his mouth.

"Ellen!" he called. "Ellen, it's Ben! You're not alone, do you hear me? You're not alone!"

Ellen thought, *Ben! Ben!* Her heart sang the word, her fingers spelled it, over and over in small secret movements against her thigh. *Not alone, not alone . . .*

In the shadows her captor raged furiously, "They have no right to spoil it! How could you let them get this close? This is our time, our place! It's not fair!"

Ellen's heart began to pound, both in reaction to his anger and with a kernel of obscure hope. What had he said before? He had seemed so calm about it . . .

"No, I can't ignore them!" he shouted. "They're spying on me, corrupting my sacred moment, my triumph. How can I ignore that?"

They're spying on me . . . They're watching us, you know, with their night-vision glasses . . .

Her heart beat faster. She looked at Daniel, who was almost lost in the shadows of the flickering flames and the self-absorption of his own outrage. *They're watching us . . .*

Charlie jerked the megaphone away from Ben. "God damn you, Bradshaw! You were supposed to talk to him, not her! I knew he couldn't be trusted."

Ben said, "I told you I don't know him and he doesn't know me! You never even told me who he was!"

Matthew said calmly, "No, it's okay. No harm done. In fact, the more he hears Ellen's name the better off we are. It personalizes her, and it's harder to kill a person than an object."

Charlie lifted her binoculars. "It doesn't seem to have done him any good. He's pacing back and forth like a caged bull, yelling at her. I don't like the look of it, Matt." She started to hand him the binoculars, then hesitated. "What is she doing with her hands? Wait a minute—is she deaf?"

"No," Ben said tiredly. "It's just a habit she has. She teaches deaf children. When she's upset or in a hurry she talks with her hands."

Matt had the glasses; he studied her silently for awhile. "She's not talking," he said. "Not to Nichols, anyway. She's just using sign language." He lowered the glasses slowly. "I think she might be trying to communicate with us."

"Of course!" Ben turned to Matt excitedly. "She knows I'm here—that's exactly what she's trying to do! Let me see!"

Matt said to Charlie, "Get me an interpreter."

Ben said, "I can interpret, damn it! Let me see!"

Matt repeated, "Get me an interpreter." But he handed the glasses to Ben.

Charlie moved off into the darkness. Ben said tightly, "I can't see. I can't see anything."

"Look away from the candlelight. Adjust the focus." Matt showed him how.

"Wait a minute. Okay, that's it. I can see her." There was a slight catch in his breath. "She's tied up. Jesus, she looks so . . ." He paused, seemed to compose himself. He was silent in concentration for a moment. "It's hard to see. The image is jumpy."

"That's because it's electronic. These things weren't designed to read a map by."

"Something dead," Ben said. "No, killed." Frustration tinged his voice. "I'm not an expert. I've gotten better since being around Ellen but—I'm not an expert."

Charlie returned. "They're sending for an interpreter." A pause. "The nearest one is a three-hour round trip."

Matthew said, "Looks like you just became an expert, Dr. Bradshaw. The only one we have."

The look Charlie gave him spoke volumes, but Matt turned away.

"Twelve people dead," Ben said. "Or he killed twelve people. Now he's going to kill me. It all happened here when I was a little girl. I saw it. All the people in the church, he cut their throats. One by one. All except me. I was hiding. Now it's my turn. That's why he's brought me here."

Charlie said impatiently, "For Christ's sake, you told him that much."

Matt said, "That's not right. He didn't kill those people in the church. He wasn't even there."

"Who *is* he?" demanded Ben, lowering the glasses. "You never answered my question. Who was the other survivor?"

"A twelve-year-old boy," replied Matthew. "According to his testimony, he wasn't in the church when it happened. He found the bodies later, and he walked thirty miles to the nearest town for help. He was in bad shape, couldn't get his story out for several days. He didn't know there had been any survivors until the story came out about Ellen. Luther Paradise was a stage name," Matthew told Ben. "His real name was Luther Nichols. Daniel was his son."

Thirty-Six

1:30 A.M.

Daniel began to empty out his backpack, carrying handfuls of candles to the front of the church.

"What are you doing?" Ellen asked.

"I'm lighting the candles, like he said," Daniel returned impatiently. "I wanted to wait till morning. I can't wait till morning. Besides, the candles will blind them. They can't see me in the candlelight."

"Listen to me," Ellen said, trying to keep the desperation out of her voice. Her hands signed the words almost more quickly than she could speak them. "You don't have to do this! It wasn't your fault, before, none of it was your fault. Brother Paradise—your father—he held your hand on the knife, I saw him do it! You didn't kill those people, he did! You're not responsible for what he made you do, and you don't have to finish what he started!"

Daniel paused in mid-stride, his hands filled with small white votive candles, and he murmured, "So much blood. Have you ever seen so much blood, Ellen?"

She whispered, "No."

346

Then he turned his head, as though listening for something once again, and then he smiled. He moved forward again. "You're a very strange girl, Ellen," he said, arranging the candles along the raised lip of the altar. "Why are you talking to me about responsibility? This is our final sacrament. It's not just our duty, but our privilege to enjoy it together."

"Pleasure—no, privilege—to enjoy it with each other," Ben said. "I can't stop him. I need help." Matt saw Ben swallow, hard, but he did not lower the glasses. "That last—was what she said, not him."

Matt looked at Charlie. "If that's true—if Paradise forced his son to commit the murders by holding his hand on the knife—that would explain a lot."

"Come on, Matt, he's lying to you! Why shouldn't he lie?"

"The kid comes out of a home life like that, a trauma like that, goes into foster care, the system tries to subjugate him, remake him—they even gave him a new first name, for God's sake—then ultimately we lose him. Where's he going to go but into the military? How else is he going to have a chance at a life? But all he really learned was how to be a better killer."

"She's starting over again," Ben said. "She doesn't know if we've been watching, or if we understand what she's trying to do. She's saying, It happened when I was a child. I saw it all. My brother—no, that's just Brother—Brother Paradise put the knife in his son's hand and put his hand on top of it and he went around the church, cutting their throats one by one. I hid under the pew and he didn't see me. And then in the end he—in the end he cut his father's throat, killed Brother Paradise. He had to. Tears. Something about tears . . . He's lighting the candles; it's hard to see," Ben said. A pause. "She says—" He stopped suddenly. He hesitated so long that Matt almost took the glasses from him, to see for himself what was happening.

"She spelled my name," Ben said. "She said, Ben, if you can see me, thank you—for being a hero. He won't wait until morning. I might not get another chance to say it."

He lowered the glasses, transferred them to the hand that was still handcuffed to Matt's wrist, and rubbed his eyes briefly, as though they were fatigued.

Charlie looked at Matt, and for the first time he saw uncertainty there. He said, "Where's Reirson?"

She looked around. "On the phone."

"Nichols is talking," Ben said, raising the glasses again.

1:40 A.M.

Daniel opened his hands and looked down at them. "Yes," he said softly. "The power is here. I have the power."

Then he looked up, an anxious expression on his face, gaze turned toward the shadows. "But you wouldn't leave me alone, would you? I still need you! You've got to see this through with me!"

348

He seemed to relax after a moment, and he said, "No. I didn't think so. I know you wouldn't."

Ellen was shaking, chilled through with the increasing depth of the unfolding horror. She tried to keep her hands steady as she faithfully signed the strange words he was uttering. Did it matter? Was anyone there to see what she was saying? Could the words make any difference to them? Did anyone even care?

"You said you'd protect me," Daniel went on. Kneeling, he struck another match and put it to a candle, then another. "I know you haven't let me down yet, but I wouldn't like to think I couldn't trust you."

Ellen couldn't stand it any longer. "Who are you talking to?"

He barely glanced at her. "What do you mean?"

"You're talking to someone." Her voice was hoarse and unsteady. "Why? Who is it?"

He looked impatient as he shook out the match. "It's Ariel, of course. Who did you think?"

She repeated dumbly, "Ariel?"

"That's right." He struck another match. "You know him."

"*You're* Ariel!" she cried. "There's no one else here! You're talking to yourself!"

"You're A-R-I-E-L. Ariel," Ben repeated. "There's no one else here. You're talking to yourself."

Suddenly he stiffened. "Oh, shit! *Shit!* He hit her! Do something, he—"

Matt snatched the binoculars from him. His knuckles shone in the dark as he gripped the casing; the line of his jaw was hard. The silence throbbed for two beats that seemed like an eternity, everyone's attention riveted on Matt, then he said, "It's okay. He backed off. She's not hurt."

Mat thrust the binoculars to Charlie and in the same, fierce, almost violent movement he dug a key from his pocket and unsnapped the cuff on Ben's wrist, then on his own. "You're free to go, Dr. Bradshaw, although I know you won't. Just try to stay out of the way."

Charlie drew in a sharp breath but before she could release it Matt started walking away, speaking into his two-way radio. "This is Agent Graham. I need crime-scene photos from the massacre twenty-five years ago and I need them now. Check the state crime lab and if that's too slow get them from the local sheriff's department. Track down the goddamn photographer and get him out of bed if you have to, but do it *now*. There's a portable fax in the crime-scene van; get the number from them. Luther Paradise. I need every shot that was taken of Luther Paradise's body. Not hours from now, not minutes, but seconds, have you got that?"

Charlie caught his arm. "Matt, what are you—"

"Ariel," he said. "It was the name of an outcast angel—according to Luther Paradise, the only kind that would ever get into heaven. It was also what he named his only son."

For only a moment she was nonplussed. "Nichols could have told Bradshaw that. Of course he would have told him that if they were working together!"

"They're not working together. They were never working together. Damn it, it's so obvious, how could I not have seen it? Nichols has a disassociative personality. The part that was Ariel—a twelve-year-old boy who was forced to commit murder at the hands of his father and who in self-defense was then forced to kill his father—that part went into hiding when the boy became Daniel Nichols. The killings, the anniversary killings, were just an inevitable eruption of repressed trauma, but they were clumsy, unsatisfactory offerings to the real demon inside the man. Because Ariel was just dormant, not dead. In fact, I wouldn't be at all surprised if we didn't find some I.D. in Nichols's possession under the name of Ariel Paradise. He wouldn't let him die, but he didn't know how to let him live. Until he saw Ellen Cox again. That brought everything back to life."

He drew in a deep breath. "I know how to get to him now. I know what to do."

Charlie looked at Ben, who was standing where they had left him, binoculars to his eyes, fixed on the church and the occupants within. She looked back at Matt, her expression troubled. "Look," she said, "I know I've been a pain in the ass from the beginning. We should have been supporting each other, working together; instead we've been on the opposite side of every issue. Most of it was my fault. But Matt, I've got to say this. You've been shaky on this from the start; you admitted you weren't ready to come back. You haven't had any sleep in days and the stress was starting to get to you before this. If you're wrong about this, if Bradshaw is setting you up or if Nichols is setting *him* up—"

Matt looked back toward the church. "I've been wrong about a lot of things on this case," he admitted. "I always teach that criminal profiling is more of an art than a science, and that at some point you have to stop and ignore what you see, and listen to your gut. I didn't want to listen before. But I'm listening now. And I'm not wrong."

He took a long, slow breath. Charlie saw his hands tighten into fists at his sides. "This one is a save," he said.

Thirty-Seven

2:12 A.M.

Matt snatched the fax pages from Reirson's hand and focused on them with a penlight. After four days at the mercy of beetles, small carnivores, and natural decomposition, there was not much that was distinguishable about the body, and the poor quality of the fax made details even more difficult to discern. But Matt saw everything he needed to know. Nondescript brown hair, not overly long, with a hint of curl, much like his own. Dark pants, a white or light-colored shirt, a dark windbreaker-style jacket, unzipped. Paradise was known to decry the vanity of fine clothes, and had often conducted services in his shirtsleeves.

Reirson said, speaking to Charlie but looking at Matt, "We got confirmation on Bradshaw. He was in Williamsburg at the time of the murder yesterday, seeing patients when Maureen Lister was killed. He's left Virginia Beach once in the past two weeks, and a woman at the Chamber of Commerce in Wintersville, West Virginia remembers seeing him with a young lady, just as he claims. I'm asked to relay to you that she was highly incensed to be awakened this time of night for such a question and intends to file a complaint. His telephone calls check out, cellular, office, and home as completely routine—family, friends, patients, hospitals, labs. There's no cellular phone registered to Daniel Nichols, by the way."

"Shit," Charlie said.

She looked at Ben, who was standing fixed and rigid in the shadow of a tree. He hadn't moved since Matt had freed him, although the binoculars hung at his side. There was far too much light inside the church for the night vision to be useful now, and far too little light for regular binoculars to reveal much more than shadowy shapes that might or might not be moving. The riflemen were as blinded as he was, and just as paralyzed with frustration.

"I guess I owe the gentleman an apology," she said, and she was looking at Matt.

Matt didn't seem to hear her, or care if he did. He swept the penlight over the last photograph and snapped it off. He straightened up and swept his eyes around the assemblage. "Hey," he said, lifting his voice a fraction. "You." He flagged an agent in a stenciled FBI jacket. "I need to borrow your jacket." He tugged his own suit jacket off and tore at his tie. "And a white shirt. Who has a white shirt?" He started unbuttoning the Oxford stripe that he wore. "And I need something—paint, charcoal, something—to cover up these letters." He took the stenciled jacket from the agent.

"What about black marker?" Reirson suggested.

"Get it."

Reirson sprinted off in the direction of the van.

Charlie began to understand what he was doing. Even understanding, she couldn't believe it. "Matt, you can't be serious."

"A white shirt, Charlie, find me a white shirt. Nichols remembers every detail of that day, he was picking victims by the kind of jewelry they wore for Christ's sakes. He's going to remember what his own father was wearing."

"Matt, you're not going down there."

An agent whose I.D. badge Matt couldn't read in the dimness came up to him. "Did you say a white shirt? I'm wearing one. It's a little wrinkled—"

"Sold."

"For God's sake, Matt, what can you be thinking of? He'll kill her as soon as he sees you clear the woods. You said yourself—"

"He won't kill her if he looks at me first." Matt's tone was grim as he swiftly exchanged shirts with the agent. "He won't do anything without my permission once he sees me."

"Great jumping Jesus, Matt, do you know what you're saying? You're going down there dressed as his father—he fucking *killed* his father!"

Matt tucked in the shirt. "Exactly."

Charlie turned away with a sharp hiss of breath. Reirson started working on the yellow letters of the jacket with the marker.

Matt walked around to face Charlie. She was rubbing her throat, staring into the distance. Her mouth was angry and tight.

Matt said gently, "Listen to me. I'm old, and I'm out of it, and I make mistakes. But I wouldn't be going down there if I wasn't sure. This afternoon, two o'clock, I'm going to be at the Richmond airport carrying the luggage of the only person in this world I give a damn about, not lying in a pool of blood on the side of this Godforsaken mountain. Okay?"

She searched his eyes long and hard. After another moment she took a deep breath. It was a struggle, but she managed to make her features relax. She nodded. "What's your strategy?"

"I'm going to try to talk him out. I think I can at least get it on a one-to-one basis, give her a chance to get away."

"Great. So instead of a civilian hostage, he'll have an FBI agent."

Matt smiled. "Not even close."

His expression sobered. "She's in trouble down there and we've been blacked out for over ten minutes. Confronting him with his dual personality was about the worst thing she could do. I'm the only one who can get close to him. It might already be too late. There's not a lot of room for debate here."

She said, "If you can't get him outside, get him near a window."

He hesitated, then nodded. He looked over his shoulder. "Reirson, neatness does not count."

"Got it." He held up the jacket.

Matthew started to pull it on, but Charlie stopped him. "Agent Graham." She held up his shoulder holster.

In a beat Matt said, "Right," and pulled it on.

"Stay in the shadows as long as you can. Circle west and come out behind the church, then ease up onto the porch. She'll only be vulnerable from the time he sees you. Let's keep that time as short as possible."

He pulled on the jacket and ran his fingers through his hair, disheveling it.

"Matt . . ."

He waited, but all she said was, "We'll be covering you every step of the way."

He said, "I know."

She pulled out her radio as he started down the hill.

2:20 A.M.

Daniel lit the final candle and tossed the matchbook away. He stood back to admire his work. There must have been thirty or thirty-five of them, flickering in an eerie, discordant symphony. Even Ellen had to appreciate how close he had come to recreating the scene of twenty-five years ago. In the candlelight the decay was disguised—cobwebs were hidden, the disarray of a quarter of a century of abandonment sank into the shadows. She could almost see them there—the mother and the baby with the teddy bear, the fat man with the cross and his wife, a gray-haired woman with glasses on a chain, the man in the plaid shirt, the woman in the red blouse, the little boy in the red-and-white polo—her family, her family.

Daniel said softly, "There. Now we're ready."

He went back to his backpack and retrieved one

last item. "I wish Ariel could see this. But you made him angry. He'll be there when I need him, though. He always is. He'll be back to help me celebrate."

Ellen's lip was swollen from his blow and she could taste blood, but she wasn't badly hurt. Not that it mattered. She thought, *Oh Ben, after all we've been through it doesn't seem fair that it should end like this, just when I've found all the answers.* Then she thought how strange it was that in the last moments of her life—because she knew that was what these were—she should be thinking about a man she had known only weeks.

She said tiredly, "He's not coming back, not this time. He's not coming back because he never existed outside your imagination."

He stood up, smiling, and came toward her. The flicker of a candle flame glinted on something metal in his hand. "I've waited so long for this, angel," he said softly. "So long."

And suddenly, out of the darkness, a voice commanded, "Stop where you are, Ariel."

Ellen cried out because she thought—just for a second she thought—that Ariel's dark angel had come for him, had come for them both, and he was silhouetted there, a darker shape against the dark of the door, having materialized in the center aisle. And then the cry turned into a choked gasp of pain and terror because in an instant Ariel was upon her, twisting her hair in his hands with a nerve-jolting jerk, snapping her head back, exposing her throat, and now the sting of cold metal on her skin, and now the trickle of something warm down her neck.

"Who are you?" Ariel shouted. "How dare you defile these proceedings! Get away from this place!"

"Don't you shout at me, boy! Who do you think you're talking to? Look at me, boy! Look at me when I talk to you!" The figure moved forward with two long, commanding strides, half in and half out of the flickering shadows cast by the candlelight.

Ellen caught her breath and began to shudder, choking back whimpering sobs of sheer terror.

It was Luther Paradise.

2:30 A.M.

"Talk to me, damn it!" Charlie demanded of the radio. "What's happening? What do you see?"

The crackle of a voice came back. "He's inside. Three of them. The girl hasn't moved. I don't know if she's alive. Wait—somebody just moved in front of the window. Shit. It's Graham."

"Hold your position," Charlie said sharply. "You are not clear to fire. Copy?"

No hesitation. "Copy."

Ben Bradshaw stood beside her. His eyes were haunted. "She could be dead."

"We don't know that." Charlie was uncomfortable around him, and there was no hiding it. She said, a little stiffly, because she had never been good at apologies, "Looks like we were wrong about you. I guess I should probably make a bigger deal about it, but I'm a little busy right now." She spoke into the radio. "Ready spotlights. I want a hundred thousand watts aimed at that church and blasting away the minute I say go."

From the radio came a staticky: "Spotlights ready."

Ben said, with only the faintest hint of a dry smile around his pale, dry lips, "You ever think about destiny, Agent Fontana?"

"Can't say that I do, no."

"I haven't been thinking about much else these past couple of hours. How I got from a bridge in Virginia Beach to headlines in national magazines to a mountainside in the middle of nowhere at the mercy of a madman. Destiny. I can't say that I like it very much."

Charlie looked at him. She tried not to, but she couldn't help softening somewhat. "Why don't you go back to the car? I'll get an officer to take you."

But he shook his head, and turned back to look down the hill at the church. "No," he said, "I'll wait."

2:33 A.M.

The pressure on the blade eased; Matt could see the slight relaxation in the muscles of Daniel's hand. His voice, small and uncertain, said "Daddy?"

Matt's heart was thundering in his chest, not with fear but with triumph, exhilaration. He could do this. He knew this man, he had studied his work for fifteen years. He knew Mayday, the creation of Luther

Paradise; he knew Luther Paradise. He *was* Luther Paradise.

He had spent a lifetime crawling around inside the heads of monsters, dreaming their dreams, thinking their thoughts, swimming naked through the black, rancid core of their souls. He had let them twist him and torture him and damn near break him. But now, now was his chance. Now it was all worth it. Now he *was* the monster; he was in command.

This one was a save.

Matt moved forward. "Let her go, Ariel. Have you learned nothing all these years? Vengeance is mine, saith the Lord!"

Daniel's hand tightened in her hair and she cried out, her eyes big and dark with fear. But the hand that held the scalpel blade against her skin was shaking. Ever so slightly, but shaking. "Yea, though I walk through the Valley of the Shadow of Death," he said, half-whispering. There was a desperate edge to his voice as he added, "Stay back." His tone had somehow lost its volume, its control. He sounded younger, much less sure of himself. "I'll kill her." A threat, not a promise. Whispering, frantic now, "Yea, though I walk through the Valley of the Shadow of Death—"

"I will fear no evil," Matt said loudly. He kept coming. "For thou art with me . . ."

Matt kept moving. Halfway down the aisle now. The hand that held the blade hadn't moved, and the trickle of blood that soaked Ellen's collar hadn't increased its flow. Perhaps it had lessened. There was panic in his eyes. Panic.

"Stop, I tell you!" There was a note of hysteria to

Daniel's voice now, and a choked sound of pain and terror from Ellen. The hand on the scalpel tightened. Matt stopped.

"You have no right to be here!" Daniel cried. "This is my time, my moment! My time to make everything right, and you can't be here! You're dead, you—"

"But I'm not dead," Matt said. His voice was cold, his words distinct. "You fool, don't you see that? You couldn't even get that right. Twelve of the faithful, the holy tribe—but this woman wasn't one of them. She doesn't deserve Paradise. You got everything else right, but you missed that. *The twelfth person wasn't her.*"

Daniel stared at him. His voice was small and uncertain. "No. It wasn't her."

"I will fear no evil," Daniel whispered again, his lips barely moving. His eyes were fixed on Matt.

Matt said, "For thou art with me."

Matt was at the end of the aisle now. A dozen steps more and he would be able to reach out and grab him. If he drew his weapon now he couldn't miss. But if he drew his weapon he would have to fire and shoot to kill, because whatever hold he had on Nichols's mind would be broken then, the fantasy shattered. And only a flex of a muscle stood between life and death for Ellen Cox.

He said, moving steadily, "You know what you have to do, Ariel. You know."

And Ariel whispered, "Yes. I know."

Matthew saw it happening an instant before it actually did. The fingers tightening on the blade, the shoulder muscles, the hand lifting, drawing back. He screamed, "Daniel, no!" and he lunged for him.

But it was too late.

"Nooooooo!" The cry, hoarse and horrible, echoed throughout the mountains like a harbinger of Armageddon, circling, swooping, piercing, shattering. Disaster. Despair. Death.

And that was the last clear thing any of them remembered. From that point on time seemed to unfold in a series of fast-forward and slow-motion vignettes, choppy, disjointed, cold with horror.

Fast-forward: Agent Fontana, shouting into her radio, "Lights!" And suddenly the desolate weed-choked collection of buildings below was illuminated in a bright white light, blinding light, and she shouted, "Take your shot, take your shot!" and the radio crackled back "I can't see!" and she cried, "Reirson, Scroggins, you're with me!"

Slow motion: Running, stumbling, holding onto the branches that tore the hands, pushing off trees, falling, getting up. Running from shadow into hot white light, and then someone caught his arms, pulled him back. Fighting, shouting, struggling uselessly. Ben stood still and listened to the harsh scrape of his own breath in and out of his lungs and watched as Agent Fontana and the two men, weapons drawn, moved in crouched position toward the church.

Agents swarmed down the hill. Charlie took the stance, shouted into the building: "FBI! Freeze!" Nothing. She moved forward, up the steps, onto the porch.

The light that flooded the grounds outside made only a dim illumination for the interior of the building. Flattening herself against the wall, leading with her weapon as she swung herself inside, Charlie did a quick sweep of the room. Rotting floorboard, misaligned pews, trash and debris swept to one side, an altar filled with flickering votive candles—Ellen Cox, tied to the throne chair, soaked with blood, her head ducked awkwardly to the side as though to avoid a blow, still and silent. On the floor behind the chair, drenched in shadows, were two figures: one prone and lifeless, the other kneeling over it, bloody hands resting palms up on his knees, just kneeling there.

Swiftly she crossed the room. She was aware of other agents behind her. Two of them went to Ellen Cox, and Charlie dropped down beside Matt. "What happened?" she demanded quietly.

Slowly he lifted his eyes to her. "I tried to stop the bleeding," he said. He lifted his blood-soaked hands a few inches from his legs, but they fell down again as though weighted. He gave a slight lift of his shoulders and finished, "Hard to stop an arterial spurt. He bled out before I could get to him."

He turned his gaze back to the body on the floor. Charlie saw his chest rise and fall with a long slow inhalation. "He turned the knife on himself. He saw his father and he thought that was his only choice."

Charlie said, very steadily, "You knew that was a possibility."

"Yeah, I knew." He looked at her. "So what does that make me?"

She was quiet for a time. "What do you think it makes you?"

He looked across at Ellen, at the agents who were untying her. He got to his feet. "Tired," he answered. "Just—very tired."

* * *

Ben watched, muscles aching, throat dry, as the two federal agents came out of the building. Agent Fontana, and with her Matthew Graham. Graham's white shirt was red with blood and so were his hands. His shoulders were bowed, his head low. He walked with a slow, defeated step. Ben thought, *No. No.*

He pulled away from the restraining arms. They released him without much protest.

"I have to see," he said hoarsely. "I have to know."

He started walking down the hill, onto the road, past the house with the big lilac bush, toward the church.

A figure appeared on the portico, a man in a black FBI jacket. He was holding someone by the arm, a prisoner. Ben kept moving, faster now, his stride stronger. The agent moved out of the shadows, and so did his prisoner.

Ellen pulled away from the agent. Gripping the rail, she moved down the steps. There was blood on her face and in her hair; her dress was spattered with it. She saw Ben and she started to cry. Then she started to run.

She stumbled and he swept her into his arms before she fell. He held her close, just held her close. She wept, and finally, so did he.

After a long time she pushed herself away, and she looked up at him. "I thought it was him," she said shakily. "I thought it was Paradise, come back to life . . . and I guess, so did Ariel. Oh God, Ben, he—he killed himself, he cut his own throat, I thought he was going to kill me but he killed himself instead! The blood, the blood was everywhere. All those people dead, and I should have died too but— he died instead. I never thought I had a guardian angel," she whispered, laying her head against his shoulder. "But I guess I do."

He held her tightly, as tightly as he could without hurting her. He wanted to hold her for the rest of his life. And in the end all he could think of to say was, "Happy birthday, Ellen. Thank God, happy birthday."

Thirty-Eight

Richmond, Virginia

2:30 P.M.

The plane was late and the gate was crowded. Matthew stood, feeling self-conscious with the bouquet of sweetheart roses he held, and scanned the deplaning passengers. Then he saw her, and he forgot his self-consciousness, forgot his fatigue, forgot the horror and filth of the past ten days, forgot the blood on his hands that four scalding hot showers had not been able to wash away.

She moved like a fairy princess, frizzy red curls glinting and bouncing, long, black-stockinged legs flashing in and out among the other passengers. He was overcome with a sense of awe, of cautious, burgeoning pride that he should know such a creature, that she should belong to him, that he could claim her as part of his life. His treasure, his joy, the only woman he would ever love above all others for the rest of his life. Polly.

Then she spotted him and her face lit up. She waved to him and began to move faster, threading her way through the crowd. Clearing the congestion, she stood for a moment a few dozen feet away from him, beaming at him, and he opened his arms wide.

"Daddy!" she cried, and she launched herself at him.

Matt caught her up, laughing, crushing the roses, his daughter, his love, his life. He held her close, and he felt clean.